THE RUINS OF US

STOLEN MOMENTS BOOK III

CATHARINA MAURA

For you

Thank you for following Emilia and Carter's story, and for supporting my career. I couldn't have done this without you.

CONTENTS

Playlist for The Ruins Of Us   vii

Chapter 1   1
Chapter 2   6
Chapter 3   11
Chapter 4   16
Chapter 5   20
Chapter 6   26
Chapter 7   30
Chapter 8   35
Chapter 9   39
Chapter 10   46
Chapter 11   51
Chapter 12   56
Chapter 13   60
Chapter 14   66
Chapter 15   71
Chapter 16   75
Chapter 17   79
Chapter 18   84
Chapter 19   89
Chapter 20   93
Chapter 21   97
Chapter 22   101
Chapter 23   105
Chapter 24   111
Chapter 25   115
Chapter 26   119
Chapter 27   125
Chapter 28   130
Chapter 29   134
Chapter 30   139
Chapter 31   144
Chapter 32   148

Chapter 33   153
Chapter 34   158
Chapter 35   162
Chapter 36   167
Chapter 37   172
Chapter 38   177
Chapter 39   182
Chapter 40   186
Chapter 41   191
Chapter 42   196
Chapter 43   202
Chapter 44   206
Chapter 45   211
Chapter 46   215
Chapter 47   219
Chapter 48   223
Chapter 49   228
Chapter 50   232
Chapter 51   237
Chapter 52   241
Chapter 53   246
Chapter 54   250
Chapter 55   254
Chapter 56   259
Chapter 57   263
Chapter 58   268
Chapter 59   272
Chapter 60   277
Chapter 61   281
Chapter 62   285
Chapter 63   289
Chapter 64   293
Chapter 65   297
Chapter 66   302

Exclusive Extra Content   307
Afterword   309
Also by Catharina Maura   311
Acknowledgments   313

PLAYLIST FOR THE RUINS OF US

Emilia and Carter's Playlist is available on my Spotify. The easiest way to get to it is to google 'Catharina Maura Spotify'

Alternatively, you can find it here: https://spoti.fi/349xyUl

CHAPTER 1

milia

"God, that was exhausting," my manager says as we walk out of the client's office.

I suppress a yawn and nod. We've been working on closing this deal for months now. I can barely believe it's actually finally over.

"But hey, we did it," she adds. She holds her hand up for me to high five, and I grin as my palm meets hers.

Alice, my boss and mentor, has trained me since my very first day at the firm. We've grown together, and I wouldn't be where I am today if not for her. She's the reason I decided to specialize in transaction law, just like she did. The merger that was signed today cost us months of prep and sleepless nights, but it was so worth it in the end.

Alice puts her hand on my shoulder and smiles, radiating with pride. "Come on, let's grab cocktails. We've worked hard enough today."

I glance at my watch and burst out laughing. "It's only two in the afternoon."

Alice shrugs and drags me to the pub near the office that we frequent. We walk to our usual table and take a seat. "I'm proud of you, you know?" Alice says. "You handled this entire engagement almost entirely by yourself."

I smile at her in thanks. I definitely have come a long way in the eight years since I moved to London. The city I ran away to has become home to me. It doesn't feel like it's been eight years, though. Not even remotely.

"This year has flown by," I murmur. "Can't believe we spent a quarter of it on just this one single client."

Alice sighs and nods. "At least the holidays are only around the corner. Is your Dad coming to see you again, or are you going home this year? I don't think you've gone home once since we started working together. Don't you miss it?"

For a split second my mind flashes back to Woodstock. To the home I grew up in... and the house right next to mine. I think of *him*, and my heart twists painfully. I force my thoughts away and shake my head.

"No," I murmur, smiling tightly. "London is home to me now."

Alice looks at me with that blank expression that I hate — it's that expression she puts on when she's cracking a case. I look away and lift my glass to hers. "Cheers," I say, smiling as brightly as I can.

Even the memory of home still ruins my mood. The memory of everything I lost, everything I left behind. I've worked so hard to build myself a new life, one I can be proud of, yet I still don't think I'm strong enough to go back. It still hurts too much.

"Fair enough," Alice says, thankfully changing the topic. "How is that cute boyfriend of yours?"

I smile to myself, the aching of my heart dulling at the thought of Sam. We met at university, and we were friends for years before I finally agreed to go on a date on him. I wish I hadn't taken so long to give him a chance, because he's been nothing but wonderful. "We've been dating close to a year now, and things couldn't be more perfect," I tell her. I didn't think I'd ever be happy again, not truly, but what I feel for Sam is as close as it's going to get.

"I'm glad you're finally dating. For a while I thought you'd become a spinster, for sure. It's good to see you happy."

I roll my eyes. "Does anyone even use that word anymore? And I'm only twenty-seven, Alice."

She shrugs. "You act like you're eighty, though."

I glare at her and take a sip of my cocktail. The truth is, for a long time I thought I'd become a *spinster* too. If not for Sam's persistence, I don't think I'd ever have dated anyone. Not a single man I met could measure up. I bite down on my lip and force my thoughts away. It's stupid, but I can't even think of his name without my heart hurting. Eight years, and I'm still not completely over him.

I finish my drink and Alice glances at her watch. "Let's just call it a day. You and I have both barely gotten any sleep in the last week, so let's just go home," she says. I grin at her and shake my head. I'm so lucky to have her as my boss. She's trained me from the very start, and she always has my back.

"Thank you," I say, smiling. Alice looks at me, and she looks that way she occasionally does... like she's worried about me. Sometimes I wonder if she can see right through me, to that broken part of me that I keep hidden. Thankfully she doesn't say anything, and I breathe a sigh of relief.

I'm absentminded the entire way home. The mere mention of Woodstock has me wondering what my life might have looked like if I hadn't left when I did. Would we be married now? Would we be living in California? Would he and I have made it at all? It hurts to think of everything we could have had.

My heart twists painfully as I walk up to my apartment

building and I close my eyes, steadying myself against my front door.

I inhale deeply before walking in, only to freeze in surprise when I realize my apartment isn't empty, as it should've been.

Sam turns around in surprise, his eyes wide and his hands filled with pink decorations. Sam has a key to my apartment, but he doesn't usually drop by without notice. "Hey, you're home," he says, frowning. "I was trying to surprise you."

I glance at the decorations in his hands in confusion. "I thought you'd still be at the hospital?" I murmur.

He shakes his head and smiles. "I swapped shifts. I'm free all night today. Didn't expect you to be back anytime soon, though."

Sam walks up to me and presses a kiss to my forehead. "Did you have a good day?"

I smile up at him and nod. "What's all this?" I ask, and his smile drops.

He inhales deeply and shakes his head. "You forgot," he says, all the cheer leaving him instantly. I bite down on my lip and glance around, my eyes widening when realization dawns.

"No, of course not," I murmur, trying to play it off. "Happy Anniversary," I whisper. How could I have forgotten? I glance at the flowers on my dining table and the heart shaped balloons on the floor. I'm the worst girlfriend ever. I didn't even get him a card. Scratch that, I didn't even remember.

"You *did* forget," he says, and the accusation in his voice is heart wrenching.

I sigh and drop my forehead to his chest. "I'm sorry, Sam," I whisper. "It's just been such a long week at work. I've barely had time to sleep. I'm just so tired."

I know it's an excuse, and I think he knows it too, but he lets me get away with it nonetheless. Sam wraps his arms around me and presses a kiss to my temple.

"I know, honey. It's all right. I know how busy you've been

this week," he says, and I feel even worse. Sam is a doctor specializing in neurosurgery — he's far busier than I've ever been, yet he nods in understanding.

"I love the balloons," I murmur, smiling up at him. Sam shakes his head, and my eyes roam over his bright green eyes and his sandy brown hair. He looks as tired as I probably do, yet he's smiling up at me with so much love in his eyes. How did I get this lucky? I need to do better. Sam deserves the world, and it's past time I try to give it to him. I can't keep living in the past.

CHAPTER 2

arter

I sigh and run a hand through my hair. I'm so fucking exhausted. I've worked fourteen-hour days every single day this month, and I need a fucking break. I can't, though. Not now. Not anytime soon.

I walk up to my car and yawn. How long am I going to be able to keep this up? I've already employed half the town, but it seems like I'll need to hire even more people soon. The company is growing quicker than I anticipated, and Asher and I can barely keep up.

I pull up in front of John's house without even realizing it. I'd been planning to go straight home, but I ended up here nonetheless. Every once in a while, I find myself back here without realizing it. I step out of the car and shake my head. Since I'm here, I might as well say hello and drop by my parents' house next door too. I ring the bell and lean back against the wall as I wait for John to open the door.

He glares at me as the door swings open. "Boy, I gave you a key for a reason," he says, scowling. I smile and follow him in, my eyes lingering on the photos of Emilia and John in the hallway. I've memorized every single one of these photos, yet the memory of her fades more and more with each passing day. When I close my eyes, I struggle to remember what her smile looks like. I struggle to imagine the way she used to look at me, yet I can never forget the way she's always made me feel. I tear my gaze away and follow John into the living room.

"How have you been, old man?"

He looks frail and tired. The dialysis keeps getting harder on him, yet he's refusing my help.

"Fine."

I sigh and drop down on the sofa. "You're obviously not fine. I'm pulling every string I can, John, but I've only barely been able to move you up the transplant list."

John smiles at me, and for just a second, I see the man he used to be. I never expected it to happen, but when Emilia left, John and I ended up becoming closer. I felt so bad for the sacrifices she'd made for my family that I wanted to make sure to take care of her Dad in her absence. It started with me offering to get a drink together, and John having to take me home, wasted and in tears over his daughter. Ever since then, he's slowly but surely become a second dad to me. It kills me that I can't help him. I've got all the money in the world, yet I can't get him a kidney transplant. Not legally, anyway. I'm not above sourcing one elsewhere if he doesn't have one when time starts to run out. There isn't much I won't do to save his life.

"You chased the latest nurse away, I heard."

I keep hiring him nurses, and he keeps finding new ways to chase them away. I finally learned where Emilia got her wild streak.

"The fake eyes in jars were a nice touch. I got a call from Officer Oliver this afternoon, telling me they had to come in and search your house because your latest nurse reported that

7

you were harboring body parts. I was told she feared for her life."

He chuckles and I inhale deeply. I pinch the bridge of my nose and close my eyes. He's just as stubborn as she is.

"I don't need help," he says, crossing his arms. "I'm not a child, Carter. I don't need a caretaker."

I bite down on my lip and shake my head. "I don't get why you're being so difficult. I have money, John. Why won't you at least let me hire you a chef that can create a diet for you that works with your treatment? Every time I see you, you look thinner. And what's with chasing away the nurses, anyway? They're here so you can do your dialysis at home. Do you really want to go back and forth to the dialysis center every single time?"

John looks away, falling quiet. I look up at him in surprise. He always has a retort ready for me, but not today, it seems. He glances at his phone in his hands for a few seconds, and then he nods.

"I'll take you up on your offer," he tells me, his eyes steady and calm. I'm startled. I haven't seen that look in his eyes in years. He looks confident and just a little... *calculative.*

I look at him with raised brows. "Which one of my offers?"

He smiles, and my shackles are raised. When he looks at me like that, he looks just like the fearsome prosecutor he used to be.

"I'll move into that ridiculous mansion of yours. You have a perfectly good chef, don't you? And you have space for all the equipment and supplies I'll need if I want to have in-home dialysis. Besides, you have that nice little gym of yours. I'm supposed to keep working out to stay healthy, but it's getting too cold to go for walks."

I blink at him in surprise. I've been asking him to move in with me for months now. Why is he suddenly agreeing?

I nod slowly, feeling blindsided somehow. I'm not certain what he's up to, but he's got something up his sleeve for sure.

8

"Okay, great. I'll make the arrangements, and I'll attempt to hire another nurse, if there's even a single agency left that'll still take my calls. I'll have everything ready for you in a week or so, all right? I'll send my assistant over to help you pack and coordinate the move."

John nods and claps me on the back as he walks me out. "Thank you, Carter," he says. "You know, I've never said this to you, but you're the son I never had."

I grin at him as I walk out, but I can't shake the feeling that I just got played. I'm still feeling off as I walk up to my parents' house.

"Mom?" I shout as I walk in. I hear the clattering of pots and pans and follow the sound into the kitchen. She looks surprised to see me and walks up to hug me.

"My baby, you're home," she says, beaming. I nod and tighten my grip on her, lifting her off the floor with ease. "Your dad just went to bed. Did you go see John?"

I nod. "Yeah. He finally agreed to move in with me, you know?"

Mom smiles. "It's about time. I'm worried about him staying in that house all by himself. Every time I try to go over to keep an eye on him, he ends up shooing me away. At yours at least he'll have staff around at all times. It'll probably be easier for him to accept some help that way."

I nod in agreement and glance over at the mess she's made in the kitchen, but I know better than to ask questions. When she's baking up a storm it usually means she's worrying about Kate again.

Kate moved to London years ago, and part of me wonders if it's because she wanted to follow Emilia. As far as I'm aware, the two haven't spoken in years. I wonder why she chose to go there of all places.

"You staying over?"

I nod and yawn again. I might as well. I'm here now, anyway.

I kiss Mom goodnight and walk up the stairs to my childhood bedroom. I walk in and pause by the door, my eyes lingering on the view from the window. My heart still aches every single time I look into her room. John has left everything untouched, and every time I'm here, memories assail me. It's so easy to fool myself into believing that she'll walk up to her window any second now. I haven't seen her in years. I don't even know who she is anymore, yet my heart still aches at the thought of her. It's foolish, but even after all these years, Emilia owns a little part of my heart.

CHAPTER 3

milia

I'm nervous as I cook dinner, intent on wowing Sam. I still feel horrible for forgetting about our anniversary last week. Sam hasn't said anything, but he's been different all week. I know he's disappointed in me, and all I want to do is put a smile back on his face.

I'm anxious as I wait for him to come over. With my luck, he'll end up having to work late, or there'll be some emergency he just won't be able to walk away from. I love his heart, but being a doctor's girlfriend isn't easy.

I exhale in relief when my front door opens. Sam walks in, and his eyes widen when he sees me. I dressed up for him tonight. I put on a tight black dress that hugs my figure and makes me feel sexy, and the way his eyes roam over me tells me he likes it.

"All this, for me?"

I bite down on my lip and nod. Sam walks up to me and I hug him tightly. "I'm so sorry," I whisper. "I know this isn't much, but just let me spoil you tonight?"

Sam smiles and nods, his eyes twinkling. I grin up at him, relieved to find him smiling so genuinely. I grab his hand and drag him to the dining table. "Take a seat. I'm serving you tonight."

He grins and raises his brow. "Serving me, huh?" he says, his voice husky. I blush and look away shyly.

"*Food*," I murmur. "I'm serving you food."

He laughs and shakes his head just as I place the food on the table. "That's not all you're serving me tonight, Emilia."

I chuckle and shake my head. "Behave," I tell him. Sam looks at the food and smiles happily.

"I love this, Emilia. I love having dinner with you after a long day. I love coming home to you. I think I want this for the rest of my life, you know?"

My heart skips a beat and for just a second, panic grips me. I push it down and force myself to nod. I should want this too, and I do. *I do.* Sam is perfect.

"Come on, try it," I say, trying my best to sound excited. He chuckles and takes a bite under my watchful gaze.

"Delicious," he says, grinning, and I smile back at him. "I meant it, you know. I think I want to spend the rest of my life with you, Emilia. I know we've only been dating for a year, but we've known each other for eight years now. Honestly, I knew you were the one for me the second I saw you. How about we stop paying rent on two properties and just move in together?"

I inhale sharply. I knew this was coming. It was only natural, and I have no real reason to say no, but somehow, I still don't feel ready. I'm not ready for that type of commitment.

Sam's expression drops when I don't answer and he looks away. "You don't want to."

I shake my head furiously. "No, that's not it. I'm just surprised, that's all." I inhale deeply and nod. "Of course we should move in together," I say, even though my heart isn't in it.

I won't ever meet a man that's more perfect than Sam is. I need to stop holding back and commit to him fully.

"Really?" he says, his happiness palpable. "If you're not ready then that's totally fine, Emilia. I would love for us to move in together, but I don't want to pressure you into doing anything you're not ready for."

I shake my head. How did I get this lucky? "I'm ready," I tell him — and myself.

Sam rises from his seat and walks up to me, pulling me to my feet. Just as he's about to kiss me, my phone rings, the ringtone loud and entirely unique to my dad. I jump in surprise and glance at my phone.

"It's my dad," I tell Sam.

"I spoke to him yesterday," Sam says. "I called to ask his blessing before asking you to move in together. It's a bit old school, I guess, but it seemed like the right thing to do."

I grin at Sam and shake my head. "You didn't," I say, wide-eyed.

Sam grins and nods as I pick up the phone.

"Hi Daddy," I say, a smile on my face.

"Princess," he says, and I sit back down, my heart twisting painfully. I miss him. "How are you?" he asks.

I nod, even though he can't see me. "I'm good, Dad. I miss you, though. How have you been?"

My dad and I were never close as I was growing up, but that has changed over the years. When I moved to London, he started calling me as often as he could, and over the years we've been able to mend our relationship. It makes staying away even harder.

"I actually have something to tell you, Princess."

I grin and glance at Sam. "Me too, Dad," I say excitedly. "Sam and I are moving in together!"

Dad is silent, and I frown. I pull my phone away from my face to check if we're still connected, but we are. "Dad?"

He clears his throat. "I see," he says, and my smile drops. I thought he'd be a little bit more excited than this. He seemed to like Sam just fine when I introduced him last year during his annual visit.

"Princess, I need you to sit down for a second, okay?" he says, worrying me. I look at Sam with wide eyes, and he lifts his brows in question. I shake my head to reassure him, but my heart is racing.

"I'm sitting, Daddy."

Dad inhales deeply before speaking. "I have end-stage renal disease, Emilia."

"End-stage renal disease?" I repeat numbly, the words not even registering. Not truly. Not until Sam looks up at me in shock, his expression morphing into horror.

"I... that... kidney failure? That's what it is, right? Please tell me you're joking, Dad."

Sam drops down to his knees beside me and grabs my free hand, offering me all the support he can. I tighten my grip on his hand in an attempt to stop trembling.

"I'm not joking, Emilia. I wish I was, Princess. It's pretty bad. It's been a few months, and I'm not sure I can even get a kidney transplant. I hate to ask this of you, but Princess, I really want to see you. Please come home, Emilia."

I swallow hard and I don't even realize I've started crying until Sam wipes away my tears. "Of course, Daddy. I'll be home as soon as I can. How long have you known? Why didn't you ask me to get tested? I should be a match, right? How does that work?"

Dad sighs. "I just want to see you, Princess. I don't want your kidney, baby girl. I'd never accept, so get that thought right out of your head. I just want to see you."

I sniff loudly and nod. "I'll be home as soon as I can."

Sam wraps his arms around me and I hold on just long enough for Dad to end the call, and then I let myself fall apart.

Sam strokes my hair and holds me tightly, trying his best to console me, but my tears just won't abate.

"I didn't even know," I sob.

Sam tightens his grip on me and presses a kiss to my hair. "You know now, honey. I'll check with the hospital if I can take some time off, okay?"

I nod and pull away. I see the insecurity in his eyes. He knows just as well as I do that I'll be away for months. Sam presses a kiss to my forehead. "Everything will be okay, Emilia. Be strong for your Dad, okay?"

CHAPTER 4

arter

I walk into John's dialysis room after a long day at work to find him staring into space, a lost expression on his face. He's settled in just fine at my house, and he seems to enjoy all the facilities and the staff he now has access to, just like I knew he would. I don't know why the old man is so damn stubborn. We could have done this months ago.

He looks up at me and smiles. "Carter, my boy," he says, patting the seat next to his. I walk up to him and sit down, turning on the massage function on both our chairs. I got him top of the line equipment and furniture, since he spends four hours in this room every single day.

"How was your day?" I ask. His expression crumbles, and I regret asking the question immediately.

"Spent half the day hooked up to this," he says, holding up his arm, the tubes all still connected, his blood flowing in and out.

I sigh, wishing I could do more. John smiles at me and shakes his head as though he knows what I'm thinking.

He straightens in his seat and looks up at me with a serious expression, and I tense automatically. "I told Emilia that I'm sick," he says, and my heart drops. He rarely mentions her, and every time he does, my heart aches.

I nod at him, but my mind is on Emilia. I wonder how she took the news. The girl I used to know would've probably burst into tears the second the words left John's lips. I hate the idea of her being all by herself over there, especially because it's all my fault that she's there, and not here with her father.

"I asked her to come home."

I freeze and look at him with wide eyes. Emilia hasn't been back here since the day she left. For years I hoped she'd come back one day, that I'd run into her somewhere, but with every year that passed my hopes died a little more.

"What did she say?" I ask, my voice soft.

John smiles. "She said she'd come home, of course."

Emilia coming home? I feel nervous at the mere thought of it. I haven't seen her in years. Will she still smile at me the way she used to or will she treat me like a stranger?

John clears his throat and smiles tightly. "I'd very much like her to stay with me," he says, his voice soft and pleading. He looks up at me and I know what he's going to ask me before he even says it.

"Can she stay here with me? Would that be okay with you?"

I inhale deeply and let my eyes fall closed as my head falls back on the massage chair. Emilia, living in my house? My heart beats just a little faster at the thought of it. It's been eight years since I last saw her. I have no idea how she feels about me and my family, but I doubt there's even one remotely positive feeling left. Not after everything we put her through. Not after everything my mother and sister have said to her. They broke her spirit right before my eyes, and I stood by and watched it happen.

"I'm not sure she'd be willing to, John," I tell him honestly.

"But if that's what you want, then yes, of course Emilia is welcome here."

He smiles at me gratefully and I try my best to smile back, but I can't manage it. I've been surviving on the memories I have of Emilia, and I wonder what it'll be like to see her again. Does she still think of me the way I think of her? Does she ever wonder what our life together might have been like? Does she ever miss me? I've always hoped that she does, and that I still own part of her heart the way she owns part of mine. I wonder if she'll shatter all of my illusions.

Having Emilia around, having her in my house... I have no idea what that might be like. Am I ready to see her again? For as long as I can remember, she's been *my person*. Now all I am to her is someone she used to know.

I sigh and run a hand through my hair. I've waited years to see her again, but now that it's finally happening, I don't know how to feel. So many times I've booked a ticket to London, only to cancel it at the last minute. She asked for a clean break, and after everything my family and I put her through, that's the very least I owed her. Yet I selfishly wished to chase after her. Sometimes I still do.

"You okay, son?"

I blink and glance at John. "Yes, of course," I murmur, forcing a smile onto my face. John looks at me, and something about the look in his eyes makes me wonder if he orchestrated this. I've been asking him to move in with me for months, and he finally agrees shortly before telling me Emilia is returning? What is he thinking?

"It'll be good for her to be here," he tells me, and something about his tone puts me on edge. "It's time for her to come home."

He says it with such decisiveness that I can't help but frown. I'd like to think he just wants her back here because he's sick and he misses her, but I know him better than that. No, he's got something up his sleeve, and I have a feeling it involves both Emilia and me.

CHAPTER 5

milia

I'm a wreck as I disembark the plane. Multiple times I end up apologizing because I find myself standing still when I'm willing myself to walk. I don't think I've even slept in two days.

All I've been able to think about is Dad, and everything he's been through by himself. I can't believe I wasn't there when he received his diagnosis. I can't believe I haven't been there for his first dialysis appointments. Sam walked me through everything Dad must have been through, and everything that's yet to come. No one should ever have to go through something like this by themselves. I'm Dad's only family, and I wasn't there.

Bitterness courses through me at the thought of Dad suffering by himself. I should never have stayed away for as long as I did. I never should've even left. Kate didn't deserve it. I shouldn't have been the one to sacrifice my family to save hers. If I could go back in time, I'd undo that choice.

I bite down on my lip and shake my head. What's done is done. All I can do now is be there for Dad going forward. I can't make up for lost time, no matter how much I might wish to.

I inhale deeply as I walk out with my luggage, my heart racing. I look around me, feeling nostalgic. The airport has changed so much, yet simply standing here after so many years still feels like coming home.

"Emilia!"

I turn around, surprised, my eyes finding Dad.

"Princess," he says, opening his arms wide. I drop my bags, my eyes filling with tears instantly. I walk into his arms and hold him tightly, a sob tearing through my throat.

"Daddy," I murmur, choking on my sobs. He looks so thin and frail. When did this happen? How could I not have noticed? What kind of daughter am I?

Dad chuckles and tightens his grip on me. "God, Emilia. I'm not dead yet, you know?" he says, and I cry even harder. Dad pulls away and holds me by my shoulders, a pained smile on his face. "You're still an ugly crier, huh? I missed your ugly little face."

I pout and try my best to stop crying, but my attempts to rein in my tears only make him laugh. "It's not funny. None of this is funny," I tell him.

Dad nods and hugs me tightly. "I know, honey. But like I said, I'm not dead yet, okay? None of this crying nonsense, all right?"

I nod, trying my best to get a handle on my emotions, and Dad wipes my tears away carefully.

"What are you doing here, Dad? I thought we agreed I'd rent a car and drive down?"

Dad smiles and brushes my hair behind my ear. "Couldn't wait to see my little girl again."

My heart warms and fresh tears runs down my cheeks. I inhale deeply and sniff. "Dad, are you even supposed to be driving?" I ask, my voice wobbly.

He chuckles and shakes his head. "I'm mostly fine, sweetheart. So long as I don't miss my dialysis appointments I'm fine. Don't you worry."

Sam did say that most people can go on to live for years so long as they receive regular dialysis, but Dad doesn't look *fine*. He looks sick and frail.

Dad grabs my hand and pulls me towards his car. I frown and glance at him. "New car?" I ask, taking in the Range Rover. It's stunning, and it's not something Dad would usually drive.

Dad grins and shakes his head as he checks his watch. "It's not mine," he tells me. "We'd better hurry. My new nurses are a bit strict," he says, shaking his head. "I'm pretty sure Carter hired them as payback."

I freeze, my heart twisting painfully. "Carter?" I whisper. A wave of longing goes through me at the mere mention of his name and I bite down on my lip as I strap myself in.

Dad nods as he starts the car. He falls silent as he drives us home, and I look at him. "Why would Carter hire you a nurse?" I ask, my voice trembling slightly. His name sounds foreign on my lips. It tastes forbidden. I've kept myself from thinking of him for so long now. Even speaking his name feels wrong somehow.

Dad smiles tightly. "Carter has been a pillar of support unlike no other. He's built me an entire treatment room with every piece of equipment I could ever need, so I don't need to travel outside of town for my treatments. He's arranged dieticians and chefs to curate my diet, and he's given me access to his home gym so I don't have to walk outside in the cold. But more than that, Emilia, he's become like a son to me over the last couple of years."

I blink in disbelief. "A *son*?" I repeat numbly, the mere thought of it horrifying me. Dad chuckles. He looks at me, his eyes twinkling.

"Well, sort of," he says. "I'll take him as a son-in-law too. I'm not too picky."

I stare at Dad in disbelief, my heart bursting with longing. Carter as Dad's son-in-law?

My heart feels funny at the mere thought of that, and I look at my dad through narrowed eyes. I raise my brows, ignoring his remark. "How? How did this happen? You haven't mentioned him in years. How could you two possibly be close enough for him to do all of that?"

Dad smiles at me. "Princess, this is Woodstock, not London," he reminds me, as though that's sufficient explanation.

I sit back and glance out the window. Carter and Dad being close surprises me. I've forced myself to think of nothing but Dad, and I assumed Carter would still be in L.A. I've seen him and his company on the news a few times, and from the little bit I know about him, he seems to be wildly successful.

I didn't think I'd even see him here at all. I can't help but wonder if he's with someone else now. If he's happy. If he ever thinks of me at all. My heart twists painfully at the thought of him having moved on.

I'm probably just a reminder of everything Kate went through, a part of their lives they'd rather forget about. I wonder how long it'll take before I run into her. I wonder if she's happy now, if she's healthy. I bite down on my lip harshly and force myself to turn my thoughts back to Dad. No one matters but him. I've put others above him in the past, and I've lost precious years with him because of it. I won't ever make that mistake again.

"We're here," Dad says, and I look up in surprise. Dad drives up to giant gilded gates, and they open automatically. I stare out the window wide-eyed and glance at Dad.

"Where are we?" I ask, my heart hammering in my chest. "This is *not* our house."

Dad looks slightly nervous as he glances at me, a tight smile on his face. "This is where I've been staying," he tells me. "Remember, I told you about the nurses and the chef?"

I stare at Dad in disbelief as he parks the car. I look up at the sprawling mansion in front of us, my heart in disarray. Slowly but surely, all the puzzle pieces are falling into place.

I'm about to question Dad further and object, when his phone alarm goes off, and he stiffens. Dad deflates, a sad expression on his face. He turns off his alarm and looks at me. "It's time for my dialysis," he tells me, and the despair in his eyes guts me.

I don't have the heart to argue with him about him staying here, or about everything he seems to have kept from me. The last thing I want to do is hinder his treatments in any way.

I grab his hand and follow him to his treatment room, my eyes widening when two nurses in uniform greet us as we walk in.

I look around the room in surprise. It just looks like a luxurious sitting room, with some expensive looking equipment by the wall. I'm pretty sure those chairs are massage chairs too. Just how expensive is everything here?

I sit down in the chair next to Dad's, and I flinch when the nurse inserts a needle into his arm. His blood starts to flow through the tubes, and I look at it in horror, my eyes filling with tears all over again.

Dad grabs my hand with his free hand and squeezes. "It's okay," he tells me. "It's fine."

I shake my head and sniff, trying my best not to cry. "It's not, Daddy. Let's go to the hospital tomorrow. I want to get tested. If I can, I'd like to donate my kidney. I just want you to get better as soon as possible."

Dad looks at me, panicked, and he swallows hard. "Absolutely not," he says, sounding angry. "I will never accept that, Emilia. Get that off your mind right now. If you so much as dare to even get tested against my wishes I'll put you back on a plane myself."

I sigh and lean back, my head dropping to his shoulder. I knew he'd be stubborn about this. It seems like I'll have to ease him into the idea of accepting a kidney donation from me, if I'm even a match at all. He looks grumpy, but he presses a kiss on top of my hair, and I smile to myself.

Dad turns on the huge TV on the wall and I smile when he puts a chick flick on, obviously for me. He wraps his arm around me and I lean against him as we watch the movie. I'm exhausted from the endless worry in the last couple of days, and the flight on top of that, but it's so good to be here with dad. I know there isn't anything I can actually do right now, but just being able to hold his hand while he's undergoing dialysis seems to make him happy.

"Tell me everything, Dad. Sam filled me in on what to expect, but tell me how it's been. Tell me how you feel, and tell me what I can do. Tell me how to make you feel better."

Dad presses another kiss on top of my head as he fills me in on all the medical procedures I had no idea he even underwent. I can't believe there's so much I missed out on, so much I wasn't there for. I need to make sure I'm by his side for everything from now on. I can't believe he's been going through all of this by himself. What kind of daughter am I? How could I not have known? How could I not have been there for him?

CHAPTER 6

milia

I wake up in a familiar bed and smile happily. How many times have I been here? How many times has my mind taken me back to these precious moments? I've had this exact dream for years now, and I still can't get enough of it. It replays in the exact same way every time, as though I'm watching a highlight reel of my favorite memories.

I turn over and trace the edges of the pillow next to mine with my fingers. I grin and scoot over to his side of the bed. It's still warm, so I know he can't have been up for long. I bury my face in his pillow and inhale deeply, my lungs filling with his scent, the butterflies in my stomach set ablaze. Carter.

It's only in this dream that I feel this alive. I can't tell if any of these memories, these dreams, are even real. I don't know if they're a figment of my imagination, a glorification of the past. They must be, because real life can't ever have been this good. The happiness I feel when I have this dream... it can't be real.

I sigh and sit up, the sheets falling to my waist. Even though he was with me just moments ago, I miss him already. My heart feels empty, the yearning heartbreaking in the best way. I bite down on my lip and rise to my feet, the floor cold underneath my feet. My eyes fall to the hooks we put on the door together, my robe hanging from one of them. I slip it on and tie the sash around my waist, grinning all the while, because I know it won't stay on for very long.

I walk out of our bedroom, our apartment so tiny that his eyes find mine the second the door closes behind me. Carter is standing in the kitchen, wearing nothing more than boxers. My eyes roam over his body, a pang of longing coursing through me.

He catches me looking and smirks as he leans back against the kitchen counter, his body on display for me. I walk up to him, and his hands thread through my hair the second I'm within reach. His lips find mine, and I rise to my tiptoes, my hands sliding over his shoulders and around his neck. Carter's lips feel soft against mine, and the gentleness he kisses me with make my heart overflow with happiness. I pull away and he drops his forehead to mine.

"Morning, Minx," he whispers.

My eyes flutter closed and I inhale deeply. His voice, his touch, the nickname that's exclusively his to use... I tighten my grip on him and hug him tightly, loving the feel of his body against mine. Standing here with him makes me feel like everything is right in the world.

Carter hugs me back, and I press my lips against his neck. I kiss him softly, and a shiver runs down his body. I smile to myself and kiss him again, teasing him.

"Minx," he warns.

I giggle and pull away. Carter looks at me, his hazel eyes filled with wonder. Every once in a while, he looks at me as though I can't be real, like he can't believe we finally made it, that we finally ended up together.

He shakes his head and hands me a cup of coffee. I glance at the cup, and my heart starts to race.

"Coffee in your favorite mug," he tells me, and I take it from him *with a smile, my eyes dropping back to the cup he asked me to be his girlfriend with.*

"Thank you, babe," I murmur, lifting it to my lips. Carter grins, and I narrow my eyes, the cup pressed against my lips. I pull it away and lift it to his lips instead. "Actually, I don't trust you. Taste test," I tell him, and Carter bursts out laughing.

"Damn it, Minx," he says, his eyes twinkling with mischief. "What gave me away? I promise this time I didn't do anything too weird. I love you too much for that. No salt or anything. I just didn't put sugar in, that's all."

I shake my head and keep the cup lifted up for him. "Nope," I say, trying my best to look stern, and failing because he makes me feel so incredibly giddy.

Carter laughs, and the sound goes straight to my core. I've never considered anyone's laugh to be sexy, no one's but his. I watch him as he takes a sip from the coffee, and he shrugs.

"Told you, baby," he tells me. "It's just coffee, sans the sugar."

I purse my lips and take the cup back, taking a teeny tiny sip, cautiously.

Carter laughs and wraps his hands around my waist, my robe coming undone. "I love you so much," he says, his voice soft.

I lean in and press a quick kiss to his lips. "I love you more, babe."

Carter lifts me onto the counter, and I almost spill my coffee. "Careful," I warn him. "I love this t-shirt."

He glances at the t-shirt I stole from him and shakes his head. "Minx, I have dozens of those t-shirts," he says. "Matter of fact, I think I should get you out of this one."

I wrap my legs around his waist, a thrill coursing through me when I feel his hardness against my inner thigh. Carter takes my coffee cup from me and puts it down on the kitchen counter.

In one fell swoop he's got me in his arms, his arm underneath my knee and my head lying against his chest.

Instead of supporting my back, his hand clutches onto my ass, and he squeezes tightly. I giggle as he carries me back to our bedroom.

I lift my hand to his face, my fingers tracing over his face, from his forehead down his nose and over his lips. I smile and wrap my hand around his neck as I pull him closer. My lips brush against his, and he inhales sharply. I grin and graze his lower lip with my teeth the way he likes, and he groans.

He sits down on our bed with me in his lap, and I pull his face back against mine. I kiss him, properly this time.

Carter doesn't kiss me back. Instead, he freezes, his grip on me becoming painfully tight. I whine in discomfort, the dream slowly slipping away.

My eyes open, and my heart stills when they settle on hazel-colored eyes. Somehow, I'm in Carter's arms, and this time, it's not a dream.

CHAPTER 7

 arter

I'm quiet as I walk into my house late at night. I've been unable to focus on work all day, much to Asher's dismay. All I've been able to think about is Emilia. Just the thought of seeing her again makes me nervous. I've been overthinking everything. I have no idea how she feels about me, how she's feeling about her dad's diagnosis, how hard it might be to be back here, to see my family again. I don't know what to say to her, how to even greet her. Do I even still have the right to call her Minx?

The entire house is silent as I walk to John's treatment room, and I check my watch. He should be finishing his dialysis right about now. I hesitate before I enter the room, my hand against the doorknob. I freeze in the doorway, my eyes finding her immediately. I stand there and just stare at her speechlessly. Emilia is fast asleep in the chair beside John's, and I can't tear my eyes away from her. She's even more beautiful than she used to be, even with those dark circles underneath her eyes. My heart races yet aches at the same time, a thousand different feelings slamming through me.

When I finally manage to tear my eyes away from her, I find John looking at me with a knowing smile on his face. I inhale deeply and shake my head. I'm willing to bet that the only reason he finally agreed to move in with me was because he knew she'd be coming back soon. I don't know what he's thinking, that crazy old man.

"She's asleep," John whispers. "She sleeps like the dead, but she'll hurt her neck if she spends all night here. Why don't you carry her to her room?"

It's on the tip of my tongue to tell him that the chair she's in flattens to a full-on bed, but I shake my head instead. It's not like I'd actually leave her here anyway. I nod at him and approach her silently, my heart hammering in my chest. It's been years since I've seen her. This all feels so surreal. I always thought I might run into her again one day, but never like this.

I sigh and lift her into my arms carefully. Emilia stirs in my arms, but then she sighs and rubs her head against my chest. I smile down at her subconsciously. Just having her back in my arms messes with my heart. All these feelings that I thought were gone came rushing back the second I touched her, and I wish I could just keep her in my arms. I wish the walk to her room was just a little longer.

I carry her to the room I prepared for her, the one right next to John's, and she moves in my arms restlessly. Emilia drags her nose along my neck and a delicious shiver runs down my spine. I freeze, my eyes falling closed. She sighs and presses a soft kiss to my neck, and I bite down on my lip to suppress a groan.

I'm about to put her down on her bed when she wraps her arms around my neck, holding on tightly. For a second I think she's woken up, but she hasn't. She's still asleep, but she's restless, a frown on her face. I sit down on her bed with her in my lap.

"What has you frowning like that in your sleep, Minx?" I whisper. She sighs at the sound of my voice, and her expression softens. Within seconds she's calm and fast asleep again. I look at her for a couple of seconds, her beautiful face, those lips that I've always loved, her blonde hair that's still in the same style she's always had it. Looking at her like this, it's so easy to imagine her the way she used to be. Back when she was still mine.

I turn to put her down, and Emilia stirs. Her lashes flutter and she smiles. I inhale sharply, my heart racing. It's been years since I've seen her smile. The countless pictures I have of her can't compare to the real thing.

Emilia sighs and tightens her grip on me, her palm flat on the back of my neck. I wonder what she's dreaming of. I wonder what's making her lips tip up in a faint mischievous smile like that.

She pulls me closer and my eyes fall to her lips. How long has it been since I kissed her? I still remember the way she used to groan every time I'd tease her by withholding a kiss, my lips hovering over hers the way they are now. She'd glare at me and then she'd pull me in, kissing me like there's no tomorrow.

I bite down on my lip and tear my gaze away from her. I'm so tempted to steal a single kiss from her, but I can't. I won't.

I'm surprised when Emilia pulls me closer, her lips brushing against mine. Emilia kisses me softly, gently, her lips soft against mine, and I freeze, my entire body tense.

Emilia pulls away, a dissatisfied frown on her face. Her lashes flutter, and she blinks lazily, her eyes finding mine.

Not even the videos I've got of her do her eyes justice. They can't capture the beautiful specks of golden brown in her eyes, or the way her lips turn up just slightly when she looks at me.

"Carter," she whispers, and my heart starts to race. How long has it been since I last heard her say my name? She smiles up at me dreamily, and I'm taken right back to the countless times I've woken up to her, this exact same expression on her face.

Emilia blinks a couple of times, disoriented, and then she stiffens. She sits up, still in my lap, and looks at me in shock. "Carter," she repeats, her tone entirely different. She pushes away from me and rises to her feet, practically jumping off my lap, her eyes wide.

"Emilia," I murmur, leaning back on her bed. My eyes roam over her body and I bite down on my lip. I knew seeing her would impact me, but this is unreal. My heart races, and I'm oddly nervous. When is the last time I was nervous?

Emilia stiffens as she wraps her arms around herself, and I tear my eyes away from her.

"I…" she says, clearly uncomfortable. I take her in, truly this time, and I can't help but frown. She just got here, so why is she wearing a pencil skirt and a blouse? She can't be comfortable in that, and the Emilia I used to know never would have travelled wearing something like that.

I rise to my feet and smile at her. "You fell asleep in your dad's treatment room," I tell her, and she nods.

The way she's got her arms wrapped around herself screams discomfort, and I hate that I'm someone she feels uncomfortable around.

"Your dad asked me to carry you to your room," I explain, wanting to reassure her, and Emilia nods again. She clears her throat and looks at me, and it's like I'm some stranger she's only just meeting for the first time. There's no familiarity in her eyes, and the physical distance she's keeping from me speaks volumes.

"Thank you," she says, nodding politely. "I understand you've taken great care of my father, and I'm beyond thankful, Carter. I had no idea you've been doing so much for him. Truthfully, I had no idea you two were close at all. I have no idea how to repay you for everything you've done."

I shake my head, my heart twisting painfully. I'm not sure

what I was expecting, but I thought that when we finally ran into each other again, it'd be different somehow.

"I'm happy to do it, Emilia. Over the years your father has become someone I consider to be my family. You don't need to be thankful in the slightest."

She nods and tightens her grip on her upper arms, her skin turning red just slightly. "I don't know what to say, truly. I'll do my best to stay out of your way. I know Dad wants me to stay here, but it's probably best if I stay at my old house. I don't want to inconvenience you in the slightest."

I shake my head and look at her. "Don't. He's been so optimistic lately, and having you around is going to help. If you go back to your old house, he'll want to follow. I can't stop him if he wants to do that, but the level of care I can provide him with here is far higher."

Emilia nods and looks around the room, her eyes lingering on some of the decorations. Some of it is stuff she bought when we first moved in together, and I could just never bare to get rid of it. I guess I expected a reaction of sorts, because disappointment fills me when I don't see recognition in her eyes.

"I'll leave you to settle in," I tell her, even though the last thing I want to do is walk away from her.

Emilia nods at me, and I turn to walk away, my heart in disarray.

CHAPTER 8

milia

I wake up just as the sun rises and get ready on auto pilot, the way I have for years. I could barely sleep last night. All I could think about was Carter. I didn't expect to see him. I certainly didn't expect to be staying in his *house*.

I inhale deeply as I make my way down, tired to the bone. My mind flashes back to how I woke up in his arms last night. For a couple of seconds, I thought I'd still been dreaming. I was so close to reaching out and kissing him. I wanted to thread my hand through his hair and lose myself in him, the way I do in my dreams. My heart clenches painfully and I shake my head. Being here, being around him is already messing with my mind, with my heart. I've spent years convincing myself that I'm over him, and right when I was ready to let go and move in with Sam, life pulled me back to him.

I walk into the kitchen, the first couple of rays of sunlight brightening the room, and I look around in awe. Like everything else in this house, the kitchen is amazing. I run my hands over the marble counter with a smile on my face. A small part of me wonders what it might have been like to decorate a house with Carter. I still remember how much he enjoyed the little changes I made to our bedroom in his small apartment, and it hasn't escaped my notice that some of the candle holders and decorative pillows in my bedroom are identical to the ones we used to have. My traitorous heart can't help but be a bit excited at the thought of Carter holding onto some of our things. It makes me feel like a small part of him might be holding onto *me*. I know I shouldn't want that, I shouldn't even be *thinking* it, but my heart is foolish.

I sigh and make myself a cup of coffee, the smell of fresh coffee waking me up just slightly. I'm startled when a door opens behind me, and I turn in surprise, my heart skipping a beat.

Carter is standing in the doorway wearing nothing but his swim shorts, his hair still wet, and my breath catches. He lifts a towel to his hair and I watch as a drop of water runs down his chest. "Carter," I whisper.

He looks surprised to see me and his eyes run over my attire, his brows rising. I look down and stare at my clothes in confusion. I'm dressed appropriately in suit trousers and a blouse, my makeup done perfectly, yet Carter somehow looks disappointed.

"Emilia," he murmurs, pausing in front of me. I look into his stunning hazel eyes, and my heart starts to race. Carter smiles at me and reaches past me to grab a coffee cup. His proximity makes my heart skip a beat, and for a second I'm tempted to reach out and touch him. Carter helps himself to a cup of coffee and I bite down on my lip.

"I, um, I didn't realize you were up, or I'd have asked your permission before using your kitchen," I murmur awkwardly.

Carter frowns and looks at me, and I hate that I can't read his expression. He's still Carter, but he's far from the twenty-two-year-old I used to be in love with. The man standing before me is all hard lines and unreadable smiles. He's so close, but he feels so far away.

"Since when do you ask for permission for anything? Besides, I told you that you're welcome here. Just make yourself at home."

I blink and then smile. He's right. When it came to Carter I've never once asked for permission to barge into his room and wreak havoc, but we aren't kids anymore. Besides, we haven't seen each other in so long that I find it hard to read him. I can't tell if he's just being polite, or if he's actually fine with me being here.

I glance around the room and lean back against the counter, trying my best to keep my eyes off his body. He looks amazing. He's far leaner than he used to be in college, and his muscles are so clearly defined that I can't help but wonder what they'll feel like underneath my fingertips. He's even more handsome than he's always been in my dreams. Reality isn't meant to be better than dreams are, but with Carter it always has been.

"So, this is your house, huh? It's astonishing, Carter. I always knew you'd be successful one way or another, but this is beyond my wildest dreams."

He leans back against the counter opposite me, and the way he looks at me makes me feel on edge. There's something about that look in his eyes that makes me feel like I'm somehow letting him down.

Carter pushes away from the counter and puts his coffee cup down before walking towards me. My heart starts to hammer in my chest as he cages me in, his arms on either side of me. I can't think clearly when he's so close.

"W... what are you doing?"

He grits his teeth and takes a step closer, his body only inches from mine. I'm so tempted to close the distance, to pull him against me. I can't help but wonder what he'll feel like, pressed against me. A thousand feelings I thought I'd buried come rushing back the second he's near me.

"For years I've wondered what it might be like if we were to run into each other, Emilia. *Years.*"

I gulp and look into his eyes, my heart pounding. Part of me wonders what he'd say if I admitted that I've always wondered the same thing.

"Yet here we are. Fucking strangers to each other. I always thought I'd one day see you again, and you'd still be mine. We'd still be *us.*"

Carter sighs and pulls away from me. He shakes his head and runs a hand through his wet hair. He turns his back to me, and my entire body is screaming for me to walk up to him, to run my hands over his body and pull him back. He still affects me like no one else ever has. He still has a hold over me.

"Make yourself at home here," he says. "I imagine you'll be here for a while."

I nod and smile tightly. "Thank you. I'll be here for a few months at least, but I'll try my best to stay out of your way."

Carter frowns. "A few months?" he asks. "So, you have every intention of returning to London if your father gets better?"

I look away and cross my arms. I have no idea how long I'll be here, but I know I can't stay. "I— yes, of course. My boss is aware that I'll be away for a few months, but she's expecting me back. My whole life is in London, after all."

"Your whole life, huh?" Carter says. "I see."

He shakes his head and turns to walk away, and somehow, I'm left feeling devastated.

CHAPTER 9

milia

I'm tense as I walk into the local clinic a few days later. Dad has been vehemently objecting to me donating one of my kidneys, and he won't even discuss it with me. He wouldn't even let me go in to get more information. I've had to pretend that I was running to the grocery store.

I'm anxious as I sit in the waiting room. I want to get these tests over with as soon as possible. It kills me to see Dad suffering every single day, especially since there's a chance I might be able to help him, to save him.

I walk into the doctor's office and much to my surprise, I recognize the doctor. "Layla?"

She looks up at me, shocked. "Emilia? What are you doing here? I thought you were in London?"

She and I were never close. I mostly remember her as Tony's little sister, and Gabby's friend. But still, I expected a slightly warmer welcome from someone I went to school with.

"I came back to spend some time with my father. That's actually why I'm here. I wanted to discuss whether it'd be possible for me to donate a kidney." She looks shocked as she sits back down and I smile at her. "So, you became a doctor, huh? That's amazing."

She nods, but it's like she doesn't even hear me, and I sit down awkwardly.

"I'm actually still in training. I mostly just get to do consultations like these," she tells me, smiling tightly. I nod. I figured as much.

She seems shellshocked to see me, and I guess that shouldn't be surprising. I haven't been back here in eight years. Not even once.

"Where are you staying?" she asks, her voice soft.

I blink, surprised. "I'm staying with my dad," I tell her, a polite smile on my face.

She swallows hard and looks away. "So, you're staying with Carter."

I forget that everyone knows *everything* in small towns. Everyone probably knows that my dad is staying with Carter, so it won't take long before they realise that I am too.

Layla shakes her head and inhales deeply. "Right, so, you want to discuss kidney donation? For women the main risks relate to childbearing. If you ever want to have children, then that's something to consider, and it's something I have to mention, but the risks are low."

I nod and take notes as she runs me through everything I need to know. I squirm just a little as she takes my blood, and before I know it I'm on my way again. In just a couple of days I'll know for sure how compatible my dad and I would be. I can't help but think about children as I drive back to Carter's house. I have no idea whether I even want them, but I do think I'd like for it to be an option.

I think back to when Carter and I were dating, my heart heavy. We'd told each other that we'd want children together one day. I remember wanting that with him, yet now I'm not sure I want any at all anymore. I certainly can't imagine having children with Sam.

———

———

I walk into the house absentminded, my thoughts on children and what my future might look like. When I imagine what my kids look like, I still imagine them the way I used to, with dark hair and hazel eyes... Carter's eyes. I sigh and walk into the kitchen, only to pause when I find the chef standing in the kitchen, in full uniform. He looks surprised to see me, and for a second, we both just stare at each other.

"Madam," he says politely, and I smile at him.

"Hi, Enzo," I say, greeting the chef. "Are you ever just going to call me Emilia?"

Enzo smiles and shakes his head. He's so formal — all of Carter's staff is. Enzo has done a great job taking care of Dad's diet, but I'm feeling mostly useless here, and I want to spoil Dad *myself* for once. There's so much staff taking care of his every need that there isn't much left for me to help with. I'm going half-crazy doing nothing all day.

I smile at Enzo pleadingly. "Do you think you could let me cook today?" I ask. Enzo smiles at me and shakes his head.

"Are you trying to steal Enzo's job?"

I whirl around and come face to face with Carter.

My heart hammers in my chest just at the sight of him. I haven't seen him in a few days now. Not since he walked into the kitchen, dripping wet. He's still every bit as handsome. If anything, he looks even better now. There's an edge to him that didn't use to be there, almost as though life has made him jaded. It's in his eyes, in the way he holds himself. He makes me nervous.

41

Even though it's been eight years, to me it all still feels so recent. I'm worried I can't be around him without acting awkward. I don't want to make him feel uncomfortable in his own home. I've been trying my best to stay out of his way, but it's been so hard. I keep wanting to reach out to him, when I know I shouldn't. I tried discussing me moving into our place with Dad, but just like Carter expected, he threatened to move back with me if I do so. He'd actually do it too; I have no doubt.

Carter looks at me, and the fact that I can't read his expression breaks my heart. I don't know the guy standing in front of me, yet I'm still clinging to who he used to be. I smile tightly and look away.

"Enzo, please give us a minute," Carter says.

The chef nods at Carter and walks away, leaving the two of us standing here. I look up at him wide-eyed, and he smiles at me. "Were you planning on making dinner?"

"I...yes... I thought it might be nice to make Dad a home cooked meal. I hope you don't mind."

Carter frowns and walks up to me. He places his finger underneath my chin and lifts my face up. I look into his eyes, surprised. Just having him this close makes my heart race, and it's got me feeling flustered.

"Emilia, do whatever the hell you want. You want to cook dinner? Do it. Honestly, just make yourself at home here. If I didn't want you here, you wouldn't *be* here."

I nod and Carter smiles. I breathe a sigh of relief when he takes a step away. I can't breathe when he's this close to me. "Do you need any help?" he asks, and I shake my head. "All right. I'll check in on your dad, and we'll both join you for dinner soon, okay?"

I nod and collapse against the kitchen counter the second he walks out. I close my eyes and inhale deeply. This is ridiculous. It's crazy that I still can't be around him.

I'm absentminded as I cook, and it isn't until I put the

lasagna in the oven that I realize I made Carter's favorite food. Or, well, what used to be his favorite food. I have no idea if it still is.

I'm nervous as I walk to the dining room. It's still odd for me to see Dad and Carter laughing together. Dad never even mentioned Carter in all the years I was away. Not even once. I had no idea they were close enough for Dad to *move in* here, and I feel oddly left out. Carter seems to have become such a huge part of my dad's life. How could I not have known?

I place the lasagna on the table and my eyes meet Carter's. For just a second, I see the guy I used to know, the one I used to love. He looks up at me in excitement. It's an intimate and adoring look, and my heart skips a beat. I blush and look away.

"It's vegan," I murmur. "Even the cheese is vegan. I only put in ingredients that are easy for your body to process, Daddy."

Dad nods and smiles up at me. He digs in as soon as I've served him a slice, and Carter drops his cutlery to his plate loudly. He's staring at Dad in disbelief and crosses his arms.

"What the fuck, John?"

Dad looks at him and shrugs.

"Months. For *months* I've been trying to get you to eat vegan cheese. You said you'd rather die than eat that crap, but the second Emilia puts it on your plate you eat it like it's fucking bacon. What the fuck?"

Dad looks at him and shrugs again before smiling up at me. "Delicious, Princess."

"Delicious? *Delicious*?" Carter repeats. "When I gave you the exact same thing you spit it out," he says, his eyes narrowed.

I burst out laughing and walk up to Carter. I put a serving of lasagna on his plate and drop my hand to his shoulder.

"I can ask Enzo to make you something else if you want?"

He shakes his head and grins at me. His smile still makes my heart skip a beat. "Nah, it's fine. Lasagna has always been my favorite."

I nod and sit down next to Dad, opposite Carter. For a few moments, the three of us eat in silence, and it's oddly nice. I haven't had a family dinner in so long, and I've missed this. I've purposely been missing dinner under the guise of still being unable to get used to the time difference, or being tired. All in an effort to avoid Carter.

My phone lights up on the table and I glance at it in surprise.

"Who's Sam?" Carter asks, his eyes my phone. There's an edge to his tone that makes me nervous, and I instinctively shake my head. My heart is racing and I'm panicking internally, but I can't quite figure out why. I grab my phone and silence it. It'll be much easier to call Sam back after dinner, in the privacy of my room. I haven't found a way to explain what's going on yet. Back when Sam and I were still friends, I told him all about Carter. There's no way he's going to be okay with me staying here.

"Sam's her boyfriend," Dad says, and Carter stiffens. "You said you two were moving in together, didn't you, Princess?"

I bite down on my lip and look down, avoiding Carter's burning gaze. "I'm not really sure when that's going to happen. I'm not sure how long I'll stay here. There's a lot to think about."

Carter crosses his arms over each other and stares me down. "That explains why you said your *entire life* is in London," he says, his voice harsh.

Dad glances at Carter and raises his brow. "That reminds me, how is Layla?"

My stomach sinks and I look at Carter in disbelief. "You're dating *Layla*?" I ask, my heart twisting painfully. So that's why she seemed so unhappy to see me this morning. The idea of Carter being with someone else wrecks me.

Carter grits his teeth and sends Dad a warning look. Dad

holds his hands up in surrender and Carter shakes his head. "I'm not dating her," he says.

Dad bursts out laughing. "Right. You're just shagging her, huh? Boy, after all this time you might as well make it official."

I feel sick. I can literally feel the color drain from my face. My heart aches at the mere thought of Carter with Layla. I knew he would've moved on, I just never expected it to be with someone I know. The two of them must be the town's golden couple. The successful entrepreneur and the doctor.

I rise to my feet and grab my phone. "Excuse me, I should really call Sam back."

Why do I suddenly feel like crying? It shouldn't matter to me that he's dating. He shouldn't matter to me at all. It's Sam I should be focusing on.

CHAPTER 10

milia

I lean back against my closed bedroom door and inhale deeply. What is wrong with me? Why am I this upset? I haven't even seen Carter in eight years. How could he possibly still affect me this much? So what if he's dating Layla? I shouldn't care.

I sink down on my bed and try to calm myself. It's just all these memories that are throwing me off, that's all. Besides, it's not uncommon to be curious about your ex. I clutch my phone tightly and scroll through my contacts until my finger hovers over Sam's number. What am I supposed to tell him?

I inhale deeply and press dial. He picks up almost immediately, and I feel even worse for not picking up during dinner.

"Hey," I whisper.

"Emilia, is everything okay? I tried calling you a few times, but I couldn't get through."

I bite down on my lip and nod, even though he can't see me. "Yes, everything is fine. It's just all been a lot. Dad seems okay, but he's hooked up to a machine for four hours every single day. It's really hard to see."

Sam sighs. "I looked up your hometown, and it looks like the closest dialysis center isn't even in your town. The commute must be exhausting for him too."

I freeze and fall silent, my heart racing. I can't not tell him, but I'm worried about letting him down. I feel like all I ever do lately is letting him down one way or another.

"There's something I need to tell you, Sam," I whisper. "But don't overthink it, all right?"

It's Sam's turn to fall silent, and for a second neither one of knows what to say. "You're worrying me, Emilia. What's going on?"

I inhale deeply and close my eyes. "I didn't quite realize, but while I've been away, my dad seems to have gotten quite close to the neighbors — to Carter. I'm not really sure if you remember him at all. I think I might have mentioned him once or twice, years ago. Either way, it seems like Carter offered to help with my father's treatment, and he has this room in his house that he's pretty much transformed into a private dialysis clinic."

I can hear Sam inhale deeply, and I can just imagine him pinching the bridge of his nose. "Carter, your ex? The guy you were so in love with that you wouldn't even give me a single chance for *years*?"

I shake my head as though he can see me and squeeze my eyes closed. "No, it wasn't because of him," I say, knowing full well that I'm lying to both him and myself.

"Emilia," he whispers. "I don't know what to say. I thought he was just someone you dated at college. You never even told me he's someone from your hometown. What does this mean? Do you see him every day now? How come you're only just bringing this up now? You've been there for a week."

I need to tell him the full truth, but I didn't think it'd be this hard. "I... about that... actually, before I even got here, my dad had already moved in with Carter. He's got this chef that cooks for my dad in accordance with his doctor's instructions, and he's got a personal trainer too. I've been meaning to tell you, but our conversations have been so short, with the time difference and all. I guess I also just didn't want to worry you needlessly."

My heart beats loudly as I wait for Sam's reply. I feel like I'm letting him down, and I hate that.

"Carter... he's not Carter *Clarke*, is he?" Sam asks, sounding tense.

I inhale deeply before replying. "I— yes."

"Your ex-boyfriend is the CEO of one of the most influential technology companies of all time? Clarke Reed is headquartered in Woodstock, isn't it?" he whispers, seemingly more to himself than to me.

"Technically, yes. But I don't care about any of that, Sam. He's just Carter to me. Besides, I barely even see him. And it's only you I want, Sam."

The words come out rushed, and I worry that he won't believe me. I swallow hard as he falls silent.

"I'm not comfortable with this, Emilia. I'm not comfortable with you staying in his house. Because that's where you're staying, isn't it?"

I fall back on my bed and sigh. "Yes. I'm sorry, I should've told you the second I got here. But honestly, all I've been able to think about is my dad. I've barely even seen Carter. We've spoken maybe a handful of sentences to each other. It's not a big deal, I swear. Besides, he's got a girlfriend anyway," I say, thinking of Layla.

"Not according to Google, he doesn't," Sam says, sounding angry.

"Are you seriously googling him right now?" I run a hand through my hair and sigh. "According to my *dad*, he does have a girlfriend. Not that it even matters. If I wanted to be with him,

I'd have come back home years ago. I didn't, Sam. I need you to trust me, okay?"

He inhales deeply before replying. "I do. I do trust you, Emilia. But I can't help but worry, nonetheless. I'd be insecure if he *wasn't* who he was. The worst thing is that I actually look up to the guy. The medical research his company is doing is phenomenal, and I hate that, you know? I hate everything about this."

"I know," I whisper. "I wish things were different too. I want nothing more than to be in London with you. I wish my dad was fine and none of this was happening. But it is, Sam."

He groans. "Shit, I'm sorry, Emilia. I'm being ridiculous. Put your dad first, okay? I'm sorry. I wish you weren't staying with *Carter Clarke*, but I'll deal with it. I know you're mine, and I know you're loyal. Besides, I was able to get a few weeks off next month, thanks to the endless overtime I've worked, so I'll come see you and your dad, all right?"

I bite down on my lip, a twinge of unease settling in the pit of my stomach. Sam and I agreed that he'd come visit as soon as possible, but that was before I realized I'd be staying with Carter. "You don't have to spend your entire annual leave on a trip here," I say carefully. "But I'd love to see you. I'd love to show you the town I grew up in."

Sam chuckles. "I can't wait to see it, and to meet the people you grew up with."

I inhale deeply. Is there even a single place I could take him where I don't have memories with Carter? I shake my head in an attempt to clear the memories. I can't go down memory lane.

"I can't wait," I tell him.

"I can't wait to see you," he says. "I love you, Emilia."

I stare up at my ceiling blankly, my heart filled with a dull ache. "I love you, too," I murmur, but for the first time in a long time, I'm questioning my feelings. If I love him like I've convinced myself I do, why don't I miss him? Why don't I need him when things are so tough? Why don't I crave his arms?

CHAPTER 11

arter

I walk into the kitchen at six in the morning, only half surprised to find Emilia standing in front of the coffee machine, dressed in that prissy way she likes nowadays. A tight black skirt that hugs her ass beautifully, and a pink blouse that I'm sure will cup her breasts perfectly. I'm already anticipating her turning around so I can get a better view.

I lean back against the wall and watch her for just a couple of seconds. I barely even recognize her. She doesn't smile the way she used to, and she no longer has that mischievous look in her eyes that I used to love about her. It's like time has chipped away at everything that made her so *her*. I wonder if she even owns any jeans anymore. I know for a fact that she rarely leaves the house, yet she wears these stuffy clothes and those hot fucking heels every single day.

I push away from the wall and Emilia turns, surprised. Her eyes widen when they land on me and I bite back a smile when her gaze roams over my body, lingering on my abs. She bites down on her lips, and I swallow hard. Looks like she enjoys my *fresh from the gym* look.

"Morning," I murmur, my voice gravely.

Emilia snaps out of it and looks up at me, her cheeks pink. "Good morning, Carter," she says, and the tone she uses irritates me. Everything that comes out of her mouth sounds so fucking formal. I look at her with raised brows and walk towards her to grab myself a cup of coffee.

"Where are you going this early in the morning?" I ask her, my eyes running over her body. I fucking knew it. Her breasts look amazing in that blouse. Why the hell is she still this beautiful?

Emilia blinks up at me. "Oh, nowhere. I have no plans. I was thinking of having breakfast with my dad, and then I'll have to see. I thought it might be nice to go into town."

I frown and lean back against the counter as I take a sip of my coffee. "You have zero plans, yet you're dressed like you're going to work. What's up with that?"

Emilia looks away, a flash of annoyance lighting up her eyes. "I can't very well walk around in my pajamas."

I bite down on my lip and her eyes follow my every move. "Hmm, I recall you lounging in my t-shirts all day, back when we lived together. If I recall correctly, you once tried to convince me that bras are torture devices concocted by misogynists." My eyes drop to her breasts and I lick my lips. "Looks like you've had a change of heart, huh? Here you are, *definitely* wearing a bra, *voluntarily*. You certainly don't need to on my account."

When my eyes travel back up to hers, she's staring at me wide-eyed. I grin at her and she blinks, her cheeks reddening. "I... that's... what?"

I bite back a smile. "I said you don't need to wear a bra on my account. If anything, I prefer you without the damn things on."

Emilia looks shocked, and I can't help but chuckle. That's

more like it. At least that damn prissy expression of hers has cracked. She glares at me and crosses her arms over each other, covering up her breasts.

"What would Layla think if she heard you say that? Do you have no respect for your girlfriend, Carter?"

I take another sip of my coffee and look at her leisurely. "Why should I care what she thinks? I've only ever had one girlfriend, and it was never her. It never will be, either, and she knows that," I say. I see the surprise in Emilia's eyes and I love it.

"So, like Dad said, you're just *shagging* her?"

I burst out laughing. "Shagging?" I repeat. "That word sounds ridiculous coming out of those pretty lips of yours."

Emilia looks away, the edges of her lips tipping up just slightly. I push away from the counter and walk up to her, pausing right in front of her. Emilia looks up at me and I place my finger underneath her chin, keeping her eyes on mine.

"Yes, I was *fucking* Layla. It didn't mean a thing. But you... you're moving in with some guy, aren't you? What's next? You marrying him, Emilia? Are you dreaming of becoming his little wife?"

I lock my jaw in anger at the mere thought of her living with someone else. Does that asshole get to wake up to her? Spend lazy Sundays in bed with her?

"*Was?*" she repeats. "You *were* fucking her or you *are?*"

Out of everything I just said to her, that's what she's focusing on? Interesting. "Does it matter?"

Emilia takes a step away from me and grits her teeth. "No, I guess not. She seemed pretty damn upset to see me yesterday, so if you're still with her, you might want to reassure her or something."

I freeze. "Where did you see her?"

Emilia looks away. "I went in to get my blood tests done. I

know Dad won't agree to it easily, but if I can, I'd like to donate my kidney."

My heart fucking drops. She got the blood tests done already? She's only been here for a little over a week. "You can't. I'll find a solution, Emilia. You aren't doing that."

She crosses her arms over each other and stares me down. "It's my choice, and my mind is made up."

"I'm sure Layla will have told you this, but for women the main risks are related to pregnancy. Are you aware that women who get pregnant after donating a kidney have a lower likelihood of full-term deliveries and a higher likelihood of fetal loss? What about those two kids you told me you wanted to have? A boy and a girl, right?"

I still remember her lying in bed with me, dreaming out loud about the children we'd one day have. She told me they'd have my eyes and her nose, and that our son would be a mini me. I remember how fiercely she wanted all of that. I know not every woman wants to have children, but the Emilia I used to know was close to picking their damn names.

She glares at me, a flicker of something dark in her eyes. "Layla told you all that? I'm well aware. Sam is a doctor too, and he ran me through all the risks. I'm fine with it."

She's dating a doctor, huh? Why couldn't he have been some sort of fuck up? Why did it have to be a fucking doctor? I inhale deeply and shake my head.

"No. You aren't doing this. I'm not having you risk your health like that, and neither will your dad. The recovery will be brutal, and the health-related consequences will impact you for the rest of your life. I'll find a black-market donor before I ever let you risk your life."

She looks at me with those stubborn eyes of hers and I almost grin at her. She's still got that spark. She just keeps it hidden.

"You're crazy if you think you can tell me what to do. There's nothing I won't do to save my father's life. He would've done the same for me," she says, pushing past me.

She slams the kitchen door behind her, and I sigh. There's no way I'm going to get her to change her mind. If nothing else, I need to keep her from getting her hands on those blood tests. For now, at least.

CHAPTER 12

milia

I'm still reeling from my conversation with Carter this morning.
I hate all these memories that are suddenly assailing me. I've
never once imagined myself having a child with Sam, but I
wanted children with Carter. I wanted it so badly that I could
even imagine what they'd look like. I wanted everything with
him. I wanted him to propose and I wanted to call him my
fiancé before finally getting to call him my husband. I wanted
to be Mrs. Emilia Clarke, yet I can't even imagine being Mrs.
Emilia Holden. I guess it's because I'm older now. I don't have
time for childish fantasies anymore.

"What are you thinking about so hard?" Dad asks.

I blink at him and adjust his blanket. He's hooked up to his
dialysis machine, and according to the clock we only have a
couple of minutes left. I shake my head and smile at my dad.
"It's nothing, Daddy."

Dad smiles at me and brushes my hair out of my face. "You
know you don't have to sit here with me every day. It just makes
me feel bad. Why don't you help Carter out with work? That

boy has done so much for me, but I can't repay him myself. Why don't you spend a few hours a day working with him? I won't feel so guilty about leeching off him, then."

I'm about to make an excuse, but dad holds up his finger. "And don't give me that crap about your work contract in London. You're a lawyer. Find a loophole."

I sigh. He's not leaving me much choice, and he's right. I can't even imagine how much all of this equipment costs, and then there's the nurse, the chef and the personal trainer. Carter has gone all out.

"Fine. I'll talk to him and check what he might need help with. I just wanted to spend as much time with you as possible, Dad."

The timer goes off and Dad yanks the needle out, startling his nurse. She runs up to him and shakes her head anxiously, and Dad sits back in annoyance. I glare at him and cross my arms over each other. "Let her do her job," I warn him.

"Fine, but I'm tired of staying in. Let's go for a drive, shall we? I need to pick up some stuff from the house anyway."

I nod and lead Dad to the front door, but he pulls on my hand and shakes his head. "This way," he tells me. He walks me to a garage that houses five different cars. All supercars, it seems. Dad grabs a set of keys from the hook by the door and walks straight up to a red car. He throws the keys my way and I shake my head.

"Dad, I don't think we should be driving any of these. I've been borrowing your old car. It's parked out front."

Dad shrugs and gets into the red sports car without a single worry. "It's fine," he says. "Carter won't mind you driving this."

I bite down on my lip nervously. There's no reason for Dad to lie to me, but I'm anxious nonetheless. These cars all look really expensive, and I wouldn't put it past myself to accidentally dent or scratch them.

"Come on, Emilia," Dad shouts, and I jump into action. I get into the car and just sit there for a minute. It isn't until Dad snaps at me again that I finally drive out of the garage.

I smile up at our house and park right in front of it. My full focus has been on Dad since I got here. I haven't even visited my old house yet. I'm excited as I step out of the car, only to freeze when the door to the house next to ours opens.

Helen walks out with a wide smile on her face, and my heart twists painfully. I look away, hoping we can both just pretend we didn't see each other, but Dad waves at her.

"Helen, darling, how are ya?" he shouts, and I grimace. It's been eight years. Of course, he's on good terms with our neighbors. I'm sure she's looked out for Dad in the time that I wasn't here to do it myself, but I can't stand to look at her nonetheless. I still vividly remember her handing me her credit card and asking me to move out of the place Carter and I shared. I remember her telling me that I shouldn't make things harder on Carter by staying. I always thought of her as the mother I never had, but in the end, blood is thicker than water.

I nod at her politely and tug on my dad's arm. "Emilia," Dad murmurs. "Come on, let's drop by and say hi."

I look up at him, my eyes flashing with rage. "No. I will not keep you from greeting our neighbors, but I refuse to join you in doing so," I tell him defensively. I know I'm hiding behind the lawyer persona I've built for myself, and it isn't fair on Dad, but I can't help myself either. I do it without thinking. "I'm happy to wait in the car for you, or alternatively, you can let me into the house," I add, my voice soft.

Dad looks at me, and for a second he looks so defeated, that I almost want to give in. But then he nods in understanding and waves at Helen as he leads me to the front door. Just seeing her again ruined my entire mood. Logically, I understand her choosing her daughter's happiness over mine, but at the same time, I can't forgive her for it. I can't forgive her for all the pain she caused and all the blame she placed on me. The only sin I ever committed was loving her son. I didn't deserve to be treated the way I was, especially not by a woman I loved like she was my own mother.

I walk into my old bedroom, my entire body tense with anger, and I lean back against my closed door. Everything is still the same. I stand there for a minute, just staring into Carter's room. How many times have I stood here, watching him? I sigh and push away from the door, slowly walking through my bedroom. I rummage through my wardrobe and pause on a tee I once stole from Carter. My fingers linger over the fabric, and I carefully take it off the hanger. I try my best not to overthink it as I fold it and put it in my handbag. They're just jammies, that's all.

I frown when I hear the sound of a sports car, and for just a second I worry I left the key in the ignition. I stick my head out the window and find Carter stepping out of a sleek black sports car. He looks up, and my traitorous heart skips a beat.

CHAPTER 13

arter

I walk up to John's house, a scowl on my face. He knows damn well no one is allowed to drive my babies but me. What the hell was he thinking, taking my Ferrari out? If Mom hadn't asked me to come over tonight, I probably wouldn't even have found out.

Instead of ringing the bell, I use my key and walk straight in, fuming. I find him sitting on the sofa, and he grins up at me smugly when he sees me storm in.

"You..." I say threateningly.

"Hey, Carter," Emilia says from behind me, and I turn around to face her. "What are you doing here?" she asks.

Seeing her standing here brings back so many memories. For years I've been wishing that I'd find her here, and now that she's finally back, it's all so surreal.

"I had a near heart-attack when I heard your car. I thought I left the key in the red one and that someone was trying to steal it."

I blink at her, surprised. "Um, *you* were driving my Ferrari?" I ask slowly.

Emilia nods at me and glances at her father. "That's okay, right? Dad said it was fine. I'm sorry, I should've checked with you personally. It's probably a really expensive car."

I shake my head and smile at her. Emilia behind the wheel of my Ferrari... I bet that makes for one hell of a sight. "Of course it's fine, Emilia. It's a car. It's for driving."

John chuckles and I turn to glare at him. "I told you," he says, smiling smugly. "Carter doesn't mind you driving his cars."

This dick. He knew full well that I don't like anyone behind the wheel but *me*. He's right, though. Oddly enough, I don't mind it so much when it's Emilia. She smiles up at me, and for just a second, she actually looks giddy. "It's such a pretty car," she tells me. "I just love the color, and it feels so nice to drive."

I smile at her indulgently. "You can keep it for now," I tell her, the words leaving my lips before I even realize it. "It suits you. I don't use it often enough anyway."

I must've lost my mind. That's my favorite car. I rarely even take it out myself. John looks at me with raised brows, and I can't even face him. Even after all these years, Emilia has this crazy hold over me.

I run a hand through my hair and bite down on my lip. She still affects me so much. So many times I've wondered whether she'd give in if I went to London and begged her to give me another chance. But she was right, eight years ago. Things between my family and her will never be the same again. Things between us will never be what they used to be, no matter how much I still want her. She'll never be able to be around my mother or sister without being reminded of the pain they put her through, and I could never ask her to suffer through that for me. I stayed away for a reason, and I need to remember that.

I sigh. "It's been some time since you've been here. Wanna go for a walk?" I ask her, trying my best not to overthink it. She's been going out of her way to avoid me since she got here, so I don't even expect her to say yes, but I can't help but try either.

Emilia looks startled and glances at her father, who is staring at the TV, pretending like he can't hear us. Emilia nods and then walks out, much to my surprise. I freeze for a second and then I rush after her, my heart beating just a bit faster.

I'm so tempted to take her hand, but I can't. I no longer have the right to nestle her tiny hand in mine, and it hurts. I convinced myself that I'd gotten over her in the years we've been apart, but now that she's here, I realize I was wrong.

Emilia and I walk in silence, both of us lost in thought. It isn't until we reach the treehouse that I snap out of it. I look up at it in surprise. I've paid top dollar to make sure that it's been maintained properly, but I haven't had the heart to enter in years. Emilia stares up at it with such a hurt expression that I regret leading her here, however subconscious it might have been.

"Is it okay if I go in?" she asks me, her expression filled with uncertainty. That she's even asking me surprises me. She's always done whatever the hell she wanted, and she's never once asked me for permission for anything. I still remember how she'd put a sign over the one Dad made for us, so it read *Kate and Emilia's Treehouse,* rather than *Kate and Carter's.* Replacing each other's signs was one of the fun parts of our little feud. When she realized I wouldn't give up, she vandalized my sign, turning the C in my name into an F. Didn't take me long to take it down after that, and she ended up winning that fight.

"Of course," I say, smiling at her fondly. I wonder what she thinks of when she sees the treehouse. I wonder what her favorite memories are here.

Emilia smiles at me and carefully walks up the stairs, her

heels clicking against the wood. I follow closely behind her, terrified that she might trip. I breathe a sigh of relief when she reaches the top. Emilia's hand trembles as she opens the door, and I wish I could grab hold of her.

She stands in the entrance, a million different memories flickering through her eyes. I wonder what she's seeing. This is where we met. It's where we both lost our virginity, and it's where I asked her to be my girlfriend for the very first time. This place houses some of our most precious memories.

Emilia sighs and walks in, her expression sad as she sits down by the window, right where I found her crying over her mother, long before she and I even realized we were in love with each other. I swallow hard, my heart twisting painfully.

"Thank you for letting me come up," she whispers, a small smile on her face, and I shake my head.

"Since when do you ask for permission to enter the treehouse, Emilia? Since when do you thank me for something so irrelevant?"

I walk up to her and sit down beside her. "It's only polite," she tells me, and I smile humorlessly.

"Polite? I don't want you to be polite to me. I want the girl that would challenge me over the slightest thing. The girl that loved jeans instead of these damn skirts you wear nowadays. The girl that threw fake cockroaches in my bed and that would mess with me every way she could think of. What happened to her?"

Emilia looks at me, her expression guarded. "She grew up," she says, her voice barely above a whisper.

I look away, unable to hold her gaze. I did this to her. To us. My family and I wrecked her, and all that's left is the ruins of us.

"I've wondered about you for years," I tell her honestly. "I don't think a day has passed that I didn't think of you."

Emilia looks at me, her expression pained. I smile at her, but my heart is aching.

"Part of me wondered if we'd ever find our way back to each other. If you'd ever come back home. If you'd ever be able to forgive my family, and if you'd ever give me another chance."

I run a hand through my hair and sigh. Emilia stares over my shoulder, lost in thought. When her eyes find mine again, she looks angry, and I regret saying anything at all.

"I won't," she says. "I won't ever forgive them, and you and I... that will never happen. I'm not staying here. I'm really only here for my dad, and if it's up to me, I won't see your family at all."

I nod and try my best to keep from showing how badly her words hurt. For so long I've held onto hope that maybe someday, Emilia and I could be together again. With just a few words she took that all away.

Emilia smiles one of her polite smiles, her expression guarded.

"What's in the past is in the past. It's done, and I honestly don't even want to think about it. I *would* like to sincerely thank you for looking out for my father the way you have been," she says. "I had no idea you two were even on speaking terms. I had no idea you did so much for him while I was away. It should've been me, but I... I wasn't there for him, and that's on me."

My heart fucking shatters. She and I both know why she wasn't there. I'm the reason she's stayed away from home for as long as she did. "Emilia, I... please don't thank me for that. It's the least I could do. It isn't enough."

She shakes her head, her eyes filled with heartbreak. "Of course I should thank you. But I'd also like to repay you. I'm going through my father's insurance contracts to see whether I can reimburse you at least partly in that way, and I'll repay whatever is left myself. In addition, I'd be happy to work for you while I'm here. I know it won't offset my debt to you by much, but every little bit helps, right? I think it'll help alleviate Dad's guilt too."

I nod at her. I might not know her that well anymore, but deep down she's still my Emilia. Once she has her mind set on something, I won't be able to sway her. If this is what she needs for now, then that's how it'll be.

CHAPTER 14

arter

I'm annoyed when my assistant announces that Layla is right outside my office. She knows full well that I hate it when she drops by unannounced. Layla walks in and smiles at me. I sigh and run a hand through my hair. I'm already tired of this conversation and she hasn't spoken a word yet.

"What are you doing here?"

Layla smiles at me, but her smile wavers. She walks up to me and rises to her tiptoes, obviously attempting to kiss me. I grab her shoulders and hold her in place, not allowing her to move any closer to me. Her eyes flash with indignation and hurt, and I sigh.

"Carter," she murmurs. "I missed you."

I let go of her and sit back down. Layla leans back against my desk and looks at me, her expression unreadable.

"Haven't you missed me too?"

I frown at her. "What is this? You always knew what we are and what we aren't. Have I ever been unclear about it?"

Layla shakes her head and looks away. The pain in her eyes

guts me. She's a sweet girl, and I hate hurting her, but I can't ever give her what she wants from me. I'll never love her. I have no love left to give in this lifetime.

"Is it her? Is it because she's back?"

Layla grabs my tie and I look at her, my gaze unwavering. "Yes," I tell her honestly. Even though I know I can't have Emilia, I can't stomach the thought of being with someone else when she's this close. When she sleeps underneath my roof. I can't do it. "You and I are done, Layla. Hell, we never even were a thing, but whatever it was, it's done."

I've been meaning to end things with her in person, but I couldn't be bothered to even meet up with her. I'm glad we're getting that over with now.

Layla fists my tie and yanks on it before unraveling it. "I heard she has a boyfriend. She seems happy. Are you really going to wreck that happiness? Do you really want to be the other man?"

Her words hurt, like they intended to, but I don't give her the satisfaction of letting it show. Layla unbuttons my shirt slowly, her eyes on mine. "I guess you can probably convince her to have a little affair while she's here. She might even appreciate having someone to bang before she goes back home to her boyfriend."

Her hands run over my chest and I grit my teeth. I grab her wrists and stop her from groping me. "Whatever might be happening between her and me is none of your business, Layla."

She laughs and pulls her hands out of my grip. "You'll come running back. You've been so stuck on the idea of her. It won't take you long to realize that you've idealized the memory of her. There's no way the real thing can measure up. You'll come back to me, with renewed appreciation for what we have. Mark my words."

She pushes away from me when someone knocks on my

door, a smile on her face. "You need to stop living in la la land," I tell her, just as my office door opens.

Emilia walks in, and she freezes when she sees Layla and me standing together. The expression on her face can only be described as utter devastation, and hope soars within me. The look in her eyes... she definitely still cares, and she's not happy.

"It looks like I'm interrupting," she says. "Should I come back later?"

I shake my head and do the buttons of my shirt up carefully. "No. Layla was just leaving."

Layla grins at me as though she's well aware that I won't be able to talk my way out of the impression she just created, and she winks at me before walking out. Fucking hell.

Emilia looks angry as she walks into my office, her eyes lingering on my undone tie. She looks at me like she might actually throw something at my head, and I bite back a smile. She's jealous, and she's failing to hide it. It's not often, but every once in a while, that mask of her cracks, and I enjoy watching it happen. I leave my tie undone and lean back in my seat as Emilia approaches my desk.

"How inclined to believe me would you be if I tell you nothing happened just now?"

She crosses her arms over each other, but all that does is highlight her breasts more. I bite down on my lip and look away.

Emilia looks at me, hurt and disbelief flickering through her eyes, before she forces a neutral expression on her face. "I'm not sure why I should care either way."

I grin at her. She's so obviously angry, yet she insists she doesn't care. For a while I was certain that she was over me, but that can't be right. She wouldn't be glaring at me the way she is if she were over me.

"Hmm, if you don't care, then I guess there's no point in

telling you that I ended things with Layla. Not that there was much to end, anyway."

I see the small flicker of relief in her eyes and smile to myself. Emilia looks away and clenches her jaw. "So what was that? Break-up sex?" she asks, her voice wavering, as though the mere thought of it hurts.

I take my time studying her. She's beautiful, and she's still her. She might be hiding underneath that prim persona she created for herself, but when provoked or hurt, that facade cracks.

"Do you really think she could've walked out the way she just did if I'd fucked her on my desk? It seems you forgot what being with me is like. Would you like a reminder?"

Emilia's eyes are blazing with equal parts outrage and passion. Is she remembering what we used to be like? She's still the best I've ever had, and I pray it's the same for her.

"And before you ask, or even wonder with that twisted little mind of yours, *nothing* happened at all. I didn't even kiss her."

Emilia looks into my eyes as though she's trying to figure out whether I'm lying or not. She might be telling herself that she doesn't care whether I'm with someone else or not, but she does. She fucking does.

Emilia seems satisfied with what she finds in my eyes, because her shoulders relax and she takes a seat in the chair opposite mine.

"I told you I don't care. Fuck the entire town for all I care," she says, and I smile to myself.

"Well, at least you aren't calling it *shagging* anymore. I'm not even sure I can get it up if you're calling it that."

Emilia looks at me wide-eyed, and I chuckle. She's easily scandalised these days, huh?

She crosses her arms over each other and pins me down with a pointed stare. "Anyway," she says, "I'm here to discuss what I can help you with, as agreed."

I nod and push a stack of documents her way. I wonder if she still remembers what I told her all those years ago when I first told her about the business ideas I had — that I'd build a huge company, and she'd be my in-house council. The time I get to share with her might very well be short, but part of me is still excited to be living the dream I had years ago.

CHAPTER 15

milia

I close my dad's bedroom door quietly. He hates it when I put him to bed, so I've resorted to sneaking into his room after he's fallen asleep. I've gotten into an entire routine. I'll wait for him to announce that he's going to bed, then I'll shower and change into my jammies, and by the time I'm done, he's usually fast asleep. I just can't go to bed without seeing him asleep peacefully. I worry too much that he's up thinking about his future, or that he might be suffering by himself. So far, he's done great, but I'm worried that he might just be pretending to be strong for me.

I sigh as I walk into the kitchen, wanting a glass of water. I'm absentminded as I reach for a glass and fill it up. I've already been here for three weeks, but I still don't have the results of my blood tests back.

"Interesting choice of pajamas."

I jump at the sound of Carter's voice and nearly drop my glass. I turn around, my hand pressed to my chest. He's standing by the door, a whisky glass in hand, his chest bare. My eyes roam over his body. Looks like he isn't wearing much more than shorts that hang low on his hips. It's unfair that he still looks this good. Where does he even find the time to keep in such good shape?

"Carter," I whisper. I belatedly look down at what I'm wearing and blush fiercely. I'm wearing the t-shirt I found in my closet. The one I stole from him years ago. Carter walks up to me, and my heart starts to race. His eyes roam over my body and linger on my bare legs. His t-shirt is long enough to cover me up to mid-thigh. It's almost like a dress to me, but I really should've worn more than panties underneath.

"Can't sleep?" he asks, and I shake my head. He pauses in front of me and touches the edge of my sleeve, a thoughtful expression on his face. "Where did you even find this?" he whispers, and I look up at him with wide eyes.

I panic. "It's Sam's. I'm wearing it because I miss him," I say, lying to his face. Carter's expression is steady and he nods. I'm not sure why I expected to find at least a little bit of jealousy or anger. I guess it's because that's what I felt when I saw him with Layla. It was obvious that she's the one that pulled his tie off. He might have said that nothing happened, but he obviously let her touch him. I was burning with jealousy when I walked into his office, yet he stands here in front of me, unaffected, even though I told him I'm wearing Sam's tee.

Carter takes another step closer, and I take a step back, my hips hitting the kitchen counter. "The man has good taste," he murmurs. "How could he not, when it's you he fell for?"

Carter raises his hand and gently brushes my hair out of my face. I can't breathe when he's this close to me. I can't get my eyes to behave. I keep catching myself staring at his chest and his abs, and a depraved part of me can't help but wonder if he'll still feel the same under my touch. Will I still be able to make him shiver if I run my fingers over his abs, straying precariously close to where he always wanted me touching him? I bite down on my lip as hard as I can and tear my gaze away. Nothing good will come from wondering about things I can never ever have again.

Carter raises his glass and hands it to me. I take it from him carefully and take a sip, the liquor burning through my throat. I resist the urge to cough and take another sip. A drink is exactly what I needed.

Carter looks at me, his eyes heated, and I pray that he won't realize that my body still responds to his proximity the way it always has. I'm hyperaware of him. Carter has always been in my very veins, even when I don't want him to be. I thought time might have changed things, but it hasn't. The second I laid eyes on him every feeling I thought I buried came rushing back.

"What's Sam's full name?"

I blink, surprised at the question. "It's Samuel Michael Holden."

"Hmm," Carter says, the edges of his fingertips brushing over my chest. "Then why is it *my* initials that are embroidered on this t-shirt?"

I look down with wide eyes. How could I have forgotten about that? It's tiny, but right over my left breast there is indeed a small little monogram, a relic from Helen's embroidery phase. I blink, my cheeks bright red. Thank god it's late at night and the lights are dimmed.

Carter moves closer to me and I inhale sharply. He's far too close. Just one single step, and his body would be pressed against mine. I should move away, but I'm frozen. It's been years since he and I have been this close, and try as I might, I can't make myself push him away.

"I have newer t-shirts, you know," he whispers. "I'm surprised you haven't sneaked into my bedroom yet. There's so much shit for you to steal. I have a whole collection of hoodies that you can *borrow*, and so many t-shirts that you'll never run out of pajamas, though I much prefer you without them anyway. But if you *must* wear them, then I guess I like you best in my tees. But then again, I haven't seen you in one of my dress shirts yet. I can just imagine it... I think I might just like that better."

I'm breathing hard and my eyes fall closed just as he presses a soft kiss to my shoulder. I try my best to harden my heart and step away from him. I can't even bare to look at him. "Please," I whisper. "Don't do this, Carter. I'm in a relationship. I love Sam. I want to be with him. Don't do this. Let's not go down memory lane."

He looks up at me, anger flashing through his eyes. "You *love* him?" he whispers, and I nod. Carter smiles at me, but there isn't a trace of humor in his expression. "Does he make you laugh? Does he know how to make you sigh, how to make you moan, how to make you scream his name? Does he bring out your devious side? Does he make you lower that damn shield you've put up?"

Carter takes a step away from me and shakes his head. "You don't love him, Emilia. You *want* to love him, but you don't. He doesn't own you the way I did, and you know it."

Carter walks away and I stare after him, terrified that he might be right.

CHAPTER 16

arter

"What's wrong with you?" Asher asks.

I glance up from my screen to look at him, a frown on my face. "What?"

"You've been absentminded all day. What's going on?"

I hesitate and run a hand through my hair. He's been trying to run me through a potential acquisition he's excited about, and I should probably be paying more attention. I really should have told him. "I offered Emilia a job here," I say cautiously. "Told her we could use her legal expertise."

Asher freezes and then looks away, his expression troubled. "Are you sure you want to do this, Carter? She's got a boyfriend, doesn't she? Has she even spoken to your mother or your sister yet?"

It's been years since I've heard him say Kate's name. His wounds seem to be as deep as mine, yet we've both mastered the art of pretending like we're fine.

"I know she does, and no, she hasn't. But does it matter? Does any of that matter, Asher? I let her go years ago because I was trying to put my family first, and because Emilia was right. We couldn't have survived the total chaos our lives had turned into. But now? What's holding me back now?"

Asher looks up at me and shakes his head. "The fact that she has a *boyfriend*, Carter. She has an entire life back in London. A life she'll go back to, eventually. Where will that leave you? It took you years to get over her, man. I saw you tearing yourself apart for years, burying yourself in more work than any man should reasonably do. For years you were barely even alive. You're finally at a stage where you're happy again. I don't want to see you fall apart, man. Not again," he says, an anguished expression on his face. For years Asher was worried sick about me, and he's right. I was a fucking wreck for far longer than I want to even admit to.

"Besides, what will Emilia have here?" Asher says, his tone cautious. "Just because so much time has passed doesn't mean that her wounds have healed. Don't you remember how your mother treated her? The things your sister has said and done? Because I do. I remember Emilia crying her heart out over you and your family. Being with you means she'll have to confront all of those memories. If she's with you, she'll have to smile at your sister and your mom at every single family occasion, even if it kills her. And because it's Emilia, she *will*. She'd tear her own heart out if it made you happy. Can you put her through that during every Sunday family dinner? Can you bare the alternative, which would be either you not going at all and letting your mother down, or leaving Emilia at home and making her feel like she's letting *you* down? You can't ask any of that of her. You can't, Carter. You can't pursue her if you can't make her happier than her boyfriend can."

I look out the window and watch my red Ferrari approach. Emilia parks right in front of the building and steps out of the car, unaware of all the attention she's getting. She's always been clueless like that. She never realized how beautiful she is. How incredible she is.

I tear my eyes away from her and look back at Asher. This is exactly why I didn't tell him that I offered Emilia a job. Because I knew he'd say the very things I didn't want to hear — but needed to. "It's just a job," I say, my mood ruined. "All I offered her was a job. Besides, I told her she can work from home so she can be with her dad. She'll only ever really come in for meetings she can't miss."

Asher shakes his head. "It's never that simple when it comes to Emilia. Don't ruin the life she's so painstakingly built for herself. Don't pull her back into the life she tried so hard to escape. Don't seek out hurt, Carter."

I'm still thinking of his words hours later, when I walk into a meeting that I asked Emilia to be present for. I was planning on onboarding her myself, but thanks to Asher, that was left to Human Resources. I know he's trying to look after her in his own way, but he's irritating the hell out of me.

Emilia looks up with wide eyes as I walk in, and it takes me a second to realize that it isn't even me she's looking at with such happiness. She rises from her seat and walks straight past me, practically throwing herself in Asher's arms. He hugs her tightly and presses a kiss to her hair. "Hey, Milly," he murmurs, tightening his grip on her. She hugs him, her body pressed to his.

I look at Asher through narrowed eyes and grit my teeth. If he doesn't let go of her in the next couple of seconds, he won't be coding shit for the next couple of weeks. Hell, he won't be using his arm at all.

Asher looks at me, his eyes twinkling with amusement, and he squeezes her tighter before he lets go of her. I didn't even realize my entire body had tensed until she takes a step away from him, and I can finally breathe easy again.

"My gosh, how have you been? You look amazing," Emilia

says, sounding excited. She didn't even show me an ounce of that excitement when she saw *me* again. Matter of fact, she wasn't even remotely excited. If anything, she seemed perfectly unaffected. I've never been jealous of my best friend, but right now, in this moment, I am. I can't believe he got to hold her in his arms the very second he saw her, yet she jumped out of mine the second she laid eyes on me.

Asher places his hand on her lower back as he walks her back to her seat, and much to my annoyance, he takes the seat next to hers. The one I'd been eyeing. I bet he fucking knows what he's doing too. I know he's right. I know I should stay away from her. But fucking hell, it's *Emilia*.

I can't focus at all during the meeting and keep nodding absentmindedly, earning me a few kicks from Asher. Eight years, and my heart still races at the sight of her. She's still the most beautiful thing I've ever seen. Asher is right, though. I need to put her happiness first, and no matter how hard I try, no matter how much money I have, no matter how much I fucking love her, I can't erase the past. I can't take away the pain she suffered at the hands of my family. I can't be the one to make her happy, no matter how badly I want to. I've known Emilia almost all my life. The one thing she's always craved above all is a loving family. I can't give her that. And even if I could, it's not me she wants it with.

CHAPTER 17

milia

Something is wrong, but I can't figure out what it is. Carter seemed absentminded all day, upset even. I can't quite pinpoint how I know, but I do. I glance down at my tee and hesitate for only a second before grabbing my leggings and tugging them on.

I make my way through the giant house and pause in the living room, my eyes on the large glass sliding doors that lead to the veranda. As expected, he's standing there, staring up at the sky, a whisky glass in his hand. He doesn't seem to feel the cold, even though he's only wearing shorts and a loose tee. It's not winter quite yet, but it's definitely too cold to be standing there dressed like that.

I bite down on my lip and walk over to the sofa to grab the thick furry throw. I hesitate before walking up to the doors, and I inhale deeply before walking through them. The sound of the door sliding open startles Carter, and he turns to look at me in surprise.

I walk up to him, my feet freezing, and pause in front of him. I look into Carter's stunning hazel eyes and wrap the throw around him, gripping the ends tightly. "You'll get cold," I whisper, my voice disturbing the tranquility of the night.

Carter looks at me like I'm some sort of mirage. The way he's looking at me makes my heart race. For years I've dreamt of him looking at me like that, just one last time. Every single time that he visited me in my dreams, he'd look at me like this, and I'd wake up in tears, knowing it'd never happen again. My heart clenches painfully as Carter raises his hand to my face. He cups my face gently, and I lean into him subconsciously.

"What are you doing here, Minx?"

My eyes widen and my heart starts to race. It's been years since I got to hear him call me Minx, and I didn't quite realize how much I missed it.

"What do you mean? I'm here for my dad, of course."

Carter shakes his head and tugs the throw out of my grip. He wraps it around the both of us, his hands on my shoulders.

"What are you doing out here? Your dad isn't here. It's just me."

I look away, unsure how to reply. "I don't know," I answer honestly. Dad has already gone to bed and I've already checked up on him. I'd just been twisting and turning in bed, unable to keep my mind off Carter. "I was worried about you," I admit. "You seemed upset today."

Carter takes a step closer to me and wraps his arms around me fully, closing the distance between us. My breasts graze against his chest, and I have to resist the urge to melt into him. I look up at him, my heart beating wildly.

"You noticed I was upset, huh? No one else did. Not even Asher. How come you still read me so well, Minx? How come you still notice every little thing about me?"

I bite down on my lip as I stare into his eyes. I could get lost in those eyes of his. The specks of green and all the different shades of brown have always captivated me. "I don't know," I whisper.

Carter sighs and drops his forehead to mine, his eyes fluttering closed. He inhales deeply, and I close my own eyes, wanting to lose myself in this moment with him.

"Are you happy, Emilia?" he asks, his voice barely above a whisper. Am I? I like to think I am, and most days I can make myself believe it too. But have I been truly happy since I lost Carter? I don't think so. There's no point in admitting that, though.

"Yes," I whisper. "I am."

Carter inhales deeply and tightens his grip on me. This moment feels so precious. I can't remember the last time I wanted a moment to last forever. I guess the last time I felt this way was with Carter too.

"Sam... does he treat you well?"

My heart wrenches at the thought of him, and I feel guilty immediately. I stiffen in Carter's arms and bite down on my lip. The truth is that right here, right now, I'm happier than I have been in years. Why is it that no matter how hard I try, I don't ever feel this way with Sam? I want this so badly with him. He deserves it.

"He does. He treats me incredibly well. He's very kind and considerate. I'm very lucky to have him."

Carter tenses, and I feel bad. I wish he'd never even asked me that question, but I can't lie to him either. Sam is amazing and I'm not sure I'm even good enough for him.

"Are you?" I ask. "Are you happy?"

Carter remains silent, his chest rising and falling against mine. "No," he says eventually. "I haven't been happy since you walked out of my life, Emilia. I haven't even truly felt alive since you left."

Carter pulls away from me and wraps the throw around me, leaving himself exposed. "It's good to hear that you're happy, though. It's all I've ever wanted for you. I'm glad you found your happiness, even if it isn't with me."

I force myself to smile and nod at him. These things that I'm suddenly feeling around Carter... it's all just nostalgia. At the end of the day, I'll still go back to London, to the life Sam and I are building together. I'll still move in with him. I can't get caught up in whatever it is I'm feeling right now.

"You'll find your own happiness too, Carter," I tell him. I guess the sayings about first love are true. You never really get over your first love. I don't know how else to explain the rage I feel at the thought of Carter with someone else.

"Maybe," he whispers, but I can tell he doesn't believe it. Carter brushes my hair behind my ear and smiles at me.

"I'm glad you're back, Emilia. Home hasn't been the same without you."

I nod at him. "It's good to be back. I wish I'd come back sooner, to be honest."

Carter smiles, yet his expression is heartbreaking. "Me too," he whispers.

He clears his throat and inhales deeply. "Look, you and I... we'll always have history. But you'll be living here for the foreseeable future, and you'll be working with me too. I'd like it if you and I could try to be friends. I think your father would appreciate that too. No more sneaking around trying to avoid me around the house or at work."

I blush and look away. "You noticed that, huh?"

Carter chuckles, and the sound makes my heart flutter. "I notice everything about you," he whispers. He looks away and so do I. My heart can't take it when he says things like that.

"Yes, of course," I murmur. "We should try to be friends. We were friends before we were ever anything else."

Logically I know that's true, yet I can't think of a time that I wasn't in love with Carter. Were we ever even truly friends? Even before I realized it, I considered him to be mine.

Carter smiles and nods, and that's that. We're *friends*.

CHAPTER 18

arter

I'm still thinking about Emilia in my t-shirt when I walk into the office in the morning. My Ferrari was missing, so it seems my little Minx escaped before I got to speak to her. She won't be able to evade me for very long at all, and I doubt she even wants to. Asher's words threw me off, and I know there's truth to what he said... but part of me wants to prove him wrong. Even though I know he's right, I can't stay away from Emilia.

I spot her the second I walk into the office. Her eyes find mine, and a blush spreads on her cheeks. She looks away, flustered, and I smile to myself. Whether she likes it or not, she's still affected by me. She's deceiving herself if she thinking she's in love with Sam. I walk up to her, and she brushes her hair out of her face, the movement almost... nervous.

"Morning," I murmur.

She looks up at me, and my heart skips a beat. This woman, will her beauty ever cease to faze me?

"Morning," she whispers.

I tilt my head towards my office, and she follows me, a hint of reluctance in her steps.

"Asher and I are considering a new acquisition, and I'd like you to accompany me as I set the deal in motion. The CEO of the company I've been wanting to acquire has been hesitant to sell to me, but he's suddenly turned around and agreed late last night. I want to close this deal as soon as possible, before he has a chance to change his mind again. That means there's a lot of due diligence to be done, and it needs to be done now."

I tilt my head towards the suitcase in the corner of my office. "We'll be gone for three days. I would've told you in the morning, but you were nowhere to be seen."

Emilia's cheeks redden, and she looks away. I bite back a smile and look down at my shoes, unable to wipe my smirk off my face completely. She's flustered and affected by me, and she's failing to hide it.

"The client is in New York. Our flight is in four hours," I tell her. "We'll be going with a small team, but I expect you to take the lead on the legal aspects."

Emilia nods, a serious expression on her face. Her eyes flash with determination, as though she's intent on doing a good job, and I smile to myself. She's always been this way, even in school.

"I'll see you at the private air strip," I tell her, handing her a card with the address on it. "Have Graham, my security officer, drive you there."

Emilia nods and I lean back against my desk. Three days with her... I can't wait. Even four hours seems too long, and they pass at an excruciatingly slow rate.

By the time I pull up in front of my private jet, I'm antsy. Emilia is already there, her suitcase and Graham by her side. She's looking up at my jet in awe, and I smile at her when she turns to look at me.

Graham walks towards my car to retrieve my luggage for me

and I walk up to Emilia. I place my hand on her lower back and tip my head towards the plane. "Shall we?" I ask.

Emilia blinks in disbelief. "This... are we taking *this*?" she asks, gesturing towards the plane.

I smile at her. "Well, I'm not walking, that's for sure," I say, and she looks at me through narrowed eyes.

I smile and let my hand slip down to find hers. I entwine our fingers and pull her along.

"Didn't you say we were travelling with a team?" she asks, and I nod. I walk her to her seat and take the seat next to hers.

"We are. They're flying commercial."

I see the unspoken question in her eyes, and I smirk as I lean over her to strap her in. As if I'd ever let her fly with the rest of my staff.

"Carter, it's so good to see you again," I hear the air hostess say, but my entire focus is on Emilia. "Is this your secretary?" she adds, and I look up in annoyance, only to freeze when I realize she looks vaguely familiar. Damn.

Emilia grits her teeth and looks up at the air hostess, her eyes flashing. She glances at me, her brows raised, and I look away, unable to face her.

"Tamara, is it?"

She beams and then nods. The way she looks at me makes it obvious that we have history, and I can't help but cringe. I don't even dare look at Emilia, but I can tell she's tense.

"Can I offer you some champagne?" Tamara asks. I nod, and she turns towards Emilia, who is ignoring her.

"Please get both of us a glass," I say, and she nods before walking away.

I turn towards Emilia to find her staring a hole in her shoes, her jaw clenched. My heart sinks. She looks angry, but she looks hurt too, and I hate that I put that expression on her face.

I clear my throat awkwardly. "The flight won't take long," I tell her. "We'll be there soon."

She nods, avoiding my gaze. I grab her chin and turn her face towards me. "What's wrong?" I ask.

Emilia grits her teeth and forces a smile on her face. "Nothing," she says, her eyes flashing with anger.

I nod awkwardly and pull away when Tamara returns with two glasses. She glances from me to Emilia, disappointment evident in her eyes. She hands us our glasses quietly and then walks away, giving us privacy.

Emilia empties her glass in a matter of seconds and puts it down before crossing her arms over each other. I bite down on my lip, unsure what to even say to her.

She undoes her seatbelt and rises the second we're in the air. She turns towards me, an unreadable expression on her face. "Is there a bathroom here?" she asks, and I nod.

"Use the one in the bedroom," I tell her, my head tipped towards the door opposite us.

Emilia blinks, her eyes widening. "There's a bedroom here?" she asks in disbelief. She looks up, her eyes settling on Tamara, and then she laughs. "Of course there is," she says.

She turns and walks away, and I bury my hands in my hair in frustration. I hesitate for half a second before following Emilia, catching the bedroom door just before it closes.

She turns to look at me in surprise when I enter the bedroom, and I grab her, pushing her against the closed door. I take a step closer to her, my body flush against hers. Emilia melts against me, her cheeks reddening.

"It didn't mean a thing, Emilia. I won't lie to you and tell you I didn't try to fuck you out of my system, because I did. But it didn't mean a thing. No one but you has ever meant anything to me."

She looks into my eyes, and for the first time since she got here, I see rawness in them. I see her hurt, her jealousy, her longing.

She bites down on her lip and nods. Her eyes fall closed,

and she drops her forehead against my chest. Emilia inhales deeply, and then she pulls away from me.

When she looks at me, her mask is back in place. She smiles at me, but there's not a trace of emotion in that smile. "I'm not sure why you're telling me this," she says. "I couldn't care less who you sleep with."

I smile at her and brush her hair out of her face. "I see," I murmur. "Okay. I guess you won't mind if I hook up with someone in New York, then?" I say, teasing her.

Emilia blanches, and I grin, shaking my head. I pull away from her and smirk. For the first time since she walked back into my life, I'm truly filled with hope.

CHAPTER 19

milia

I'm still distraught by the time we reach the hotel. I know I'm overreacting, and I hate that I can't seem to hide how hurt I am. Why would I even care if Carter has been with anyone in the time we were apart? It was only natural, and considering his track record in college, it was inevitable. It's not like I've never been with anyone else either... except in my case there's only been one single other person, and it took years before I was even able to think about sleeping with someone else.

I can't help but wonder how long it took him to get over me when things ended. How long did it take before he fell into bed with someone else? How long did it take for him to remove every trace of me?

It hurts to think that there are women that know his body better than I do. That might have learned more about him than I ever have. How many women must he have been with after me? I wonder if he even remembers what we used to be like.

I try my best to shake myself out of my thoughts, but I can't. I can't stop overthinking, I can't stop hurting myself.

I feel a hand drop on my shoulder, and I look up to find Carter looking at me, concern in his eyes. He's holding up a keycard, and I blink in surprise.

"You okay?" he asks.

"I... yeah, I'm fine," I tell him. I take the card from him and turn to walk away. Maybe a little bit of distance is all I need. Lately being around him has started to confuse me. It's started to make me nostalgic, and I find myself wanting things I can never have again. Things I shouldn't want.

I swipe my key and open the door, only to stop and stare in shock. Carter walks in behind me, catching the door right before it closes. He looks at me, his expression unreadable.

"What is this?" I ask, my hands gesturing around the suite.

Carter smiles and glances at his luggage. "We're sharing this," he says. "That's your bedroom," he adds, tipping his head towards one of the doors.

I look at him in disbelief, and Carter smiles. "Chill, Emilia. We both have our own bedrooms. We'll only be sharing the living areas. Usually, your room would be my secretary's."

My first thought is of Carter with his secretary, and I can't help but wonder if he slept with her too. I can't seem to snap myself out of this vicious thought cycle. I grit my teeth and walk away, slamming my bedroom door closed behind me.

I sit down on my bed, mad and upset — and annoyed with myself for feeling this way in the first place. It took me years to get over Carter, yet a mere few weeks of being around him, and I've come undone. I drop my elbows to my knees and bury my hands in my hair. I can't keep doing this. I can't be jealous of women I don't even know. I can't feel this possessive towards a man that isn't mine anymore.

I'm snapped out of my thoughts when my phone rings, and I look at it in surprise. My heart starts to race when I realize it's the clinic, and I pick up with shaky hands.

"Emilia?"

I recognize Layla's voice, and I'm instantly filled with bitterness.

"Layla," I murmur.

"I've got the results of your blood tests," she says, and I tense. There's an edge to her tone, and anxiety almost overwhelms me. "You're not a match, Emilia. Your blood types aren't compatible."

I start to tremble, my eyes filling with tears. "What?" I ask, my voice high.

Layla sighs. "I'm sorry," she says.

I stare into space, my heart shattering. I was so certain that I could help Dad. That I could make him better. For weeks I've been hanging onto that little bit of hope, and now it seems all lost. My heart twists painfully, and air seems to evade my lungs. I try to breathe in deeply, but I fail.

"I understand you're in New York with Carter. I hope this news doesn't ruin your trip. Don't worry, there's still the donor registry, and there are other options still available to you. You could potentially do a paired donation. Come in when you're back, and we'll discuss it."

"I... yes, thank you," I manage to say.

A big fat tear rolls down my cheek, and I inhale shakily, my lungs burning from the lack of air. I feel panic creep up slowly as I end the call, and I pull my knees to my chest as a sob tears through my throat, devastation slamming through me.

What will happen to Dad now? He can't spend the rest of his life on dialysis. I see the way he suffers, the way he hides how he feels. He's a shell of the man he used to be, and it's only been a few months. I don't want him going through this for months.

I inhale and end up gasping for air, my heart breaking. Strong arms wrap around me, and I look up at Carter. He lifts me onto his lap and wraps his arms around me.

"What happened, baby? You're worrying me. What's going on?" he asks, his voice trembling.

I clutch his shirt and then throw my arms around his neck, holding onto him tightly.

"I... I'm not... I'm not a match," I say, sobs interrupting my sentence. I rest my cheek on Carter's shoulder, finding solace in his arms.

Carter buries his hand in my hair and holds me tighter. "Minx," he whispers. "I'm so sorry."

He sounds anguished, as hurt as I'm feeling, and I cry even harder. Carter pats my back, his touch soothing.

"What am I going to do?" I ask, my voice breaking. "I can't save him."

My entire body is shaking, and I can't seem to stop my tears. It's like all the fears I had have suddenly come true. It's like I was in denial, and all of a sudden, I'm thrown into reality. My dad has a terminal illness, and I can't save him.

"We'll save him, Minx. One way or another. I promise you. I'll get him a black-market organ if I need to. I won't let him die. I won't let him suffer. I swear, Emilia, so don't cry, okay? Don't cry, baby. These things take time, but we'll find a donor for him, one way or another."

He holds me tightly, and I nod, my nose brushing against his neck. I want to believe him, but what if he's wrong? What if we can't save him?

CHAPTER 20

milia

I wake up to the loud blaring of an alarm clock and groan. I blink lazily, my gaze settling on Carter. For a second I think I'm still dreaming, and then reality catches up on me. I freeze, my eyes widening. Last night slowly comes back to me, and I pull away from Carter.

He groans and pulls me back, my body flush against his. My cheeks redden when I realize he's not wearing his suit trousers like he was last night. He buries his face in my neck and kisses me where I'm sensitive. I shiver when he throws his leg over me, his hardness pressing up against me. My heart is racing, and desire washes over me.

I bite down on my lip and push against his chest. "Carter," I murmur. "We've got a meeting in an hour," I tell him. He spent all night consoling me. I woke up countless times, bursting into tears all over again, and he was there every single time I woke up. He held me and consoled me until I fell back asleep, over and over again. It's no wonder he's exhausted now.

"Just a few more minutes, Minx," he whispers. I pull away

from him and slip out of bed carefully, my heart twisting painfully, equal parts in guilt and pain. I breathe in deeply, my thoughts turning to Dad. Sadness washes over me, the feeling so intense that it almost brings me to my knees. I brace myself against the wall and inhale shakily. Carter is right, there will be a way. These things do take time. I need to have a little bit of faith.

I think back to my phone call with Layla as I step into the shower. I can't help but wonder if she called me because she heard I went on a business trip with Carter. Did she call me when she did in an attempt to ruin this trip? Surely not... she's a medical professional. She must've just called me when the tests came back in, and this must've been a coincidence. I bite down on my lip and drop my forehead to the wall, the water hitting my back. I can't be this person... I can't assume the worst of people, for no good reason.

I'm absentminded when I walk back into my bedroom, my towel wrapped around me. My eyes move to Carter, and I freeze. I expected him to have gone back to his own room by now, but instead he's sitting up in my bed. He smiles at me and runs a hand through his hair lazily. His eyes roam over my body hungrily, and I suddenly feel nervous, almost in a giddy way.

"How do you feel," he asks, and I look down, forcing myself to get my feelings in check.

"I'm fine," I murmur. "I'm sorry about last night. Thank you for staying with me. You really didn't need to."

Carter rises from my bed, and my eyes roam over his body. He's no longer wearing the suit trousers he wore last night, and I struggle to keep my eyes off him and the boxer shorts that do nothing to hide his morning erection. A fierce burst of desire courses through me, settling between my legs. Carter walks up to me and places his index finger underneath my chin, lifting my face to his.

"Minx, I'm glad I was there. I'm glad I was the one to hold

you when you fell apart. There's nowhere else I'd rather have been last night."

I look up into his hazel eyes, and my heart starts to race. How come being around him still feels like being *home*. He's still my safe haven.

"I'd better get ready," he says, his hand cupping my cheek. "We leave in ten minutes, okay?" he says.

I nod, and Carter takes a step closer. He presses a soft kiss to my forehead, and my eyes flutter closed. "Everything will be okay, Emilia. I'll do everything in my power to make it so, all right?"

I nod, and Carter smiles at me. He takes a step away and then turns to walk out, leaving me standing here breathlessly. I sit down on my bed, my eyes roaming over the clothes he left on my floor.

He's still able to take me from sadness to desire, from pain to happiness, from hopelessness to optimism, all in a couple of seconds. No one else has ever been able to do that to me. I inhale deeply and run a hand through my wet hair.

My phone buzzes on my nightstand, and I reach for it, expecting to find a text or call from Dad. Instead, I find ten missed calls from Sam, the last one just a couple of minutes ago. My heart starts to hammer in my chest, and I'm instantly filled with so much guilt that I physically feel sick. I needed Carter with every fiber of my being last night, and I didn't even think of Sam. I didn't, but I should have.

I call him back, my hands trembling. He picks up almost immediately, and my guilt increases further yet.

"Emilia, where have you been? I haven't been able to reach you in hours. Is everything okay? Did you get to New York okay?"

"Yes," I say, quick to reassure him. "Everything is fine. I'm sorry. I just... I just tuned out last night. I was going to call you, but I just... I couldn't."

Sam is silent for a beat. "What do you mean? What's going on?"

I inhale deeply, tears threatening to spill down my cheeks all over again. I draw a shaky breath before I speak. "I got a call from the clinic last night. I'm not a match," I whisper.

Sam exhales, almost as though in relief. "God, I thought you were going to tell me something happened with Carter," he says, and I frown.

I bite down on my lip harshly before speaking again. "Did you even hear a word I just said? I cried myself to sleep over and over again last night, and the news still wrecks me, yet your first reaction is to worry about *Carter*?"

A spark of anger ignites within me, and I clench my jaw. I understand where his worries stem from, but at the same time I'm hurt that he's glossing over what I just told him.

"Shit, I'm so sorry, Emilia. I just... I don't know. My first thought was just *God I hope I don't lose her*. What you told me didn't even register until now. I'm so sorry, honey. I'm sorry to hear the news, and for the way I reacted."

I grit my teeth and try my best to calm myself, my anger turning into fury. I shake my head, feeling disappointed and hurt. "I gotta go," I tell him. "I need to get to work."

"Emilia, no. Please, honey. I'm sorry. Don't hang up like this."

I shake my head. "Bye, Sam. I'll speak to you later."

I can hear him still speaking as I pull the phone away from my ear, but I end the call nonetheless. I'm hurt, confused, and heartbroken in so many ways. Sam calls me back, but I reject the call instantly before turning my phone off entirely.

Part of me feels relieved about not having to speak to Sam. He's the one I should be reaching for, the one that should be my greatest support in these trying times. Yet it's someone else that soothes my soul.

CHAPTER 21

arter

Emilia has been distant and quiet all day. I'm worried that she's thinking about her Dad, that she's keeping in her sadness in order to get the job done.

"You all right?" I ask, my hand on her lower back. Emilia looks up at me, and guilt flashes through her eyes.

I grit my teeth and carefully brush her hair behind her ear. Looks like it isn't her dad she's thinking about... it's Sam.

Waking up next to her this morning was amazing, it was everything I've been wanting for years, yet to her, I was likely just someone who was in the right place at the right time, someone to confide in when she received devastating news.

Emilia nods, and I lead her to our table, when the very last thing I want to do is have another fucking business dinner. I want to take my Minx back to our hotel and draw her a bath or book her a massage. I want to take care of her, if she'll let me.

"Carter," Chris says. I nod at the man whose company I'm trying to acquire, but tonight all my attention is on Emilia. I pull her seat out for her, and she smiles up at me. I don't know what it is about today, but I'm feeling far more protective than usual. I'm worried about her and I want to be the one that makes her feel better. I don't want her thinking of anyone but me.

"Is this lovely lady your girlfriend?" Chris asks, Emilia's hand in his. I drop my arm behind her chair and shake my head, wishing I could *yes* instead.

"She's my lawyer."

Emilia smiles at Chris and nods politely. She's got bags underneath her eyes that betray how rough last night was for her. She woke up countless times, crying. It broke my heart to see her that way. The only other time I've ever experienced her crying while fast asleep was when Kate tore her apart. I hate that she's going through this again. Even worse, yet again, there's nothing I can do about it.

I can barely focus on what Chris is saying, even though his company is highly valuable, and highly coveted. I spent almost an entire year convincing him to sell to me, but now that I'm this close, I just want to go back home. I want to put Emilia on a plane and take her back to her dad. I feel horrible for taking her away from him in the first place.

Emilia places her hand on my upper arm and tilts her head in question, and I realize I must have missed a question. I smile at Chris in apology, but much to my surprise, he's smiling at me. He's always been incredibly short-tempered, but today he's being very... pleasant.

"Emilia just reassured me that none of my staff will lose their jobs," he tells me, and I glance at her, nodding.

"That's right," I tell him. "One of the things that makes your company so invaluable is the company culture, the bond and the vision everyone seems to share. I'd be a fool to take that away."

Chris nods in agreement. "I never thought of you as a family man, Carter. For as long as I've known you, all I've seen is a ruthless business man. Tonight, I'm seeing a different side of you," he says, glancing at Emilia. My eyes follow his, and Emilia looks into my eyes, her eyes twinkling. Every once in a while, she looks at me the way she used to, back when she was mine. I tear my gaze away and smile at Chris politely.

I refill Emilia's wine glass and try my best to focus on what Chris is telling me about his company, but my eyes keep finding Emilia's. By the time dessert comes around I'm antsy and ready to get out of here.

The waiter places our desserts in front of us, and I shake my head, stopping him. "I'm sorry," I say, "but she doesn't like anything that's strawberry flavored," I add, my head tipped towards the strawberry tart.

Emilia looks at me in surprise, as though she can't believe I remember that about her — like I could ever forget anything about her. She smiles, and this time, it's a real smile. It's that type of intimate smile that we always used to share, the one I didn't think I'd get to see again.

She puts her hand on my shoulder and shakes her head. "It's fine," she says, her voice soft. "I'll have this."

I shake my head and have the waiter replace her dessert. I lift my hand to her face and gently brush her hair out of the way. She smiles at me in thanks, and my heart skips a beat.

"I'll sell to you, Carter," Chris says, and I turn to him in surprise. I expected to have to go through far more groveling. He glances at Emilia and then smiles at me. "Family is at the heart of my company. Family, love, respect. Those are our core values. Until recently I didn't think you'd be a good fit for us, but I was mistaken. I'm not getting any younger. It's time for the next generation to take the lead, and I think you'll achieve exceptional things without losing the values the company is built on."

Relief rushes through me and Emilia grins at me. I smile back at her and nod at Chris. "Of course. Your legacy is safe in my hands, Chris," I tell him, before glancing at Emilia. "Emilia will personally take care of all the paperwork."

She nods and that's that. I'm still in disbelief when we walk out of the restaurant. The second we walk around the corner, Emilia grabs my shoulders and throws herself in my arms. "Oh my gosh," she says, squeezing tightly. "We actually did it!"

I laugh and lift her off her feet, twirling her around. She giggles, and I lift her higher, my arms on her upper thighs. She looks down at me, her eyes sparkling with joy and pride. It's the happiest I've seen her in a while.

"I always knew you'd go far, Carter, but wow... you've surpassed every dream, every wish I've ever had for you. I'm so proud of you," she says, her arms around my neck. I lower her to the floor slowly, her body still pressed against mine.

"*Every* dream?" I ask, my voice playful.

She narrows her eyes and giggles. "Carter," she admonishes, grinning from ear to ear.

I reluctantly let go of her and grab her hand. She looks startled, and I smile. "It's cold, Minx," I murmur, putting both our hands in my pocket. I entwine our hands, and Emilia looks at me with such longing... this is exactly what I wanted. I want to be the only one on her mind. I want to fill her every thought, so that there's no room left for sadness or heartache.

"Let's go for a walk," I murmur, and she nods, looking happy. She's probably the only person I know that can set aside the things going on in her own life to be genuinely happy for me. I'm going to do whatever I can to keep that smile on her face, to keep her sadness at bay.

CHAPTER 22

arter

I've got Emilia's hand in mine as we slowly make our way back to the hotel, purposely going the long way around. Despite the terrible news she received, she seems so much happier here, where it's just the two of us. Being so far away from everyone makes it easy to pretend like life didn't tear her away from me.

She sighs happily and I turn to look at her. She's staring up at the sky, and I'm staring at her. "You're still the most beautiful woman I've ever laid eyes on," I tell her without thinking. Emilia looks at me, her eyes wide. She blushes, and I like that look on her. I like throwing her off, I always have.

Her eyes roam over my face, and her cheeks darken even further. Her eyes drop to my lips, and she looks away.

She tries to pull her hand out of mine, and I shake my head, tightening my grip on her. I tuck our hands back into my pocket, my thumb stroking over the back of her hand, my face tipped up at the sky. Stolen moments... that's all I'll ever have of her, but if that's all I can have, I'll take it.

Emilia's cheeks are crimson and her eyes are sparkling in a

way I haven't seen in years. We both have smiles on our faces as we continue our walk.

Emilia flinches when a snowflake falls on her face and she looks around as snow comes pouring down around us. She giggles and looks up at me, and I wish I could just capture this moment.

My fingers brush past the edges of her coat, and I zip her all the way up, half her face hidden behind her collar. She looks up at me, her gaze intense. I can't help but wonder if she's feeling what I'm feeling. Does this moment feel precious to her too?

I throw my arm around her shoulder and keep her close as we continue our walk, snow surrounding us. Emilia pauses and then grins at me. "Let's grab a bottle of champagne," she tells me, and I frown at the liquor store we're standing in front of. "We have something to celebrate, after all."

Emilia pulls me along, and I laugh. "Minx, you do realize I can afford to order us champagne at the hotel, right?"

She pouts at me and shakes her head. "It won't be the same," she tells me. Emilia grabs my hand and pulls me into the store.

We emerge with a couple of bottles of cheap champagne, and Emilia all but drags me back to the hotel. She's shivering by the time we make it back to our suite.

"Shall I draw you a bath, Minx? You're freezing."

She looks at me and shakes her head. She grabs one of the bottles of champagne and smirks. "You pop this, I'll be right back."

I shrug out of my coat and do as she says. Minutes later Emilia returns to the living room with her entire duvet wrapped around her. I bark out a laugh as she runs up to the sofa and pats the seat next to hers. I smile and take off my suit jacket before joining her, two glasses in one hand, a bottle of champagne in the other.

"I didn't work this hard to have cheap champagne," I tell her, shaking my head. Emilia shrugs, the duvet dropping off her shoulders. She holds it out for me to crawl underneath and then covers me up. My eyes fall to the clothes she changed into, and I grin as I pour her a glass of champagne.

"Oh-kay, Mr. High and Mighty," she says, rolling her eyes. "You know what we call people that say stuff like that back in London?"

I shake my head as I tap my glass against hers. "Tossers," she says. "You're acting like a total tosser. Cheap champagne is *wonderful*, I'll have you know."

Whenever she talks about London, her accent turns a little more British, and it's hot as hell. "You know what we call *you* here?"

Emilia sits up, her hair still windswept, and her eyes filled with excitement that's become foreign to me. "A thief," I murmur, my fingers tracing over her collarbone. Emilia looks down at the hoodie she stole from me and blushes.

"Well, you did say you had more interesting stuff for me to steal..."

I smirk and take a sip of my champagne. "It's fine, I guess it does look better on you than it does on me."

She blushes and grabs the remote control, zapping through channels until she finds some sort of telenovela, for a lack of better word.

I look at her with raised brows and she looks back at me, a challenge in her eyes. "Let me guess," she says. "The amazing Carter Clarke is too good for Spanish soaps."

I purse my lips and tug my tie off. The truth is that I'd watch anything with Emilia, I'd do anything to spend some time with her, just as she is right now — no shields up, no hiding behind the person she thinks she's become.

Emilia shifts positions, bringing her knees up, and I pull her legs towards me, settling her feet in my lap. "God, Minx.

Your feet are freezing," I say, alarmed. I rub my hands over them, massaging her and warming her up at the same time.

A small moan escapes her lips, and I have to reposition her feet in my lap to keep her from finding out just how much she still affects me. A single moan from her, and I'm rock solid. Emilia tries her best to focus on the soap she's allegedly watching, but her eyes keep dropping back to mine. She follows my every movement as I undo the first few buttons of my shirt, her tongue darting out to moisten her lips, and I get even harder.

I clench my jaw and try my best to watch the soap she put on, but I'm struggling. I so badly want to pull her closer. I want her in my lap the way I had her last night, but this time I want her smiling at me, I want her arms wrapped around my neck, her lips on mine.

I circle my thumb over her ankle, and another gasp escapes her lips. I love all of these little sounds she makes. I fucking wish I could massage the rest of her body too, but she'd just pull away from me entirely if I tried.

I try my best to focus on the TV and end up reading the subtitles just to keep my mind off the things I want to do to Emilia. I narrow my eyes and then look at Emilia. "What the hell does that even mean, *outraged in Spanish*," I say, and Emilia bursts out laughing, her body shaking. I can't help but laugh too.

I want more of this. More of these moments with her, where we're both who we used to be. I want more of these moments where I truly feel happy once again. I can't help but fear that this bond we seem to have recovered here in New York will fall apart the second we set foot in Woodstock tomorrow.

CHAPTER 23

arter

Emilia walks into the office wearing the stuck-up clothes she's come to love so much, when most people at the office are in jeans and tees. I guess it only makes sense, since she's a lawyer, and not a techie.

I pause what I'm doing and look up at her, my eyes trailing her across the room. She's so fucking beautiful. Our trip to New York is still fresh in my mind. It's been years since she and I have been so close. It feels like I've got her back now, even though she isn't mine.

"Pay attention," Asher snaps, and I look back at him sheepishly. He narrows his eyes and shoots me a warning look, which I ignore. I don't understand why he feels the need to run over every single business decision ten times. His risk appetite decreases every freaking year, and it drives me insane.

"Let's move forward with this," I say, pointing at the least risky investment. We'd stand to make so much more money if we went with any of the other two options, but I just know Asher is going to be anxious as fuck if we do.

I'm excited about this new project. It means I'll get to spend some more time with Emilia, getting all the due diligence and paperwork done. I might even be able to invite her for another trip.

It's like Asher can read my mind, because he crosses his arms over each other. "I'd like to take point on this one," he tells me, and I shake my head.

"Hell no," I say, glancing back at Emilia.

Asher follows my gaze and shakes his head. "Carter, I warned you."

I sigh and look back at him. "I know. I know, Asher. I'm not doing anything. I'm not pursuing her. When the time comes, I'll let her go. But she's here now. I just want to spend a couple more moments with her."

He looks so hurt on my behalf that I almost wish I didn't speak at all. He nods and looks away. "Just be careful. In trying to protect her heart, you'll end up breaking your own all over again. I'm the one that's had to keep you together in the last couple of years. I don't want to have to do it again, man."

He's right, of course. I was a fucking mess for years, but that's one of the main reasons our company is so successful. Working is the only thing that kept my mind off her.

I sigh as I walk towards the meeting room, pausing by the coffee machine right outside it. I frown at the stack of documents and Emilia's bag and phone on top of it. Where the hell did she even go?

I grab her phone and it lights up, the background photo one of her and John. What would I have done if she had a photo of her and Sam on the background? Back when she and I were dating, we always had pictures together as our screensavers.

I bite down on my lip and try to unlock it. I hesitate before trying her old password, a combination of her birthday, mine, and our dating anniversary. Much to my surprise, it unlocks. She's still using the same code after all these years? I grin to myself and think about all the mayhem I can cause with this knowledge.

The very first thing I do is download the most obnoxious song I can think of and set that as her ringtone before taking her phone off silent. I grin to myself. I can't wait to find out what expression she'll have on her face the next time her phone rings.

Her phone buzzes as she gets a text from Sam, and I freeze. I hover over the notification with my finger, my stomach turning. He's her boyfriend, and she says she's happy with him. I can't help but wonder what she's like with him. She's so closed off these days, and I wonder if Sam gets the version of her that I miss so much.

I click on the message without thinking, expecting the worst. Instead, all I find is the most mundane text messages imaginable. All she and Sam ever seem to talk about is how their day was or what they ate. Yet when she was with me, I could never open my messages in public, because I never knew what kind of naughtiness she was getting up to that day. I clutch her phone tightly and click on the photo icon, my entire body tense. Maybe this is exactly what I need to get her out of my mind. I just need to see something I can't unsee.

I scroll through her photos, and sure enough, there are some cute ones of her with Sam that I fucking hate, but none of the type of photos she'd always send me. I can't imagine being away from her for weeks and not having her keeping me on my toes. Has she really changed that much or was she just different with me?

I'm so caught up in checking out the contents of her phone that I don't even realize that she's returned until she snatches her phone out of my hand.

"What the hell, Carter?" she says, her eyes flashing.

I grin at her and cross my arms over each other. "You should really change your access code."

"You— are you insane? That's such an invasion of privacy. How... how... uncivilized."

I chuckle, I can't help it. "Uncivilized?" I repeat, amused. "That's the best you can come up with?"

She grits her teeth and crosses her arms over each other, pushing her breasts out unknowingly.

"Can't believe how boring you've become. You were never like that with me," I murmur, my voice husky. "*What did you have for dinner? Really?*"

Emilia holds her hand out and I frown at her. "Phone," she says, angrily. "If you get to go through mine then you'd better damn well believe I'm going through yours. Give it to me."

I shrug and place my phone in her palm. I watch her as she tries to unlock it and succeeds in one go, my password still identical to hers. She looks up at me in wonder for a brief second, and I lean back against the wall as she scrolls through my phone. I know she won't find a thing. There were some messages Layla sent me that I wouldn't want her to see, but I deleted that entire message thread the day I called it quits with her.

The few things that I absolutely don't want her finding are locked up in an app I created myself. I don't entirely put it past her to manage to get into that too, since the password is her birthday. I really should've picked a more secure password, but then again, no one but her would ever dare touch my phone, or like Emilia just did — straight up demand it from me. I'm nervous as she scrolls through my apps. I really don't want her to find out that I still have old photos of her and of the two of us locked away.

She glances at me before clicking on the photo gallery icon, her eyes filled with insecurity. She frowns as she scrolls through my photos, finding nothing other than photos of documents and family. She goes through my texts next, and I can't tell if she's disappointed or relieved when she finds that they're equally boring.

She hands me back my phone, her lips forming a pout that's far too cute on her. "And you call *me* boring," she murmurs, amusement dancing in her eyes.

I shrug and put my phone in my pocket. "You're always welcome to do something about the boring contents of my phone," I murmur, winking at her. "Matter of fact, I can already imagine it. Some hot photos, even hotter text messages..."

Emilia looks at me through narrowed eyes and brushes past me. I grin as I follow her into the meeting room. My phone buzzes just as I sit down, and I frown at it in surprise when I realize it's a text from Emilia. I glance at her, but she's staring at her phone, an amused smile on her face.

I open the text to find a photo of red chili peppers, along with at least a hundred emojis of fire and chilis. I snicker, I can't help it. "So lame," I tell her, and she giggles. "Seriously, so lame," I repeat, but I can't get the smile off my face. I've missed her. I've missed this. Lame jokes and that smile of hers.

I can't keep my eyes off Emilia throughout the meeting. This has got to be the most boring meeting I've been in, but she's taking notes as though she's scared she might miss a critical piece of information. It's so her. She was like this at school too. Her notes were always ridiculously detailed. It's no wonder she became a lawyer.

I bite back a yawn as the meeting wraps up and scroll through my contacts, pausing on her phone number. I glance at her, wondering just how pissed off she's going to get when I do this, and then I do it anyway. I press dial, and all of a sudden, *Crazy Frog*, the most annoying song known to mankind, starts to play. Emilia jumps in shock, and it takes her a good couple of seconds to realize that it's *her* phone that's ringing. I burst out laughing, her expression too priceless, and she looks at me.

Emilia shakes her head, her lips opening and closing in

shock, and then she bursts out laughing too. The two of us just sit there, chuckling like two school kids, *Crazy Frog* playing in the background. I have a room full of employees staring at us in shock, but I couldn't care less. This is the happiest I've felt in forever.

CHAPTER 24

milia

The prank Carter pulled on me in today's meeting still has me smiling to myself. It's been years since I've felt even remotely playful. I forgot how it feels to laugh like that. I kind of want to retaliate. I want to make him laugh the way he made *me* laugh.

"What are you smiling about, Princess?" Dad asks.

I grin at him and shake my head. Dad is hooked up to his machine, his hand in mine. "Oh, it's nothing. Do you remember that really annoying ring tone everyone was downloading back when I was a kid? It was called Crazy Frog. It was the worst."

Dad laughs and nods. "Yes, I remember. You and the Clarke kids drove me half insane with it."

I giggle. "Well, today Carter managed to change my phone's ringtone to that song. Then he called me in the middle of a meeting. I had no idea whether I should be mortified or amused," I say, laughing. "I can't believe he's still so childish."

Dad smiles at me indulgently. "He still makes you laugh, huh?"

I nod, thinking back to the two of us sitting in that meeting, both of us laughing. "He's the CEO of such a huge company, yet he still does stuff like that. He really should take himself a little more serious."

Dad grins knowingly. "Oh, he does, Emilia. He does, around anyone that isn't you. You're the only one that gets to see that side of him. The only one that brings it out."

I look up at Dad, startled. I smile tightly and shake my head, but before I can even deny it, Dad interrupts. "I assume you're going to get him back for this?" he says, an amused look in his eyes.

I giggle. "Of course, Daddy. Who do you think I am? I went straight to the little toy store in town and bought myself a set of supplies."

Dad laughs, his entire frame shaking. "That's the spirit, Princess," he says. The way he's looking at me warms my heart. It's like he hasn't seen me in forever, even though I've been with him for weeks now.

My phone buzzes and I glance at it, tensing when I realize it's Sam. "Sam just messaged to say that he's booked his tickets," I tell Dad. He glances at my phone, his expression guarded. I should be eager to see him again, but things haven't been the same between us in a while now. I keep feeling like he doesn't understand me, like he doesn't truly care about what's going on. Everything he says grates on me, and we keep arguing.

"It'll be wonderful to have him here for Thanksgiving and New Year's. But we don't have plans, do we?" I say, trying my best not to let my agitation show.

Dad purses his lips and shakes his head. "I usually spend Thanksgiving with the Clarkes and then I come see you for Christmas. Carter has been hosting Christmas here for years now, but I always spend it with you in London."

My expression falls. How could I have forgotten that he usually spends Thanksgiving at Carter's house? He rarely talks about it, but he's mentioned their invites before. The last thing

I want to do is spend Thanksgiving with Helen, and I doubt she'd even have me. I bet I'm still just a reminder of what happened to Kate. I bet she still blames me.

I've tried my best not to wonder about Kate. I know she doesn't live here anymore, or I'd have run into her weeks ago, but she'll probably come back for Thanksgiving, and maybe even Christmas too. Both are huge affairs at the Clarkes. I don't want to see her. I might want to avoid Helen, but that doesn't even come close to how badly I want to avoid Kate. When everything went down with her and I left, I'd just felt hurt. But now? Now I'm mad. I'm angry that I loved both of them so much, yet I was treated like some sort of pariah. I'm mad at them for hurting me the way they did, but I'm even more mad at myself for letting it happen for so long. There were always signs. Little things Kate would say or do that I'd just ignore.

"So, Sam and you are quite serious, huh?" Dad says cautiously, snapping me out of my thoughts. I look at him and nod. I guess we are.

"Do you think he's the one?"

I stare at Dad in surprise and laugh nervously. "Dad, where is this coming from?"

Dad tightens my grip on my hand and sighs. "Well, you said you two are moving in together. I guess the next step is marriage, isn't it?"

I nod, but the mere thought of that gives me anxiety. I can't imagine getting married. I love Sam, and I love my life back in London, but I just can't imagine it all being so... permanent. The thought of it terrifies me. I feel panicked just thinking about walking down the aisle and finding Sam waiting for me.

I bite down on my lip and shake my head. "We haven't even moved in together yet, Daddy," I murmur. "I do like the idea of you walking me down the aisle, though."

Dad finally smiles and nods. "I'll be there to do that, Emilia."

I tighten my grip on his hand and nod. I really need to go to the clinic to discuss a paired donation, and any other options, but I've been avoiding going back in to see Layla. I can't even look at her, knowing she's had everything that used to be mine.

"I never asked you, Dad, but what do you think of Sam?"

Dad sighs. "He's a nice man, Emilia. He's well educated, and from what I can see, he treats you very well."

"Why do I feel like there's a *but* there?"

Dad looks at me, his eyes filled with sorrow. "Because there is, Princess. I might like him, but he doesn't make you come alive. Maybe I'm biased, because I only spent three weeks with you last year, and I met him only a handful of times... but I can tell, Emilia. I want you to be so happy that it radiates around you, and with Sam, you just appear to be *content*. I want more for you than that, no matter how good of a guy he might be."

"No, Daddy," I say, trying my best to reassure him. "I love Sam. He *does* make me come alive. I guess I might have just been busy with work the last time you visited. He'll be here soon, and you'll understand then."

Dad nods, but it doesn't look like he believes me at all. I never knew. I had no idea that Dad was thinking any of this. I don't want him worrying about me. When Sam gets here, I'd better make sure that he sees just how good we are together. I never really consciously thought of it, but I guess Sam most likely *is* the guy I'll end up marrying. I want Dad to like him. It might be hard due to the distance, but I'd really like for Dad and Sam to develop some sort of bond. I'm my dad's only family, so whoever I marry will definitely have to be good to Dad too. I know Sam will be great with Dad, but I'm starting to wonder if he and I are just too far away from Dad. I'm not sure I can bare to leave Dad behind to return to work in London, and I don't know what that means for Sam and me.

CHAPTER 25

milia

I wake up exhausted on Sunday morning. I've been overthinking things all weekend, and I haven't slept a wink. The longer I'm here, the more I think I want to stay. I'll need to talk to Sam, but I don't even know if I *want* to ask him to move here with me. I walk into the kitchen, irritated.

"You look cute."

I freeze and look up to find Carter leaning back against the kitchen counter in nothing but his swim shorts, his hair still wet. He's got a coffee cup in his hands and raises it to his lips. I hate that he looks so good. I hate that I still find him so damn attractive. Freaking Carter.

"More stolen goods, huh?" he murmurs, his eyes roaming over my body. I was so tired this morning that I stormed out in nothing but Carter's tee. I glance down at my outfit, my cheeks heating.

Carter holds up his coffee cup for me and I take it from him gratefully. I take a huge gulp and sigh in delight. Carter chuckles and brushes my hair behind my ear. "You're still fucking terrifying before you've had your coffee in the morning," he murmurs, and I look up at him in surprise, my lips tipping up in a smile. "I feared for my life in New York, you know?"

"Shut up," I murmur, making him laugh.

Carter takes a step closer and steals his coffee back from me, earning him a glare. "Just one sip, Minx," he whispers. My heart still skips a beat when he calls me Minx. I didn't think I'd ever get to hear that again.

I pull on his hand, wanting his coffee back, and he chuckles. I take the coffee from him, and Carter cages me in, his arms on either side of me. I look up at him cheekily as I take another sip of his coffee, and Carter laughs.

That's how Dad finds us, standing in the kitchen, being petty over a cup of coffee. He grins at us, and Carter takes a step away. Dad's eyes drop to my coffee cup, and he frowns before looking at Carter.

"I thought you said that was your cup? Every time I try to use it you throw a fit."

I look at it — truly look at it — and my face drains of color. This... this is the same cup Carter asked me to be his girlfriend with, isn't it? I look up at him in question, and he looks away, a slight blush tainting his cheeks. "Why do you still have this?" I whisper.

He smiles tightly and looks away, robbing me of an answer. He joins Dad on the chairs by the kitchen counter and I sigh. "You're gonna get the chairs all wet," I murmur, shaking my head. "Why don't you change into something else? Something warm, maybe? You'll catch a cold like that."

Carter looks at me, his eyes twinkling with amusement, and shakes his head. Dad glances from me to him and smiles to himself before turning to Carter. "You're going home for Sunday lunch?" he asks, and my heart twists painfully. Sunday lunches at the Clarkes feature in some of my best memories.

Carter nods, and Dad sighs. "Come with me," he tells Dad. "Mom has been asking about you. I think she's worried, and I know you miss playing cards with Dad. Why don't you come with me?"

Dad glances at me and my heart sinks.

"Carter is right, I *have* missed Sunday lunch at the Clarkes. I'd really like to go, Emilia, and I'd really like it if you joined me."

Dad looks so hopeful, so pleading. It's been so easy to forget that he's sick, because he never acts like it. But he is, and it's my turn to take care of him. I nod very subtly, as though I'm scared to even commit to it. Since coming here I haven't done anything for Dad, not anything meaningful anyway. The staff robs me of every opportunity. But this, this is something I can do for him.

I glance at Carter, my smile so tight that it feels unnatural. "If my father wishes for it, I'll join you. I'm not certain if your mother would be happy to host me, though. If not, then I'd be very grateful if you could take him, instead."

Carter looks worried and shakes his head. "No, Mom would love to have you. She's been wanting to come over and speak to you, but I... I thought it might not be a good idea. Please, come."

I nod, and that's that. I try my best to delay as much as I can, but a couple of hours later, we're standing in front of the Clarkes house. I consider coming up with an excuse and bailing, but I can't. I can't, because Dad is holding onto my hand tightly, looking more excited than I've seen him look in weeks.

I had no idea I'd been keeping him away from his usual routine. I didn't come here to disrupt his life. I can manage to smile and nod for one afternoon. For Dad, I can do that.

The door opens and Helen appears, her eyes bright and excited. She greets Carter, and then Dad, before finally smiling at me. I try my best to return her smile, but I fail.

"Thank you for having me," I tell her through gritted teeth, and she nods at me, flustered. I follow the boys in and glance around in surprise. Almost everything has changed. The entire house looks renovated. A lot of it has a similar feel to it as Carter's house. I guess his parents probably didn't want to move, so he did the house up instead.

Carter's dad, William, rises from his seat when I walk in. He walks up to me and ruffles my hair, and my heart warms. He's always been as good to me as he could be. Even towards the end he tried his best to remain impartial. I take a seat at the dining table, and I don't even realize I've sat down in what used to be my usual spot here until Carter and Helen both look at me, their eyes filled with what can only be described as nostalgia. I regret it immediately. I'm not here to reminisce. I try to eat in silence, but Helen and William don't make it easy. Both of them keep trying to involve me in the conversation, and it hurts. It hurts that they all moved on with their lives, that they all seem to be so happy after they asked me to rip my heart out for their daughter's happiness.

I breathe a sigh of relief when my phone rings, and I excuse myself. Even a small reprieve will give me the breathing room I crave.

CHAPTER 26

arter

Everyone falls silent when Emilia leaves the room, and Mom visibly deflates. "She hates me," Mom says.

Dad shakes his head. "No, she doesn't. Emilia doesn't have it in her to hate anyone."

I know Dad, and I can hear the unspoken remainder of that sentence. *But if she did, she would definitely hate you.*

I smile at Mom as best as I can. "You haven't really seen her in years, and it's probably strange to be back here and to find everyone acting like nothing ever happened."

I don't really know what I expected of my mother, but it certainly wasn't this — pretending like she never hurt Emilia. Like she didn't blame her for Kate's actions, like she didn't ask her to leave. Mom hasn't even acknowledged the past, let alone apologized, and I want her to do both. It won't undo the pain Emilia went through at our hands, and it won't erase all the nights she cried herself to sleep in our apartment, but it might give her a small amount of closure. That's the only thing we can still offer her.

"Excuse me," I murmur, rising from my seat. I know Emilia, and she never takes calls during dinner. She doesn't even pick up when it's Sam. Her leaving mid-dinner just now can only mean two things: it's either truly urgent, or she's running.

I walk into the hallway and find her standing on the middle of the stairs, her phone to her ear. She grazes the edges of the photo frames along the staircase with her fingers, slowly walking up the stairs, absentmindedly. I follow behind her and watch her slip into my bedroom. I thought she might go into Kate's room, but I should've known better. Of course it's mine.

Emilia leaves the door ajar, and I lean back against the wall just outside my room, my eyes fluttering closed.

"Yes, it's been quite hard. Just seeing him hooked up to that machine for hours every day... I can barely take it. There isn't much I can do either. The only thing I can really do for my dad is stay strong and just be there."

I wonder who she's talking to. Her voice sounds warm and caring, whoever she's speaking to is obviously someone she's close to. Is it Sam?

"Did Sam tell you that?" she asks, sounding somewhat shy. "Yes, we're planning on moving in together, but honestly, we haven't really talked through the logistics yet. We're both renting, so we could either find something new together, or just move into either one of our apartments. I guess that's something we'll need to figure out when I'm back."

So not Sam, then. Emilia laughs, and I smile to myself. I've always loved the sound of her laughter, and even now it affects me.

"He said that? Yes, your son is usually so romantic, Nancy, but when asking me to move in with him he literally just blurted it out over dinner."

I freeze, my smile melting off my face. The person she's talking to is Sam's mother? My heart twists painfully. I want this for her. I want her to gain a whole new family when she eventually gets married, but fucking hell, it hurts. It hurts to know that once upon a time, all of this could have been mine. It hurts to know the girl in my bedroom used to be mine.

I try my hardest not to blame my sister for the way I lost Emilia, but with every year that passes, it becomes harder to remind myself that Kate was sick. It's becoming harder and harder to keep from resenting her.

Emilia ends the call and I inhale deeply before walking in. I find Emilia sitting on my bed, a lost expression on her face.

"That's nice, that you're close to Sam's mom."

She looks up at me, startled, and smiles stiffly. "I didn't realize you were there. I'm sorry, I shouldn't have gone into your room. Honestly, I did it without thinking."

I sit down next to her and look around the room. This room is filled with memories of her. I fall back on my bed and stare up at her. "That's okay," I murmur. "It isn't even really my room anymore. I only stay over every once in a while."

She nods and looks around the way I just did. I wonder what she sees. It's been years since she's been in here. Her eyes fall to my bed, and I'm certain I see a flash of jealousy and possessiveness in them.

"You know, you're still the only girl I've ever had in this bed," I murmur, my voice barely above a whisper.

Emilia's eyes widen, and her eyes roam over my body. I lift my arms and put them behind my head, my t-shirt riding up to reveal the v-line Emilia has always loved.

"Is that so?" she whispers.

I nod. She looks beautiful today, and I really want to pull her closer. I want her straddling me the way she used to, her lips on mine. I need her with such intensity that I have to force myself to look away. My heart refuses to acknowledge that she's no longer mine. I inhale deeply and close my eyes.

I want to ask her if she missed me. If she still has feelings for me. If part of her heart still beats for me. But I can't. It wouldn't matter anyway. She's with someone else, and in a few months at most, she'll be going back to him. I can't mess with her happiness in the slightest. I won't.

We both tense and sit up when a soft knock sounds on my bedroom door. Mom walks in, and she looks surprised to find us sitting together like this. Emilia stiffens beside me and looks away, as though she can't even stand to look at Mom. I can see that it hurts Mom, but I can also see how hurt Emilia still is.

"Emilia," Mom murmurs, her eyes flickering between us. "I... I would like to apologize. I know it's too little too late, but you deserve an apology. I didn't want to remind you of the past, so I remained silent earlier, but that isn't right. You deserve better than that.

The way I behaved after Kate came home from the hospital — there's just no excuse for that. I felt like I'd failed as a mother, and rather than take responsibility for that, I looked for someone to blame. And Kate, being as vicious as the drugs had made her... she convinced me it was all your doing, even though I logically knew better.

I'm not asking for your forgiveness, because I wouldn't dare, but I do want to offer you my sincere apology. I've always loved you like you were my own, and I still do. Not a day has gone by that I didn't think of you. I always hoped you were doing well, and every time your dad told me about you, I'd be so proud of you. I want you to know that. I want you to know that I still love you the way I always have, and it won't make things better, but I live with deep regret over the way I've treated you."

Mom turns to me, her eyes filled with sorrow. "And you too, Carter. I'm sorry. I'm sorry for asking so much of you. For asking you to sacrifice your relationship with Emilia, when I should have stood with you, when I should have defended both you and Emilia. I hope you'll find it in your heart to forgive me someday."

I nod at Mom, but her eyes are on Emilia. Emilia is glancing out the window, her entire body trembling. I shake my head at Mom subtly, and she leaves quietly. A tear drops down Emilia's cheek as soon as Mom closes the door behind her, and I wrap my arms around her.

Emilia sniffs and turns in my arm, clutching me tightly as she bursts into tears. I tighten my grip on her and stroke her hair, my own heart breaking. I can't take it when she cries. Every tear she sheds leaves a mark on my soul.

"I... I'm sorry," she cries, and I cup her head gently. Emilia turns her face so she's hiding in my neck, her lips grazing my skin. "I don't want to cry," she whispers through her tears, and I clutch her tightly.

"I know, Minx. It's okay. It's just me." I kiss her hair gently and try to keep my heart from breaking. I inhale deeply before speaking. "I actually never even realized I wanted an apology from my Mom, you know? I've never consciously blamed her for what happened, but it does feel like a huge weight off my shoulders," I whisper.

Emilia nods and sniffs. "Me too. I just felt... I felt so betrayed. I loved her so much."

I lift her onto my lap and wrap my arms around her fully, wrapping her in my arms. Emilia rests her head on my shoulder, endless tears still streaming down her face.

"Just let it all out, Minx. It's years overdue, just like Mom's apology. It was just easier to forget about all the ways my family and I wronged you — easier to pretend it never happened. I guess it was easier to live with the guilt that way."

Emilia pulls back to look at me. She shakes her head and looks into my eyes. "Not you, Carter. Never you. You never wronged me."

I drop my forehead to hers and close my eyes. "I did. I should've chased after you. I should've chosen you over everyone else, especially when it was so clear that you never did anything wrong. I should've stood by you."

Emilia cups my cheek and I bury my hand in her hair. "No, Carter. You did the right thing. And it's not like I actually gave you a choice at all. I left to the one place I knew you couldn't follow without giving up on your scholarship, your education, and the company you were building. I needed a clean break. It's not your fault."

I look into the sky-blue eyes that I've loved for as long as I can remember and shake my head. "I wish I'd followed you as soon as I was sure that Kate would be fine. I thought letting you go was the right thing to do. I thought I couldn't chain you to me, knowing how much resentment there was between my family and you. Some days I even convinced myself that I was over you, you know? But fuck, Emilia, you're back now, and I..."

I shake my head and look away, my heart shattering. Emilia buries her hand in my hair and turns my head back towards her. "You what?"

"I look at you, and I wish you were still mine. I've never regretted anything as much as letting you go. You will probably always be the love of my life, but I'm glad that I don't seem to be yours. I just want you to be happy, Emilia. I'm glad you are."

She smiles tightly and pushes away from me. She turns her back to me and wipes her tears away, and I regret my words instantly. It's not fair of me to tell her this, and I don't want to make her uncomfortable around me. I shouldn't have said anything, but as always when it comes to her, I couldn't help myself.

"Come on," she says, smiling the fakest smile I've yet seen her attempt. "Let's go down. Dad was so excited to be here today, let's not ruin it, okay? I'll try my best too."

I nod and follow her out the door, but all I want to do is take her home, away from anything that might hurt her.

CHAPTER 27

milia

I sip my coffee, unable to calm my nerves. I'm supposed to pick Sam up today, and rather than being excited, I find myself being anxious.

I jump when Carter walks into the kitchen and I check my watch, surprised. He should've already been at work by now. I've done my best to avoid Carter ever since he told me that he regrets letting me go. I've been battling the guilt I feel, because in that moment, all I could see was Carter. I wasn't even remotely thinking of Sam. Being here has been confusing for me, and I hate it.

"You're done avoiding me," he tells me, and I look up at him in surprise, a small smile on my face. He's so cocky these days. His entire vibe is different.

"Who said I was avoiding you?"

He crosses his arms over each other, the fabric of his shirt stretching along his muscles. I hate how good he looks in a suit.

"Weren't you? We've had coffee together almost every morning this last month, but you were suddenly nowhere to be found all of last week. Forget what I said, Emilia. It was just being in my old bedroom with you that caused me to overshare. You don't need to act so uncomfortable around me."

I bite down on my lip and look away. If only I was actually *uncomfortable*. That's how I should be feeling, but it's not. I'm flustered and excited to know that he still has some lingering feelings for me, and that just isn't right.

"I'm picking Sam up today," I murmur, my heart racing.

Carter locks his jaw and looks away, his hands balling into fists. "I see. I'll get Graham to drive you."

I shake my head and hide my trembling hands. "I can drive. I prefer to go by myself."

Something flashes in Carter's eyes, and though I can't quite identify it, I know it hurts my heart.

"I see. Which car are you taking?"

"I thought I'd take my dad's."

Carter pulls a hand through his hair and shakes his head. "Take the Range Rover. It has more space," he says, sounding tired.

I nod, not wanting to argue with him. The entire atmosphere is suddenly so tense. Carter looks like he's about to speak, but then his phone rings. "I'll see you later, Emilia," he says. He sighs as he walks out, and I somehow feel horrible.

I can't shake that feeling all the way to the airport. My heart is constricting painfully and I'm feeling completely out of it. I try to force myself to smile as I wait for Sam by the exit, but I can't.

I straighten when he walks out, a huge smile on his face. I wave at him, and he drops his luggage, running up to me. I laugh when he lifts me into his arms and twirls me around.

"Emilia," he murmurs, his lips dropping to mine. I stiffen involuntarily, unable to kiss him back.

"Hey," I murmur, pulling away. "How was your flight?"

He sighs and drops his forehead to mine. "I missed you, darling. It's been so long," he murmurs, and I hug him tightly.

"I missed you too," I whisper. This is probably exactly what I need, a reminder of everything I have and everything Sam and I have built, so I can stop focusing on what I lost. "Come on," I say, leading him to the car.

Sam whistles as I open the trunk for him. "Nice car. Your dad has great taste," he says, and I freeze. I should probably tell him that this is one of Carter's cars, but I don't want to ruin Sam's mood.

"I can't wait to see the home you grew up in," he says. He grins as we drive off and leans into me. "And share your bed," he adds, his hand finding its way to my thigh.

I smile at him, but my heart twists painfully. I've never even shared that bed with Carter. It seems weird somehow.

"How is your dad? Let's see him first before we do anything else."

I nod and bite down on my lip. I'd been planning on going straight to my old house, but realistically there's no way I can avoid taking Sam to Carter's house, since that's where Dad is living now. "He has his ups and downs. He's doing quite well for the most part. It's good to be here with him. There's so much of his life I missed out on. So much I didn't know about."

I try to fill him in as best as I can on the drive back but find myself avoiding all mention of Carter subconsciously. I'm wrecked with guilt, even though I haven't done anything wrong.

I'm nervous as we drive up to Carter's gate. I remember the first time I saw it, and how imposing it all felt. I can't imagine how Sam might feel. He falls silent as the gate swings open, and he's tense as I park the car.

"This is where my Dad is staying," I say quietly.

He nods stiffly. "So, this is Carter Clarke's house, huh?"

I nod and get out of the car, wanting to just get this over with already. Graham, Carter's security guy, walks out and helps Sam with his luggage, and I can tell Sam feels intimidated. I feel bad somehow, and I don't know how to make him feel better.

We're both quiet as I lead him to Dad's treatment room, and Sam and I both freeze when we enter. Carter is sitting in the seat next to Dad's, the two of them facing each other, both of them seemingly angry. They're glaring at each other, and neither one of their expressions improves when they turn to find Sam and me.

"Hey," I murmur, my eyes finding Carter's. What is he doing here? Why isn't he at work?

Carter rises from his seat and Sam straightens. I never realized that Carter is half a head taller than Sam, and much wider.

"Samuel, isn't it?" he says. He sounds polite, but his eyes are flashing dangerously.

Sam nods and shakes Carter's hand. "Carter Clarke," he murmurs. "It's an honor, truly."

Carter nods and steps aside so Sam can greet Dad. I'm surprised to find Dad so lackluster. He's always so excited when Carter comes home from work, yet Sam flew halfway across the world to visit him, and he acts like he's going to a doctor's visit. I cross my arms over each other and pin Dad down with a stare, and he smiles at Sam unconvincingly.

"What's going on?" I ask, my eyes moving from Dad to Carter. Both shake their heads, and Dad crosses his arms over each other.

"You must be tired," Dad says, glancing at Sam.

Sam yawns right on cue and nods, looking sheepish. "It's been a fairly long journey," he says.

Dad nods. "Carter will show you to your room."

I shake my head. "Oh, no, we were planning on staying at the house," I murmur.

Dad looks at me the way he used to when I was a teenager, and I suddenly feel like I'm in trouble.

"No. You'll stay here, with me," he says, his voice brooking no argument.

I glance at Sam and he sighs, nodding slightly. He steps closer to me and brushes my hair out of my face gently. "We're here to spend time with your dad, after all," he murmurs. He wraps his hand around my waist before turning to Carter, a smile on his face. "Are you sure Emilia and I can stay here?" he asks, and I'm not even sure what I'm hoping for. Am I hoping he'll say yes, or no?

Carter nods briskly, his eyes lingering on where Sam is touching me. "Of course," he says, his expression blank. "Your room has already been prepared."

I'm filled with so many emotions that I can't even make sense of as I follow Carter, my eyes on his back. I'm filled with disappointment, anxiety and dread, when I should be excited to finally spend some time with Sam.

CHAPTER 28

milia

I glance at Sam and slip out of bed quietly. I've been tossing and turning all night, unable to fall asleep. My heart is in disarray.

I walk down the stairs, the marble cold underneath my feet. I hesitate as the glass sliding doors leading to the veranda come into view. I'd be lying to myself if I said that I didn't expect him to be here. Carter is standing outside, wearing nothing but long sleeping bottoms, a whisky glass in his hand. Something looks off about him, and my heart wrenches painfully. I'm instantly worried, though I can't quite pinpoint what it is that alarms me.

I slip through the sliding doors quietly, and Carter turns to face me. His eyes roam over my body heatedly, and rage flashes through them. He puts his glass down and approaches me, and I take a step away, my back hitting the wall.

"What is this, Minx?" he whispers, his fingers tracing the edges of my nightgown. "Where is my t-shirt? I know you stole a few more of my newer ones, yet you're not wearing any of them."

I gulp, my heart racing. He's standing so close that I can barely breathe. I turn and slip away from him, but I've only taken one step when he's got his arm wrapped around my waist. Carter pulls me back and against the wall.

I gasp, my eyes widening. "You're drunk," I whisper. I raise my hands to his chest, intending to keep some distance between us, but he grabs my wrists and pushes them against the wall, above my head. Carter pushes his body against mine, caging me in. My eyes shutter closed at the feel of him. How many years has it been since I've felt him against me like this? I don't even have it in me to protest. Instead, I melt against him. He's bigger now. Stronger. He's all man now, far from the twenty-one-year-old I used to call mine.

"Look at me, Emilia," he whispers, and I do. I look into his eyes, and all I find is helplessness and anger. "Did you fuck him underneath my roof?" he asks. "Did you let him touch you?"

He drops his forehead to mine, as though he can't let go of me, but can't face me either. He inhales deeply, his breath ragged. Carter loosens his grip on my wrists and pulls away from me.

I grab his hand and pull him back. He looks so tortured that my heart breaks. "No," I whisper. "No, Carter. I didn't. I wouldn't."

He buries his hand in my hair and grips tightly. "Look me in the eye and tell me you didn't kiss him. That he didn't touch your body. That he didn't fall asleep with you in his arms."

I bite down on my lip and look away, unable to do as he asks. Carter's eyes fall closed and he inhales deeply. "You say you wouldn't, but you already have. It's a kiss today, what is it tomorrow?"

He laughs humorlessly. "Fucking hell... I know you're *his*. I know it. But I can't fucking stand it."

He lets go of me and turns his back to me, and all I want to do is press my body back against his. I want to wrap my arms around him and reassure him in any way possible — but I can't. I can't, and I shouldn't.

"I can leave. I wasn't even planning on staying here with Sam," I murmur, my voice barely above a whisper.

Carter turns back to face me, his eyes flashing with anger. He laughs humorlessly and walks back to me. "What, you wanted to take him to your old house? Share your childhood bed with him? Spend some alone time with him? What exactly did you need all that privacy for?"

He grabs my waist, and before I know it, he's got me lifted up against the wall. I instinctively wrap my legs around him, and he pushes against me.

"You're not going anywhere," he tells me. "You're crazy if you think I'll let you to be alone in your old house. It isn't happening, Emilia."

I'm breathing hard and my hands find their way into his hair without me even realizing it. "That isn't it. I just thought it'd be easier," I whisper.

I want to be unaffected, but my heart is racing from just having him so close to me. I subconsciously tighten my legs around his waist. If he'd held me just a little lower, he'd be pressing right up against me. I pray he won't notice just how hard my nipples are against his chest.

"Easier?" he repeats. "Fuck that. I'm not making this easy on you. I don't give a fuck that you're his. He's not touching you. He's not laying a fucking finger on you, you hear me?"

I look into his eyes and nod, and Carter relaxes just slightly. His hands drop to my ass, and he squeezes tightly, almost painfully so. Carter repositions me so I'm wrapped around his hips, and I bite down on my lip. He's hard, and my body still responds to him the way it always has. I try my best to push down a wave of intense desire and swallow hard.

"Say it, Emilia," he orders.

"He's not touching me, Carter," I whisper, my thighs quivering.

His gaze is unfocused, and I can't help but wonder just how much he's had to drink. He's been so in control since I got here. Tonight is the first night that he's truly showing me just how intensely he still cares. It's not like the few slipped words here and there. No, this is different. It's raw, it's real... it's *Carter*.

"I want to clip your fucking wings," he whispers, his lips tracing over my ear. "So you won't ever leave me again." He kisses my neck, and I tremble against him. "I want to fuck Sam up, and I want to sabotage your relationship. I want to wreck the happiness you've so painstakingly found, because I can't stand the idea of you with someone that isn't me."

Carter rolls his hips against mine, and I bite down on my lip in an effort to keep quiet, to hide how he's making me feel. "I can't stand the thought of him fucking your delicious pussy, of you screaming his name. I don't want him to ever have the honor of falling asleep with you. I don't even want you smiling at him. I don't want him saying your fucking name."

He bites down on my shoulder before pressing a kiss to it. "I want to take you away from him. I want to rip you two apart," he whispers, before pulling away. He lowers me to the floor and looks into my eyes. "But I won't, Emilia. I won't, because I fucking love you."

Carter takes a step away from me and looks away. "Run, Emilia," he whispers. "Run, because if you stay, there won't be any going back."

I look at him, my legs barely able to keep me standing. I inhale deeply and turn, running away from him, just like he told me to. With every step I take away from him, the words he uttered reverberate louder through me, over and over again.

CHAPTER 29

milia

I'm nervous when I walk into Carter's office building the next morning, Sam by my side. I regret saying yes when he asked me for a tour of the office. I'm worried Carter won't like it.

The security guard stops me and asks me for my employee card, but I forgot to bring my wallet, so I don't have any form of identification with me either.

I'm about to walk back out when Asher walks up to me. "Milly!" he says, smiling.

Sam grins and leans into me. "Milly? Really?"

I elbow him and roll my eyes as he laughs at my childhood nickname. Asher offers Sam his hand, and I see the exact moment that Sam realizes who Asher is. He blanches, and his smile stiffens. "You're the Chief Technical Officer of Clarke Reed," he says, looking just a little flustered.

Asher grins and nod. "Yeah, I'm Asher Reed, the CTO — but you can just call me Asher. You must be Sam. Emilia has told me all about you," he says, glancing at me. I look away guiltily. I haven't told him a thing about Sam, but I probably should have.

"Only good things, I hope?" Sam says, smiling.

Thankfully, Asher smiles and nods. "Of course. Sometimes I can't get her to shut up about you. I'm so glad you're finally here. Now I won't have to hear her complain about how much she misses you."

Asher turns to me and wraps his arm around my shoulders. "Did you forget your access card, Milly?" he asks, ushering us in. What is with him? I never once said that I miss Sam. I'm pretty sure that Asher and I haven't spoken about him at all.

Asher walks us to his office, and I freeze when I spot Carter in the hallway. Last night is still fresh in my mind, and my heart starts to race. The things he said to me... the way he held me, and the intensity he showed me last night. I inhale shakily and try to ground myself. He was just drunk. That's all. At least, that's what I desperately need to make myself believe. It can't be more than that.

Carter pauses when he sees Sam and me, and he glances at Asher. "Emilia, Sam," he says, nodding at us politely. I can't spot a single trace of embarrassment or awkwardness in him, and suddenly I wonder if I read too much into what happened last night.

He looks at Sam and smiles at him. "I've been meaning to invite you to come see my office," he says. "Would you like a tour?"

His offer surprises me, and I look up at him with wide eyes. Just last night he told me he didn't even want Sam saying *my name*, but today he's offering him a tour of his office?

"I'd love a tour," Sam says, and I sigh as Carter leads us deeper into the building. "I badgered Emilia into offering me one, but having you as my tour guide would be even better."

I spot the brief flash of irritation on Carter's face, but thank-

135

fully, Sam misses it. He's is enraptured by what Carter tells him about the origins of the company, and truth be told, so am I.

I remember sitting on the floor in the small apartment that Asher and Carter shared. Everything Carter has achieved was merely a concept back then. It's astounding how much he has accomplished in just under a decade. I wish I'd been there every step of the way. I wish I could've supported him throughout this journey. For a brief second, I can't help but wonder what those years would have looked like for us.

Carter and Sam pause by a large glass wall that overlooks a lab. Sam looks through the glass in awe, and I take a better look. "This is the stem cell research you're doing, isn't it?" he mutters, clearly impressed.

Carter nods and smiles, but his smile is pained. "Yes, but the research isn't moving quick enough."

Sam frowns. "What do you mean, *not quick enough*? Your team found a way to create *organoids* in almost no time at all. Your team is literally creating mini organs. It's groundbreaking."

Carter nods and sighs. "Yes, but I need full-sized organs. This isn't good enough."

Sam stares at Carter, his brows furrowed. "Come to think of it, you probably started this research around the same time that Emilia's father received his diagnosis."

I look at Carter with wide eyes. "You did this for dad?"

Carter bites down on his lip and shakes his head. "Not quite. Him falling ill is what gave me the idea. I just figured that there must be a way to help people like him, so I funded the team that was closest to reaching a break-through."

So, yes. He *did* do this for Dad. I inhale deeply, my heart twisting painfully. I try my best to blink back my tears. I've done my very best to remain strong since I got here. I've tried my hardest not to cry, even when I've had to see that lost and hopeless expression on Dad's face when he's forced to his machine every day, but this... this guts me.

Carter looks at me as though he knows exactly what I'm feeling, and he smiles tightly. I bite down on my lip as hard as I can, trying my best to keep my tears at bay, and the expression on Carter's face mirrors how I feel. He looks heartbroken.

Thankfully, Sam requests to speak to one of Carter's researchers, and I lean back against the wall, needing a moment.

"You okay?" Carter murmurs, his voice soft. I nod at him and try my best to smile. Carter runs a hand through his hair and inhales deeply.

I look up at him in surprise and try my best to smile. I was intent on keeping him at a distance after what he said to me last night, and the way he touched me. A shiver runs down my spine at the mere memory of him pressed against me, my legs wrapped around him.

I told myself I should be mad at him for his behavior, but how can I stay mad at a guy that tells me he loves me, and then shows it by doing everything in his power to save my father's life — to the extent of funding groundbreaking research.

"You were out of line last night," I murmur.

Carter sighs and pulls a hand through his hair, his eyes on mine. "I'd say I'm sorry, but I'm not. I meant every word," he says. Carter looks away and bites down on his lip. "I won't let it happen again, though. Sam seems like a great guy, and I won't mess with your happiness. I guess I just need a distraction or some shit."

I freeze and look up at him. "Don't," I say without thinking. "Don't find a distraction."

Carter looks surprised, a smile tugging at his lips. "Tell me you'll be mine, and I won't ever stray," he says, his eyes blazing.

I bite down on my lip and look away. "I can't," I whisper. "You know I can't."

If Carter wants to call Layla tonight then there isn't a thing I can do about it, because I just have no rights to him. I stare down at my feet as devastation devours me. If he truly feels the way he told me he did, then there's no way he'll last. Not with Sam here. He won't just sit there and watch me be with Sam. He'll go looking for a *distraction*. It might not be Layla, but there'll be someone. And that someone won't be me.

CHAPTER 30

arter

Emilia is quiet as she walks into the kitchen and I frown at her. The way she's looking at me puts me on edge. There's fear and accusation in her eyes, and I wonder if she's still thinking about what I said to her — that I needed to find myself a distraction.

She avoids my eyes as she walks towards the coffee machine, and I grab her arm. "Sit down. I'll make you a cup," I murmur.

She looks up at me briefly, and the bags underneath her eyes match mine. I sigh as I make her a cup of coffee, hating the tension between us now. I never should've said a thing to her. I never should've told her how I feel. I hesitate as I make her coffee, and I think back to the day she moved into her student dorm. I smile to myself and put a tablespoon of salt in her coffee, just like I did back then, just for old time's sake.

I hand it to Emilia with a serene expression, and I watch her as she takes a sip. Her eyes widen and she looks up at me as she forces the sip she took down. Her lips transform into a beautiful smile, and she bursts out laughing.

"Wow, that's a nostalgic little prank," she murmurs.

"Hey, you can't go wrong with the classics," I tell her, laughing, and her eyes flash with amusement. I breathe a sigh of relief. I was so worried that I'd ruined everything between us.

"Classics, huh?"

I look at her, alarmed, and hold my hands up. "Not the cockroaches," I whisper, pleading with her, and Emilia giggles.

"I'm going to get you back for this, you know that, right? I let you get away with the *Crazy Frog* song, but you only get one freebie."

I grin at her. I love seeing her eyes flash like this. Lately she's been looking so stressed out and worried, and I'm glad something as simple as this still makes her smile. I love seeing her laugh.

"I'm looking forward to it," I murmur, a twinge of excitement running through me. Emilia is capable of some utter mayhem, and I really shouldn't encourage her, but if it gets her to take her mind off her dad, I'll do it quite happily.

Sam walks into the kitchen, and I stiffen. I can't get my mind of the two of them spending the night together. My fucked-up mind keeps imagining his hands on her body, and I only barely manage to keep my anger in check.

Emilia has her back to him and glances at her coffee cup, shaking her head. She smiles up at me, her eyes lighting up. "Seriously," she says. "I'm outraged in Spanish."

I burst out laughing, and so does she. Sam frowns and wraps his arm around her waist, pressing a kiss to her cheek, and my amusement is instantly gone. Emilia seems startled, and it's obvious she hadn't noticed him. How very interesting... she's always hyper-aware of me.

"What does that mean, darling?" Sam asks, and Emilia stiffens.

"Oh, it's nothing," she says. "It's from a TV show."

Sam looks at her in confusion, a flash of uncertainty in his eyes, and I breathe a sigh of relief. I don't want her to let him in on any of our inside jokes. There aren't many parts of Emilia that are still mine, and I want to hold on to the ones that are with all my might.

I inhale deeply and try my best to smile at Sam, catching him off guard. "Your house is rather impressive," he says, and his British accent grates on me. I wonder if it's one of the things Emilia loves about him.

I smile in thanks and sigh. "How about I show you around?" I say, hoping he'll say no.

Sam grins at me and nods. "Oh, I'd love that. I've been curious about this mansion of yours. I must admit that I've never been in a property quite as grand as this one."

He looks at Emilia and smiles at her. I watch as he walks up to Emilia and takes her coffee mug out of her hand. Just that small act pisses me off. Emilia is a clean freak, and all our lives, I've been the only one she's ever shared food or drinks with. "Let me have a few sips of this, darling," he says, pressing a kiss to her cheek.

"Oh no, don't," she says, her eyes flashing with panic. She takes the cup back from him, and he frowns. Emilia smiles nervously and brushes her hair behind her ear, her hand trembling. "I, uh, I accidentally put salt in it," she tells him, and it's my turn to frown. I shouldn't be surprised that she keeps our pranks from him, but it annoys me nonetheless.

Sam smiles at her and shakes his head. "Sleepyhead," he murmurs, amusement twinkling in his eyes. I grit my teeth when he places his hand on the small of her back and smiles at me. "I'm rather wretched without a cuppa in the morning, but I think I'll be fine," he tells me, and my goodwill is instantly gone. Well, that lasted long. I glance at my watch and sigh. Ten seconds, or so. That's how long I lasted before wanting to punch him in the face. Even his fucking voice irritates me. I'm tempted to mimic him, but I resist.

I see Emilia bite back a smile, and I unintentionally glare at her. Surely, she doesn't like that dumb accent of his? I shake my head and inhale deeply. I really need to get a hold of myself.

Sam asks me a million questions as I show him all the different rooms in my house. I pause in the theater room and sigh. I designed this room with Emilia in mind. It's basically a much more luxurious set-up of what I arranged on her sixteenth birthday. It's crazy to think that that's over ten years ago now. Here I am, standing in this room, with the man that has everything I've ever wanted.

I shake my head absentmindedly and lead Sam to the next room. The worst thing is that he's actually a nice guy. He's tried his best to help with John too, and he seems to treat Emilia well. I can tell that he feels intimidated by me, but he's nice nonetheless. He's a little too nice, in my opinion. I can't understand what Emilia sees in him. He's so fucking dull. I haven't seen him make her laugh even once.

"You might like this," I tell him, unlocking the door to my safe room. His eyes widen as we walk into the room, and I have to admit that even I am impressed every time I walk in. "It's completely secure, with its own generator and satellite connections." I click the security feeds on, and all angles of the house are covered. "The only rooms that don't have cameras are the bedrooms and the bathrooms. I have a security team that monitors my property and my office, but I do keep copies for reference too."

Sam looks impressed and I smile at him as he plays around with the multiple controls. I was exactly the same when I got it all installed the first time around. Sam frowns at one of the screens, and I follow his gaze, my eyes narrowing.

"Oh dear, what is she doing?" Sam asks, confused. I zoom in on Emilia to find her kneeling in my dining room, something that looks suspiciously like glue in her hands.

"What is she doing?" Sam asks, frowning.

I shake my head at him and lean in closer, curious. "Is that... a whoopee cushion?" I murmur, amused as hell. "Where the fuck did she even get that?"

Sam looks more stressed out by the second, but I just find it amusing as hell. She even found one that matches the color of my chairs. I watch as she glues it to my usual seat in the dining table, a huge smile on her face. She did warn me that there'd be payback...

"I have no idea if that's even going to come off. My god, I can't believe she's doing this. That's destruction of property. How much are those chairs?"

I laugh when she pushes against the pillow and bursts out laughing. I love seeing her like this.

"Two thousand dollars each," I tell him. Worth it. That smile of hers is worth far more than a measly chair or two. I glance at Sam, the outrage on his face, the stiffness in his every move. I can see why he'd like the version Emilia portrays of herself in his presence, but the real her? He could never handle the real Emilia.

"Don't worry about it," I tell Sam. "For Emilia, this is quite a mild prank. Hell, it's probably one of her lamest. I guess it's the best she could do without time to prepare. Just pretend like you don't know. I don't care about the chair."

All I care about is the smile she's got on her face right now... the smile that *I* put on her face.

CHAPTER 31

milia

"How are you feeling, Daddy?"

He looks tired, and he's really struggling to stay awake these days. He's taking longer naps, and he seems less cheerful than he was a few weeks ago. Sam checks his equipment and questions his nurses, and Dad follows Sam's movements with a frown on his face.

"I'm fine, Princess," he says, but he doesn't sound fine. My heart is breaking. I hate that I'm so helpless. That there isn't anything I can do to help.

"I really am fine, Emilia," Dad says, smiling at me. "Go on. Just go to bed. I'll see you tomorrow morning, all right?"

I nod and look back at him one more time before walking out of his treatment room. I hate leaving him here by himself, but he seems uncomfortable having Sam around. I guess he doesn't like looking weak, which is understandable. It doesn't help that Sam keeps treating Dad like he's one of his patients.

I walk into the bedroom that I've shared with Sam for the last week and a half and sigh. Sam smiles at me and pulls me closer. "Hey, we should just get an early night," he murmurs, leaning in. I stiffen when he tries to kiss me and pull away from him.

Sam frowns. "What's going on, Emilia? I get that you're worried about your dad, but you won't even kiss me. You haven't even properly kissed me back *once* since I got here. We haven't seen each other in weeks. Haven't you missed me? Bloody hell, I've been dreaming about being in bed with you. Haven't you?"

I'm filled with dread at the mere thought of it. I bite down on my lip and look away guiltily. "This is all just so strange to me," I admit. "Seeing my dad lose more and more of his spirit every single day is killing me, and being in someone else's house isn't exactly helping. So no, I *haven't* been dreaming about that."

Sam looks at me angrily. "It's Carter, isn't it? I can't even bloody blame you, because he's Carter Clarke. The man is filthy rich, he's handsome and quite a bit more muscular than I am, and he takes amazing care of your dad. Bloody hell, even I'd be in love with him."

He runs a hand through his hair and looks away. "Just tell me that you're mine, Emilia. Lie to me if you must, but tell me that you're still mine. Tell me that you're coming home with me when your dad recovers, and that whatever is going on here will stay here."

I look at him with wide eyes. "What?" I whisper.

Sam grimaces, and I don't think I've ever seen him look this hurt. "I see the way you look at him, Emilia. You've never looked at me that way before. I see the way you two interact as though you can tell what the other is thinking, and you and I have never had that. It's obvious that even your dad likes him better, and I can't even fault him for it. I'm trying my best to help with his treatment, but that's nothing compared to everything Carter has done for him."

I shake my head and wrap my arms around his neck. "No, Sam. That just isn't true," I whisper, willing myself to believe it too.

"Isn't it?" he murmurs. "Emilia, I saw you superglue a *whoopee cushion* to Carter's dining room chair. I looked it up, just to be sure. Those chairs are two thousand dollars each. Carter just stood there and watched you do it, a smile on his face. What the hell is up with that? Since when do you play pranks like that? I've never seen you as giddy as you were while you were doing that. Not even once. You were so excited while you were *destroying* Carter's property, and he *let* you. How can you tell me there isn't anything going on? No sane man would ever let you do something as crazy as that — with a smile on his face. I don't even recognize the person you are around Carter. You're so different, and I hate it. Did you think I didn't notice the inside jokes? The way you won't even explain whatever the hell being outraged *in Spanish* even means?"

I stare at him wide-eyed. "I... I was just trying to get him back for a prank he pulled a little while ago. I'd gotten so busy with Dad that I forgot about it, but then I saw the bag from the toy store," I ramble, trailing off.

Sam crosses his arms over each other and frowns. "What the hell are you even talking about? What could he possibly have done to warrant you destroying his property like that?"

I bite down on my lip and look away. "I... he... he'd changed the ringtone to my phone and then called me during a work meeting," I murmur. It sounds stupid even to my own ears, and he's right, I probably went too far with the prank I pulled in return.

"Are you crazy?" he shouts. "You did that because the guy changed your ringtone? What is wrong with you, Emilia? I don't understand what has gotten into you. You weren't this... *crazy* just a few months ago."

He sighs and starts to pace. "You're distant and you're acting irrationally. It's like I don't even know you anymore. It's like you came here, and you turned into an entirely different person. You usually hate cooking, but here you make your dad lunch every single day, and you're usually so serious, yet now you're suddenly playing pranks. *Pranks.* You say you can't sleep with me because you're too worried about your dad, but you're not too worried to play a fucking childish joke. It's ridiculous."

Sam runs his hand through his hair angrily and looks at me, his eyes flashing with disappointment. "How the hell did Carter even get into your phone? I don't even know your code."

I bite down on my lip and sigh. "He guessed it."

Sam chuckles. "He *guessed* it? So, a guy that you haven't seen in years knows you better than I do? Well, that's just brilliant."

"I don't know what you want me to say, Sam. Yes, he does know me well. We grew up together, after all. You're telling me you hate who I am here, but what does that even mean, because for the first time in years I actually feel like *myself.*"

Sam sighs and shakes his head. "I'm just really confused. I don't even know who you are anymore. I'm starting to wonder if the girl I fell for was ever even the real you at all."

I'm starting to wonder the same thing. The girl that Sam loves, is that even the real me? Or is it just who I so desperately *wanted* to be?

CHAPTER 32

milia

Sam seems absentminded and hurt, and I hate that I did this to us. He's barely spoken a word to me since our argument last night.

He's right. I've become a different person here in Wood-stock, and this isn't what I wanted. I worked so hard to become the woman Sam is in love with, yet just a few weeks here in Woodstock have made me feel like a little girl all over again.

"How about I show you around town a little? We can do dinner tonight, if you fancy it? Just you and me," I murmur.

Sam looks up at me, a spark of hope in his eyes, and my heart twists painfully. I've been neglecting him, I realize now. I've settled in so well in my life and my routine here that I haven't paid him enough attention.

"That sounds brilliant," he says, smiling. He walks up to me and cups my cheek gently, his lips brushing against my fore-head. He kisses me so sweetly that my heart feels crushed. I feel so bad for not paying more attention to him, for not putting him first while he's here.

"Come on," I say, "let's go."

He grabs my hand and entwines our fingers as we make our way down the stairs, and I find myself tensing. Carter's words ring through my mind, and a shiver runs down my spine. *I don't want him to ever have the honor of falling asleep with you. I don't even want you smiling at him.*

I bite down on my lip and shake my head, willing myself to stop thinking about Carter. I'm so lost in thought that I'm startled when Dad calls my name.

I turn to look at him, my eyes widening when I realize Carter is standing next to him. His eyes fall to Sam's hand holding mine, and he grits his teeth, anger flashing through his eyes.

"You heading out, sweetheart?" Dad asks, and I nod.

Sam grins at Dad and throws his arm around my shoulders. "Emilia is showing me around town, and we're grabbing dinner later."

Carter nods, his expression unreadable. "I'll let Enzo know not to expect you two for dinner either," he says, before turning to Dad. "He'll just be cooking for you, then. Don't even try to get him to cook anything you shouldn't be eating. I'll know."

Dad smiles and shakes his head, the camaraderie between them heartwarming.

"Are you having dinner at your parents' house?" I ask, and Carter's eyes drop to Sam's arm wrapped around my shoulder, before he looks up at me, shaking his head.

"No," he says. "I've got a date."

My heart drops and my stomach twists violently. I freeze and look up at him in disbelief before forcing a smile onto my face.

"Oh, have fun," I say, unable to look him in the eye. Thoughts of him with Layla fill my head, and jealousy knots up my stomach.

"Ah, Emilia did tell me that you have a girlfriend," Sam says. "I'd love to meet her at some point."

I bite down on my lip hard and stare at the floor, willing myself to gather my thoughts. This is for the best. I should be happy for him.

"Will you be okay having dinner by yourself?" Sam asks Dad.

Dad huffs and waves us off. "I'm not a child," he says, his tone offended, and I smile at Dad.

"We'll see you later, all right?" I murmur, just wanting to get out of here already.

"Everything okay?" Sam asks as we get into the car.

I nod at him and smile. "I don't like the idea of Dad being by himself," I end up saying, lying, covering for my true feelings.

Sam nods in understanding. "We won't make it a late night."

I nod and drive us to my old high school, wanting to show Sam some of the places I spent most of my time at growing up.

I park in front of the building and smile, memory after memory filling my mind. I try to think of some stories to tell Sam, but every single one of my memories involves either Carter or Kate. In the end, I end up driving us around town, pointing out various places, but not a single one isn't connected to the Clarkes.

By the time I pull up at the restaurant I'm mentally and emotionally exhausted. Sam smiles at me and presses a kiss to my cheek.

"That was fun," he says. "Seeing this town through your eyes."

I smile at him, relieved that he couldn't tell how distraught I was.

Sam holds my hand as we walk into the restaurant, and he seems excited as we wait for the waitress to seat us. This is exactly what we needed, just a bit of quality time. If only I could give Sam all my attention mentally too.

I smile at the waitress as she leads us to our seats, and Sam looks around happily. As we sit down, I finally relax. This restaurant... this is one of the few places where I don't have memories with Carter. When we were younger, we could never really afford to come here.

Sam reaches for my hand over the table as he checks out the menu, and I smile. He needs to be my focus tonight.

My smile drops when I see a familiar figure approach from the corner of my eyes, and my heart sinks when my eyes find Carter's.

I blink in surprise, my mind barely comprehending him being here. It's not me he's looking at, though. No, it's Layla he's with. It's Layla's hand that's nestled in his, it's her he's smiling at.

Carter pulls Layla's chair out for her, and she grins up at him. He's looking at her like she's all he can see, and it wrecks me. It kills me to see him looking at her the way he used to look at me. My heart twists painfully and I feel sick. It takes all of me to pull my gaze away and pretend I didn't see him, but unfortunately for me, the waitress seats them right in front of us, my view unobstructed. Layla's back is to me, but I can see Carter clearly.

"Everything okay?" Sam asks. I blink and nod, but I've clearly taken too long to respond, because Sam turns around and sees Carter.

The two of them nod at each other, and Carter looks at me, his expression blank. He smiles politely, as though I'm yet another acquaintance, and then he turns back to Layla, dismissing me.

"Small towns, huh?" Sam says, shaking his head. He asks me what I want to eat and walks me through some of the dishes he thinks sound interesting, but all I can focus on is Carter.

I watch as Layla leans back in her seat and slips her foot out of her high heeled stiletto. From this angle I can see the lone shoe between the legs of her chair, and it doesn't take a genius to figure out where her foot might be. I watch Carter's face as his eyes widen and he smirks at Layla, his eyes twinkling.

I feel sick as I tear my eyes away. He's going home with her, I just know it. Worse yet, he might bring her back to his house. I bite down on my lip so hard that I end up drawing blood, and I inhale deeply as I try my best to stay calm.

I barely eat more than three bites throughout dinner, but somehow, I manage to have a conversation with Sam. Somehow, I manage to keep him from suspecting that something is wrong.

My heart is hurting so badly by the time that dinner wraps up that I'm surprised I'm still able to smile at Sam. He looks happy and content, and that's all that should matter.

We rise from our seats, and I can feel Carter's eyes on me. Sam wraps his arm around my waist and leans in for a kiss. I freeze, my eyes finding Carter.

It's not me he's looking at, though. It's Layla. He looks up at me just as I let my eyes fall closed and kiss Sam back, *properly*, for the first time since he got here.

CHAPTER 33

arter

Graham nods at me politely as I step out of the car, and I need to remember to give the guy a bonus. He didn't even blink twice when I asked him to pick me up at the local bar way past his working hours.

I inhale deeply and walk into the house, needing another fucking drink. Though I doubt that'll burn away the image of Emilia kissing Sam. I shouldn't have provoked her. I shouldn't have pushed her into his arms.

I walk into the living room, my mind torturing me with scenario after scenario of what Emilia and Sam must have done after they got home. I saw the look in her eyes when she saw me with Layla. I saw the shock, the pain, and eventually, the determination. I know what my Minx is like. My impulsive jealous actions today will cost me everything. I never should have called Layla. It wasn't her I wanted anyway. All I could see all night was Emilia.

I run a hand through my hair and walk straight to the liquor cart in the corner, pouring myself a drink. I'm surprised when I notice movement from the corner of my eye, and I turn to find Emilia standing in the doorway. My eyes roam over her body and I grit my teeth. She looks fucking sexy in that nightgown, and I know it isn't for me.

"If you're standing here right now, you clearly weren't fucked good enough, hard enough. Your little boyfriend not cutting it?" I say, my tone biting.

Emilia's eyes roam over my body, lingering on my clothes, as though she's checking whether everything is still properly in place. I see insecurity in her eyes, and right at this second, I hate it. I hate that she keeps giving me hope, that she keeps making me think she still has feelings for me too.

"If you're home now Layla clearly isn't cutting it either," she says.

I laugh and look up at the clock. "It's two in the morning. Who says I didn't just spend hours fucking her brains out?"

She walks up to me, her eyes flashing with an emotion I can't quite place. "So you need to be drunk to fuck her? Interesting."

I grit my teeth and pull her closer, my hand threading through her hair. "Maybe I do. Maybe a drink or two makes it easier to pretend she's *you*. Maybe I just sank my dick deep inside her, all the while imagining it was *you* I was fucking."

I laugh mirthlessly. "Or maybe I just wanted to get laid, Emilia. Maybe I just wanted to spend a night with a woman who actually *wants* me. Who isn't dating someone else, who isn't playing with my fucking feelings."

I tighten my grip on her hair and pull her closer, her face so close to mine that I could easily lean down and kiss her. "Either way, why would you even care who I fuck, Emilia? I saw the way you kissed Sam tonight. I saw the way he touched you, the look in his eyes. Did you want him? Did you spread your legs for him tonight?"

My eyes drop down to her nightgown and I trace the edge

of her strap with my fingers. "This sexy little thing you're wearing, is that all for him?" I ask, my voice breaking. "If you were mine, you'd be too fucking exhausted to be up and about now. You never would've even gotten round to putting on a nightgown, because you'd have fallen asleep in my arms."

Emilia looks at me with wide eyes, her chest rising and falling rapidly. "I'd rip that dress you were wearing off you the second I got you alone, leaving you standing there in nothing but your underwear and your heels. I'd kis you until your lips are all swollen and you're panting, needy. I'd undo your bra, letting it fall to the floor, and your nipples would already be hard, ready for my lips."

I tilt her head up so she's looking into my eyes, and part of me feels vindicated when I see desire in her eyes. "My mouth would be hot and wet on your skin, and you'd moan for me, a shiver running down your spine. You'd already be wet by the time my fingers push your underwear aside to give you a taste of what is to come."

She's panting and I press her against the wall, my cock pressed up against her stomach. I'm so fucking hard that it hurts.

"I'd sit you down and drop to my knees, my tongue finding its way between your legs. I'd make you come just like that, with your hands in my hair and my name on your lips. And that'd be just the start of what I'd do to you."

I take a step back and pinch her chin. "But you aren't mine, Emilia. You've made it clear you won't ever give me a chance again. You've shown me you've moved on. So every single thing I just described? Every bit of passion and desire? I gave all of it to Layla, and she fucking loved it. I watched her come for me, the image burning away every thought of you," I whisper, lying to her.

Emilia swallows hard, pain flashing through her eyes. It's

nothing compared to how she's made me feel every single time I see her with Sam.

"But I'm sure you don't give a fuck about any of that, do you? For a while I thought you did. Until today. Until I saw you rise to your tiptoes to kiss him the way you always used to kiss me. I get it now, Emilia. You've moved on. It's time I do, too."

My fingers trace over the strap of her nightgown and I push it off her shoulder, just as a single tear drops down her cheek. I watch it fall, my heart wrenching painfully.

"You're lying to me," she says, her voice breaking. "Tell me you're lying to me," she pleads, and I almost give in. I almost admit that she's right.

I lift my hand to her face and wipe away her tears with my thumb. "You don't want me," I tell her. "But you don't want anyone else to have me either, huh? That's not how life works, Emilia. That's not how *love* works."

She bites down on her lip as more tears stream down her face, and it breaks my heart. Yet I remain silent. I need this. I need the distance this will create. I need her to understand how she's been making me feel. All this time I've been hoping that eventually she'd change her mind about us, but she won't. I saw the way she kissed Sam tonight, and I get it now. I lost her. She and I might have history, and she might be a little nostalgic when she's around me, but that isn't love, and it's time I realize it. It's time I take a step back, before I destroy what little of my heart is left.

"Go back to bed, Emilia. Go back to Sam. I'm done."

She swallows hard, her eyes filled with tears, and I let go of her. I turn to leave, but she pulls on my sleeve and pulls me back. I look at her, my conviction swaying already. I can't bare to see her so sad. I can't stand seeing her cry. I never could.

"Carter, I..."

"What's going on here?"

Emilia and I both turn to find Sam standing in the doorway,

and she takes a step away from me, towards him. She wipes at her tears and shakes her head, smiling at him. It's like his mere presence makes her forget I'm still standing here too.

"Nothing," she says, walking up to him. "Carter came home right as I went down to grab a glass of water. We were talking about the past, that's all." She grabs his hand and pulls him away. She looks back at me as she rounds the corner, her eyes filled with resignation.

I sit down on the sofa as her footsteps get further and further away. I inhale deeply and pour myself another drink. Maybe Asher was right all along. She's going to bed with the man she chose, and here I am, broken all over again.

CHAPTER 34

arter

I'm tense as I wait in front of the airport. I'm feeling conflicted as hell. I should've spoken to Emilia, but she's been avoiding me all week. I don't even blame her. I did everything within my power to push her away.

Kate walks out with her suitcase in tow, and she grins at me. My heart twists painfully at the sight of her. I love my sister, but now that Emilia is back, all the damage she did feels so fresh. I know better than anyone else that she's no longer the vicious little girl that she used to be. Hell, I was the one that paid for all the treatments, the psychiatrists, psychologists and even the freaking MBA she decided to do.

Kate walks up to me and hugs me tightly, and I wrap my arms around her. "Hey baby sis," I murmur, and she grins up at me.

"Missed you, Carter," she says, her eyes twinkling. She looks healthy and happy, but will she still when she realizes Emilia is back? I'm worried. I'm worried about how Emilia might react when she sees Kate again. She's been avoiding my mother since the day that she came over for lunch, and I've barred my Mom from my house for the time being, in an effort to respect Emilia's wishes.

I'm quiet as Kate and I step into the car, and she looks at me with interest. "So, she's back, huh?" Kate says, and I freeze.

I glance at her, my expression far more tense than I intended. "Stay away from her. She's going through enough."

Kate inhales deeply and looks away, hiding her face from me. I sigh and run a hand through my hair. I'm a horrible brother for feeling this way, but I wish she hadn't come back for the holidays this year. With John being as sick as he is and Emilia finally back for the first time in years... I just want Emilia to have a peaceful couple of days. I want to protect her from my family as best as I can, the way I should have done years ago.

"I'm not here to cause conflict," she whispers, and I nod.

"I know. I know that, Kate."

Even if she doesn't cause any conflict, seeing her will still be painful for Emilia.

"I'll stay with you, away from the house," Kate says, and I shake my head.

"You can't. Just stay with Mom and Dad."

Kate bites down on her lip and frowns. "Is she staying with you?"

I nod. Even merely discussing Emilia makes me uncomfortable.

"So, you two... are you back together?"

I glance at her, trying to assess how she'd even feel about that. I can't find a single trace of viciousness in her gaze, but then again, I missed it for years. "No. She has a boyfriend. He's here too."

Kate looks at me with wide eyes. "Her boyfriend is staying with you too? What the fuck, Carter?"

I inhale deeply and nod. "It's complicated," I say, wanting to keep as much to myself as possible.

Kate looks shocked and confused, and for a second I think I see devastation in her expression. I look away and focus on the road, my heart twisting painfully. If Kate hadn't done what she did, would Emilia and I be together now? I keep telling myself that we don't know if we would've made it, and that we were so young... but I believe with every fiber of my being that Emilia would still be mine, if Kate hadn't taken her from me. It would've been me she'd wake up to every day. She'd be my wife by now.

"Is it serious?" she asks, her voice trembling.

I nod and bite down on my lip. "They're moving in together once they go back."

Kate looks pale, as though the news hurts her as much as it does me, and for a second I worry that she might try and ruin this for Emilia too.

"I... I'd been meaning to apologize to her. I mean, it must've been quite obvious that I took the job offer in London because that's where Emilia is, but I just couldn't do it. I could never find the courage. I don't know how to face her."

I shake my head. "Then don't. She has a lot on her mind right now. Her father is sick, Kate. Now is not the time to remind her of the past." Kate nods, but I worry that she won't listen to me. "Promise me, Kate."

She nods again. "I promise, Carter," she whispers, and I breathe a little easier. It's fucked up that my sister's promises don't mean much to me, but it's nice to hear her say it anyway.

"Is she really dating someone else?"

I grit my teeth and tighten my grip on my steering wheel.

"Yeah, she is. She's happy with him."

Kate shakes her head. "That's not possible," she says, her eyes flashing.

I inhale deeply and stare at the road, wishing I'd just asked

Graham to pick her up instead. "I don't want to talk about it, Kate."

Kate nods and I exhale in relief when she shuts up for the rest of the journey. The upcoming holidays are going to be unbearable. I can't tell what's worse, having Emilia here and knowing she isn't mine, or not having her here at all. Everything is a fucking mess, and I can't do a thing about it.

My head is hurting by the time I pull up to my parents' house, and it starts to pound when Kate speaks again. "I'm sorry, Carter. I know asking you for forgiveness is too little too late. I know that. But if I can't say it to her, I'd like to say to you at least. If not for me, Emilia would now be my sister-in-law. We'd all be spending a couple of amazing days together, and she'd be in the kitchen with Mom, cooking up a storm the way she's always loved doing. Because of me, you lost the love of your life. Because of me, you now have to see her with someone else. Nothing I could ever do will make up for that, but I need you to know how sorry I am. if I could turn back time, I'd take it all back. It was so easy to forget that anything even happened after I got better, to just move on with life... but I know it wasn't easy for you. If anything, I'm pretty sure every day without her was just harder on you. I don't know if you'll ever forgive me, but I'll do whatever I can to make sure you're proud of the person I am now, even if you can never forgive the person I used to be."

I drop my head to my steering wheel and inhale deeply. "Kate, please... just go, okay? Just get into the house. I can't do this. I can't."

I know she means well, but I can't tell her what she needs to hear. I can't tell her that it's okay, and that I forgive her. Because I don't. I don't think I ever will.

CHAPTER 35

milia

I'm anxious as I get dressed. Things between Sam and me haven't been the same in a while now, and I feel terrible, because I know it's my fault. I've been pulling away from him when he hasn't done anything wrong. I don't know how to fix it, and I'm filled with guilt over him flying all the way here to be here with me. I'm torn between the obligation I feel to be with him and what my heart wants, what my soul needs.

Since the night Carter came home drunk, I just haven't been myself. I've avoided him ever since, unable to look at him and know he truly isn't mine anymore. My heart feels broken and I feel like I'm mourning our relationship all over again. I thought I was over him, and I thought I was happy with Sam. Until that night. It wasn't until Carter made it clear that I truly lost him that I realized how much I still care about him. Until then part of me had been taking him for granted. Until then, I thought I'd always own part of his heart.

Sam kisses my shoulder as I finish putting on my make-up, and I try my best to smile at him. Maybe a day away is exactly what we need. I feel bad about not spending Thanksgiving with Dad, even though I'm finally home for it after so many years, but I just can't face Carter. I'm terrified he'll invite Layla, and I can't do it.

Sam seems excited as we walk down the stairs, but my heart twists painfully when I see Dad standing at the bottom of the stairs, a hopeless expression on his face. He's been asking me to spend Thanksgiving with him and the Clarkes for weeks now, but I just don't think I have it in me. I offered for us to spend Thanksgiving together, just the three of us, but Dad wouldn't have that.

"Emilia," he says, and my heart aches. He looks so sad, and I hate that I did this. "Princess, are you sure you won't spend Thanksgiving with me?" he asks, his voice soft. He turns to Sam, and the expression on his face guts me. "Sam? Won't you talk to her? Please... it's been years since I've had my daughter here. I just want one Thanksgiving like the ones we used to have."

Sam is caving, I can just see it. He looks at me, distressed. "Darling, maybe we should," he whispers. He pulls me away from Dad and I sigh. "Would it really be so bad? It looks like it'd mean the world to your dad. I don't understand why you're still mad at your neighbors. It's been years. If you and Carter are on good terms, then what is the problem? Surely you can act civil for an evening?"

I bite down on my lip and shake my head, and anger flashes through his eyes. He's been tense since he found Carter and me standing in the living room, all those nights ago. He's been acting irrational and jealous, controlling even. Nothing I do or say appeases him, especially when it comes to Carter or his family.

"What does it matter, Emilia? You're with me now. We're happy. Whatever happened is in the past. Or do you still care so much about the way things ended between you and Carter that you can't even spend an afternoon at his old house? Do you really still blame them for standing between you two? Or maybe you're not over him at all. That would explain why you won't let me touch you."

I grit my teeth and glare at him. Every argument we have keeps circling back to this. He's insecure about Carter and mad that I won't sleep with him. It doesn't matter how much I avoid Carter, Sam just won't see reason. I told him exactly why I'm still hurt. I told him about everything Kate said and did, and the way Helen sided with her. He *knows* Kate will be there. He knows the pain they caused me had nothing to do with Carter, and everything to do with the love and trust I thought I shared with *them*. Yet he still acts like that's all an excuse, like it's *Carter* I'm upset about.

"Let's go," he says. "If you're over him, then let's just go. It'd make your Dad happy anyway."

I want to tell him no, but I'm tired of fighting. I'm tired of arguing with him, and truthfully, I'm just tired of being angry altogether. Maybe this is exactly what I need. Maybe I just need to face Kate and Helen. Holding onto this resentment is killing me on the inside. And maybe, just maybe, seeing Carter happy with someone else is what I need to truly let him go.

I nod at Sam and force a smile onto my face. "Fine. Let's go."

He looks relieved and smiles at me. Somehow, in his mind, my anger towards Kate and Helen is related to lingering feelings I might have for Carter, but it isn't. Carter is probably the only person in this that I don't blame. He was as helpless as I was, and he might very well have been hurt more than I was.

I follow Sam to the door, and Carter looks up at me in surprise. He glances at Dad, concern flashing through his eyes. "You're coming with us?" he asks, his voice soft.

I hesitate and then nod. We haven't spoken in days now. I haven't even seen him in what feels like forever. My eyes roam over his face hungrily, my heart twisting painfully. Relief washes over me when I realize Layla won't be joining us.

"Don't," Carter says, placing his hand my shoulder. "Kate is going to be there, Minx. I don't want to see you hurting. I don't want to see you force a smile onto your face. Don't do this if you don't want to."

Sam pulls me away from Carter with such force that it hurts, and I flinch. "Don't touch her," Sam warns. "And her name is *Emilia.*"

Carter tenses, and the look in his eyes tells me that he's close to losing it. I wrap my arms around myself and shake my head. "It's fine, Carter," I murmur. "I'm fine. Let's just go."

He glances from me to Sam, his expression tense. Whatever he's seeing in my eyes must set him at ease, because he nods and gestures for us to walk to the car. He follows close behind us, as though he's trying to keep an eye on me and Sam, and Sam grabs my hand. He holds on so tightly that my hand hurts, but no matter how hard I try to pull my hand out of his, he won't let go. I hate seeing him like this. I hate that I've made him so insecure. So angry.

Sam holds my hand throughout the journey, but rather than set me at ease, it just stresses me out even more. By the time we arrive I'm trembling. I feel helpless and hurt, and I don't want to be here. Carter looks at me with such concern that I force myself to put up a brave front. He looks worried and just as helpless as I feel, and I force myself to smile at him. I want to set him at ease. The last thing I want is for him to worry about me. Carter inhales deeply and walks into the house, and Sam and I follow behind him.

Sam lets go of my hand to shake William's and I breathe a sigh of relief. His tight grip hurt my hand, and I didn't want to agitate him further by pulling my hand out of his. He's starting to feel like a stranger to me, and I'm starting to feel guilty for causing the change in him. I don't want to, but part of me wonders if sleeping with him might make things better. The thought makes me feel uncomfortable, but I'll get over that. I must.

I'm so focused on my thoughts about Sam and my aching hand, that I don't even see her standing there. Kate. The girl who was once my best friend. I freeze, and so does she. I guess she didn't expect me to be here today. Helen recovers from her shock quicker than Kate does, and she smiles at me.

"Emilia, I'm so glad you decided to come after all."

I nod at her, but it's all too much. Being here, seeing Kate and Helen together. It hurts. It's all too much. The pain of losing Carter, of losing Kate and Helen, it all comes rushing back. Every memory that has plagued me throughout the years assaults me at once, and I almost burst into tears right then and there.

CHAPTER 36

arter

I'm only barely remaining in control of my rage as I sit opposite Emilia. She's trembling, and I can see the hurt in her eyes. I can see her visibly shrink as she sits there, her shoulders hunched and her eyes on her plate. Sam keeps touching her, and she keeps recoiling. It's so subtle that I don't think he even notices, but I do. I notice everything about her. I notice the way she avoids looking at Mom and Kate. The way she stares at her food as though she's sorry for even existing. I knew this would happen. I knew just being here would make her feel the way she did back then. Like everything that happened was her fault. Like the love she gave out so freely was destructive. Like her presence is ruining things for everyone. None of that is true, but I know my Minx, and I know she won't be able to stop those thoughts, those doubts. I can see her holding onto her anger as best as she can, but failing nonetheless.

I watch as Sam extends his hand underneath the table, probably to touch her thigh, and she tenses. She rises from her seat and keeps her head down as she excuses herself. She's shaking so hard that I have to grip the table to keep from following her.

Sam hesitates, and then he rises too. I shake my head and stand up. I don't know what Emilia needs right now, but I know it's not for Sam to follow her. He walks into the direction Emilia disappeared to, and I cut him off in the hallway. I grip him by his shirt, hard, and pin him down with a stare. "She needs space, and you're going to give it to her," I tell him, trying my best to be polite, and failing miserably.

Sam tenses and tries to pull himself out of my hold, but he can't. "What *my girlfriend* needs right now is *me*. Who the hell do you think you are to decide for her? Maybe us being here has made you all nostalgic, but you'd better remember that Emilia is mine. You don't have the right to tell me to stay away."

I grit my teeth and laugh humorlessly. "You might be right, Samuel. She's yours, but *I'm* still very much *hers*. And if I see you touch her in a way she doesn't like, if I see you hold her hand even just a little too tightly ever again, I'm going to break every fucking bone in your hand. If you make her uncomfortable even the slightest or force her to do something she either doesn't want or isn't ready for, the way you did today... then I *will* know, and I *will* fucking kill you. I'll make you disappear so quick they'll call me Houdini. I've been playing nice, but don't forget who I am. I'm Carter fucking Clarke. And you? You're no one. You'll just be another statistic."

Sam blinks, his eyes wide, and then he looks away, a shudder running through him. I let go of his shirt and take a step back before tipping my head towards the dining room. "Get back into your fucking seat, and don't fucking move until Emilia gets back."

I see a flash of defiance in his eyes, and I fucking hope he won't listen. I need an excuse to punch him in his fucking face, and I'd love for him to give me one. Unfortunately, he nods and turns to walk back, his hands balled into fists.

I sigh and lean back against the wall. If he tells Emilia what I just said to him she'll never forgive me. Me and my fucking temper. She's been distant all week. If this gets back to her, I'm done for.

"I had no idea you could be so terrifying," Kate says, and I turn to find her standing in the corner, a smile on her face.

I pinch the bridge of my nose and close my eyes. "How long have you been standing there?"

Kate hesitates and looks away. "I just wanted to make sure Emilia was okay. I wasn't going to speak to her or anything, but I just wanted to see where she ran off to. I just wanted to know if she was okay."

I look at her, trying to assess her sincerity. I'm fucking horrible, because my first thought is that she might take anything she just heard me say, and use it to drive a bigger wedge between Emilia and me.

"Stay away from her," I tell her, unable to contain my anger. I'm tired of everything today. I'm tired of being unable to protect Emilia. Of being unable to keep her from getting hurt. I'm tired of hurting, of wanting her and knowing I'll never have her.

Kate nods and smiles bittersweetly. "I will. I promise. I'm going up to my room now, and I'll stay there for the rest of the evening. It's the least I can do, anyway." She walks up the stairs and stops mid-way. "Emilia is in the treehouse, by the way," she says, her voice soft and insecure.

I nod. Where else could my Minx have gone? The treehouse has always been her safe haven. I hesitate only slightly before walking out the door. I know I told Sam that she needs space, yet I'm unable to heed my own warning.

I pause in front of the treehouse, worried that I might be overstepping. I drop my forehead to the door and inhale deeply, but in the end I can't stay away. I push the door open quietly, and my heart sinks when I see her sitting on the floor, trying her best to cry as silently as she can.

I sink to my knees in front of her, and she looks up at me through her tears. Seeing her like this devastates me. "Emilia," I whisper. "Minx, don't cry," I murmur, lifting her into my arms. She comes gladly, and I close my arms around her. Emilia rests her head on my shoulder, and I tighten my grip on her. Her entire body is shaking from the force of her tears, and I bury my hand in her hair. "Baby, you're breaking my heart," I whisper.

She clutches me tightly, but we couldn't possibly be any closer. "Carter," she whispers.

"Yes, I'm here. I'm here, Minx. Whatever you need, I'm here."

Emilia cries even harder, and my heart shatters. When she cries like this, I can only barely keep my own tears at bay. I don't think I've cried in years, but seeing her like this brings me pretty damn close. I swallow hard and press a kiss to her head.

"I'm sorry," she says. "I'm sorry. I'm so sorry. I'm ruining everything. I'm ruining Thanksgiving. I'm ruining everyone's evening. I'm doing it again."

I pull away from her a little to look at her and wipe her tears away. "Baby, you haven't done a thing. I don't think you've even spoken a word, so how did you ruin anything? My love, it might not show, but Mom is actually happy to have you here. Don't do this, okay? Don't make yourself believe these lies your pretty mind has spun. I want you here. You're wanted here, Emilia."

She looks into my eyes and nods, but I can tell she doesn't believe me. I pull her closer and press my lips against her forehead, my lips lingering. "What am I going to do with you, Emilia?" I whisper.

She visibly steels herself, and I sigh. "I'm sorry," she says again. "I... thank you for coming to check up on me. This is silly. I'm sorry, I'm overreacting. I apologize. I'll be better... I—I'll act normal. Everything is fine."

I hate seeing her like this. I hate seeing her so insecure and so broken. "Minx, if you're hurt, you're hurt. If being here is hard, then that's okay. Fuck everyone else. Fuck everyone that's hurt you in any way. Fuck them. You owe no one anything. You don't even owe them civility if you don't feel like giving it to them. You do *not* need to force yourself to sit through a night off bullshit appearances. I won't ever ask it of you, and if your dad truly understood how you feel, he wouldn't either. He just thinks he's helping you heal, Minx. But if this isn't what you want, if it isn't what you need, then we won't stay. Say the word, and we'll go. I can drive us home right now. We don't even have to say bye to anyone."

Emilia looks into my eyes and she inhales deeply as she threads her hand through my hair. When she looks at me that way my heart aches. It aches for everything we used to have. Everything I can no longer have. I close my eyes and swallow hard when Emilia drops her forehead to mine.

"I'm okay now," she whispers. "So long as you're there, I'll be okay. Let's stay."

She pulls away from me and smiles, and my heart skips a beat. Even with tear marks running down her face, she's still the most beautiful thing I've ever seen. I almost wish that she hadn't asked me to stay, because all I want to do is keep her to myself. I don't want her sitting next to Sam. I don't want to go back into that house that's filled with all the people that tore us apart.

CHAPTER 37

milia

Sam seems tense and angry as we walk into our bedroom. Attending Thanksgiving dinner has been so draining for me that I didn't realize that he's been as quiet as I have been. He inhales deeply and runs a hand through his hair as I close the door behind me.

He turns to look at me, his shoulders stiff and his jaw clenched. He's radiating rage in a way he never has before. I don't think we've had even one bad argument in the last couple of years.

His eyes look cold as he looks up at me, and I shudder involuntarily. Sam inhales deeply and walks up to me, and I tense.

"What's wrong?" I whisper, my heart racing. He's making me uncomfortable, and another shudder runs down my spine.

Sam narrows his eyes and grabs my chin, pinching hard. I flinch but don't pull away from him. Somehow, I'm sure that'll just anger him more. "Tell me, Emilia," he says, speaking slowly. "Are you sleeping with Carter? Are you fucking him?"

I freeze and look at him with wide eyes. "What?" I whisper, in disbelief. "*No.* Of course not."

"But you want to, don't you?"

I shake my head and place my hands on his shoulders. "Sam, no. What are you even talking about? What has gotten into you?"

Sam looks into my eyes as though he's searching for something, a hint of a lie, a sign of betrayal. But there are none. I may have been tempted, but I never acted on it. I wouldn't. I'm not a cheater.

Sam moves his hand to my hair and tangles his fingers through it. "I know it's him you want. He's the one your dad prefers too. Did you think I didn't notice you sneaking out of the room early in the morning, just to have coffee with him? I've never said anything because I trust you, but now I'm wondering if that trust was misplaced. If it was all so innocent, why did you stop right after I caught you standing in the living room with him in the middle of the night?"

He tightens his grip on my hair and I whimper slightly. My heart is racing, and though I want to protest, I can't make myself.

"I called your dad a while ago. I told him I was going to ask you to move in with me, and that I wanted to propose to you soon after. I asked for his blessing, but he was just quiet for a while and thanked me for calling him, but you know what... he never actually gave me his blessing. Just a day later he called you, telling you that he was sick and asking you to come here. At the time I was so worried for both you and your dad that I didn't think much of it. But now? Now it's obvious. He'd been sick for months and only just decided to tell you then. Why do you think that is, Emilia?"

I shake my head. I know what he's trying to say, but there's no way dad would do that. Dad would never scheme like that.

"And Carter... it's obvious he still wants you. He had me

fooled for a while, you know? I thought he was such a great guy, and he was so nice to me. It's like he genuinely wanted you to be happy. But that didn't last, did it? Did he make a move on you?"

I shake my head, my eyes wide. "He wouldn't," I whisper.

Sam laughs, and the sound sends chills down my spine. "If he hasn't yet, then he will. And once he does, you'll give in, won't you? Your heart is already there. I spent years fighting to win you over, but just a few months with Carter and you're bloody lovestruck. I see it in your eyes. In the way you move. The way you smile at him."

Sam works his hand deeper into my hair and pulls on it, yanking my head closer to his. His lips come crashing down on mine, and he kisses me harshly, forcibly. I try to protest, but every sound I make is smothered. I bite down on his lip as hard as I can and push him away, breathing hard.

"What the hell is going on with you?" I shout, my eyes filling with tears. I inhale shakily and wrap my arms around myself.

Sam inhales deeply and closes his eyes. "I can't do this, Emilia. I've given you the best years of my life. I pursued you for six years. It took six years for you to even consider going on a single date with me. I've done everything I could to make you happy. I've given you my all for *years*, and here we are. Just a few *months* here with Carter, and you..."

I inhale deeply and look away, my feelings conflicted. "I never asked you to spend years pursuing me," I whisper. "If anything, I made it very clear that I wasn't ready to date. That I might never be."

Sam nods. "I know. *I know*, but I was so sure we were perfect for each other... and for a while, we were. For a while, we were happy. But not the way you are here. Despite everything going on, you radiate happiness when you're around Carter. The way you smile at him, the way you laugh with him... Emilia, you've never once even *looked* at me that way, and you know it. And that playful side of you? It didn't exist around me. It hurts to see who you are with him. I didn't think you could get even more beautiful, or even more perfect... but you do, *for him*. Only for him."

I look away guiltily. I've done my best to stay away from Carter lately, to be as respectful to Sam as I possibly could be, but I can't help but be happy when Carter is around. I can't control my feelings.

Sam walks up to me and brushes the tip of his fingers over my cheek. "I can't be here, Emilia. I want to be there for you throughout this all, but I don't think I can. I can't be here and watch you distance yourself more and more every day. I can't stay and watch our relationship crumble into dust, right before my eyes."

I nod. The fact that I feel relieved makes me feel even worse. I should want my own boyfriend with me through times as tough as these, but I don't.

"I think we need a break, Emilia."

My heart stills and I look down at my feet. Sam has been my constant for years now. He was always the friend I could count on, the guy that I could depend on. I managed to convince myself that I could be with him, that I was happy... but being back here puts it all back into focus. I decided to date him because it was easy, and it was safe. My heart was never fully in it, no matter how hard I tried. Being with him meant I wouldn't get hurt again, and I could convince myself that I was okay, that I was moving on with my life.

"Sam, I think we should break up."

It should hurt to say those words, but it doesn't. If anything, it feels like a relief to set both of us free.

Sam looks at me, and the expression on his face breaks my heart. I expected to find disbelief and pain in his eyes, but instead I'm faced with reluctant acceptance.

"I'm changing my flight," he tells me. "If I can, I'll fly out tonight. Otherwise, I'd like to go tomorrow."

I nod, and a single tear rolls down my cheek. This is the man I so desperately wanted to make it work with. I tried so hard, but you can't force love into existence.

"You and I could have had it all, Emilia. We were perfect together. You can't see it now, but you're throwing away your chance at happiness. You're a fool if you think you can be with Carter. Didn't you notice Carter's sister left dinner halfway through because you were there? How long do you think you and he will last with his family standing between you like that? The novelty of being together is going to wear off soon enough, and you'll be left facing the fucked-up mess that your life together would be. You'll flee to London all over again, begging me to take you back. And I? I'll have moved on."

CHAPTER 38

milia

I stare at the sun streaming through the kitchen window in surprise. How long have I been sitting here? I didn't even realize the sun had risen already.

I bite down on my lip and try to pull myself together, but I'm feeling out of it. Sam took the next available flight back home, and I drove him to the airport knowing I'd probably never see him again. How did we go from wanting to move in together to parting ways?

It feels surreal, but I don't feel the way I did when Carter and I broke up. I feel like I might be in shock, but I'm not heartbroken. Shouldn't I be? Sam and I might have only dated for a year or so, but we've known each other for years. I haven't just lost him as my boyfriend, but as my friend too. I should be mourning the loss of that relationship, but instead I'm just... numb.

"Emilia?"

I tense when I hear Carter's voice. He's standing in the doorway in his swim shorts, and I blink distractedly.

"Carter," I whisper.

He frowns and walks towards me, a frown on his face. He looks worried, and I can't help but wonder what I must look like, sitting here in the same clothes I wore last night.

Carter grabs my coffee cup and raises his brows when he realizes that my coffee is cold. I can't even remember when I made that.

"How long have you been sitting here?"

I blink and shake my head. "Not long," I whisper.

Carter takes a step closer to me and places his hands on my shoulders. His hands feel warm on my skin, and his eyes widen when he realizes how cold my body is. "Minx, you're freezing," he murmurs. He moves his hands over my arms, rubbing them in an effort to warm me up.

I look up into his eyes, my heart stirring. I've been so focused on keeping a barrier between us, that it's like I haven't really seen him in forever. The only time I caved was when I burst into tears in the treehouse yesterday. Strangely enough, I've missed those stunning hazel eyes of his. Even after all these years, I want to be the only one he sees. The idea of him with Layla hurts more than breaking up with Sam does, and that should've told me the truth about my feelings. I should've realized sooner that what I felt for Sam was a sense of duty and gratefulness for the time we spent together, the time he spent on me. It was never love. It wasn't anything like what I still feel for Carter.

"Carter," I whisper, and he raises his brow in question. "Sam left. I drove him to the airport last night. We... we broke up."

He stares at me in shock, his hands stiffening on my shoulders. "You *what*?"

I look away and rise to my feet, taking a step away from him. "We broke up," I repeat. "He got on the first available flight."

He looks at me like he can't comprehend what I'm saying. I see concern flash through his eyes, but there's also relief.

"Are you okay?" he asks, sounding worried.

I nod. I'm a bit *too* okay, I think. I should be in tears and I should be hurting, but I'm fine. "I'm all right. I'll be fine. It's just strange, that's all."

Carter hesitates as though he doesn't know what to say, and then he nods. He grabs my coffee cup and empties it, making me a fresh cup instead. I lean back and watch him. He looks amazing in the sunlight that's streaming through the window, his upper body on display. Would it be easier to remain in control of the way he makes me feel if he'd gotten fat and obnoxious? Somehow, I doubt it would. I doubt his heart will ever change.

I take the coffee cup from him and stare at it, lost in thought. "Why do you still have this?" I ask, my voice so soft that he almost misses the words.

Carter glances at the cup and bites down on his lip. "Because it's a memory I could never let go of. Having that cup made, showing you the writing inside it... whenever I see this, those memories come with it, and it never fails to bring a smile to my face."

My heart skips a beat. If I'm honest with myself, that's probably the very same reason I've been using this cup, when there are so many others to choose from. It's a reminder of better times.

Carter freezes and looks towards the doorway, and I follow his gaze to find Dad standing there in his pajamas, a long robe keeping him warm. Dad is usually never up this early, and I can't help but worry. Is he not feeling well?

"Daddy," I murmur, trying my best to smile at him.

He walks into the kitchen, a conflicted expression on his face. "So, he left, huh? Did you guys argue?"

I glance at Carter, and he smiles at me before slipping out quietly, probably wanting to give me some privacy. I nod at Dad. "Yes, I guess so."

Dad sits down next to me and sighs. "I'm sorry, Princess. How are you feeling?"

I look at Dad and think back to what Sam told me. While Dad hasn't been pushing me towards Carter in any obvious ways, I do wonder if he might have been doing it subconsciously. Or maybe even very consciously. I always did think it was strange that he'd move in with Carter — and that he'd ask it of me too.

"Did you even like him, Dad?"

He looks startled, as though he didn't expect the question, and smiles tightly. "He's a nice man, Emilia. It was clear that he adored you, and he really seemed to have his life together. He had a good career plan, and he'd be able to provide you with a good life."

I look at him through narrowed eyes. "That doesn't answer my question, Dad."

He smiles at me and shakes his head bashfully. "I'm not sure, Emilia. Sam is very nice and I like him as a person, but you didn't look all that happy with him. He enabled you to just let life pass you by, while still ticking off all the things you thought you needed to do to be happy. You know, like dating and moving in with someone, and maybe even getting married someday. You looked very content with him, but you didn't look *happy*."

I frown and look away. I want to refute his words, but I can't. Was it obvious to everyone but me? In the end even Sam seemed to realize that I wasn't quite myself with him, so how did *I* not realize it?

Dad ruffles my hair and smiles at me. "No matter," he says. "Life goes on, Princess. I'm sure you'll find your happiness. I don't want you to settle, Emilia. You deserve the world."

I nod and wipe away a tear that I hadn't even realized had fallen down my cheek. I drop my head to my dad's shoulder, feeling lost. It feels like everything in my life has changed and I'm struggling to keep up.

CHAPTER 39

arter

I'm a coward and I know it. I sigh as I walk into my parents' house. I worked late today just to try and keep my mind off Emilia, but it hasn't helped. All day the only thing on my mind has been that she's finally single again.

I can't even go home because I can't be sure that I'll be able to stay away from her. I'll want to have a drink with her, she'll smile at me, and I'll want to get down on my knees and beg her to give us another chance. I can't be around her right now.

Kate looks up in surprise when I walk into the living room, and just seeing her guts me. Lately it's been getting easier to forget how much stands between Emilia and me. Having her in my house and around the office has made it easy to deceive myself — to forget how much pain she's already been through, just for being with me. I could never ask that of her again.

"Carter, what are you doing here?" Kate asks, and I try my best to smile at her. I feel horrible for the way I feel around her. I don't want to resent my own sister, but part of me does. Part of me will probably never be able to forgive her.

"Hey," I murmur, dropping down on the sofa beside her. "Thought I'd stay over tonight."

Kate frowns and crosses her arms over each other. "Why?"

I laugh and shake my head. "What, am I not welcome here anymore?"

Kate purses her lips and looks away. "I just didn't think you'd come back, considering that Emilia is at your house."

I stiffen involuntarily. For years neither Mom nor Kate even spoke her name. I still find it jarring when they do, and part of me takes offence to it. Part of me feels like they don't even have the right to say her name. It's fucked up and it's irrational, but I can't help it.

"Did something happen?"

I run a hand through my hair and lean back on the sofa, exhausted, both mentally and physically. Even my heart is tired. Tired of waiting and wanting. "Emilia and Sam broke up. I thought she might need some space."

Kate looks at me with wide eyes and grins. "Oh my gosh, she dumped him? I knew it!"

I grit my teeth and try my best to temper myself. "What, you couldn't stand her being in that relationship either?" I say nonetheless. Fucking hell. If this is what I'm like around Kate tonight, then I definitely can't be around Emilia. Kate's expression crumples, and for a second I see hurt flash through her eyes, but then she looks away and smiles.

"I'm sorry, Kate. That was... unwarranted. I apologize."

Kate looks at me and shakes her head. "Don't, Carter. For years you haven't said a word. For years, you've kept it all in. Never, not even once, have you told me that you blamed me for what happened. You've stood by me, and you've helped me recover. You've funded my education and all of the different courses and programs I wanted to do. You've never asked me for anything in return, other than me taking care of myself. You're the best brother I could have ever wished for, but in return I've only ever been a horrible sister."

She sighs and looks at me, her eyes filled with sorrow. "You think you hide it well, but you don't. I can tell that you haven't truly been living ever since Emilia left. Part of the reason I left to go to London was because I couldn't stand seeing you like this, knowing that I did this to you. I couldn't live with the guilt, even though I deserved to. So lash out at me all you want, say whatever you want, blame me like I deserve. I don't mind, Carter. I'm not the weak girl I used to be. I'm not sure you'll ever see me for who I've grown into, but I've fought as hard as I could to become someone you might someday be proud of. Someone you'd be happy to call your sister."

I'm filled with guilt and shake my head. I should've remained in better control over my emotions. I never should've let Kate see even the tiniest amount of resentment I feel. She's my sister, and I love her. The anger I feel towards her is something I can deal with myself. "Kate, like I said, I'm sorry. I *am* proud of who you are, and I know how hard you've worked to get where you are. I'm sorry if I haven't expressly said that to you."

She shakes her head and smiles at me. "That wasn't the point. I only said what I said because I want you to know that I understand. I understand that you're mad and you're hurting, even if you won't ever admit to it. I see it. I see that you're unhappy, and it kills me, Carter.

And you know what? That cold mask you wear has finally started to crack, and it's because Emilia is back. So yes, I'm happy that she's single again. I might not have spoken to her in years, but even I could see that the way she looked at Sam wasn't the same way she's always looked at you, the same way she still does. I'm not who I used to be, Carter. All I want is for you to be happy. I won't stand in the way of that, not ever again.

I'll do whatever it takes to make this right, I just don't know what the right thing to do is."

I smile bitterly. "It's far too late for that," I tell her honestly. My mind drifts back to the way I found Emilia sitting in the treehouse, crying her heart out and feeling the way she was made to feel years ago.

"Being with me means Emilia would have to forgive you and Mom, and I don't think she ever will. Even if I were crazy enough to tell her that I'll turn my back on my family to be with her, she'd never let me do it. I know what she's like, and she'd always worry that I'd one day blame her. She couldn't ever live with that guilt and uncertainty. Besides, her life is in London, and mine is here."

Kate looks so heartbroken that for a second I'm fooled into believing that she understands how I feel, but I doubt that's true. I doubt anyone truly understands the depth of the sorrow I live with every day.

"I'm so sorry," Kate says, her voice trembling. "I did this. I did this to both of you."

I shake my head and force myself to smile. "It's okay, Kate. Sometimes things just aren't meant to be. Some people just aren't meant to be. I guess Emilia and I are like that. Maybe one day it'll all make sense, or maybe it won't. Either way, it is what it is. I've learned to be okay with that, and you should too," I say.

But have I? Have I learned to be okay with it? I doubt it, because every fiber of my being is begging me to go home to Emilia.

CHAPTER 40

milia

"You don't have to cook dinner for Carter," I tell Enzo, my heart twisting painfully. He didn't come home last night, and I can't stop myself from thinking about him with Layla. "I doubt he'll be home tonight either."

I'm surprised when Carter walks into the kitchen, yawning. Looks like he didn't get much sleep tonight. My mind flashes back to everything he said to me, everything he told me he did to Layla. Jealousy so fierce fills me that I'm almost brought to my knees.

I'm supposed to be heartbroken over my relationship with Sam, but all I can think about is Carter. I cross my arms and look at him. "Oh, you're here," I murmur, trying my best to hide my feelings. "I was just telling Enzo that he doesn't have to cook for you, since it looked like you might not come home tonight either."

He cups his neck and looks at me, a small smile on his face. He looks like he's in a great mood, and for once, I hate that smile of his. I hate that another woman brought it to his lips. I hate that someone else caused him to be in such a good mood. I have no doubt what caused it, and I hate that too.

He smiles at Enzo cheerfully and shakes his head. "I'm here now, and I'm starving, so please do feed me," he says.

Enzo nods and gets to work. I purse my lips and lean back against the kitchen counter, my eyes roaming over his body. He smiles at me sweetly, and I can't help but grimace. He looks tired but happy, the look in his eyes one I'm intimately acquainted with. It's bliss, and it's exactly how he used to look after sex.

By the time dinner is served, my mood plummets even further. I stab my chicken harshly and then bite down on it angrily. My mind keeps replaying scenes I don't want to imagine, and I grit my teeth.

"So, the food is good, huh?" Dad says awkwardly. I look up at him and try my best to smile, but I fail miserably.

Carter grins and nods. "Yes, almost as good as the food I had last night," he says, smiling. "Now, that was delicious."

I look up at him and lock my jaws angrily. My mind automatically takes me back to him describing how he'd go down on me, before he told me he did just that to Layla instead.

"Oh, what did you eat?" I ask, my voice monotone. I must be a sucker for punishment. Why the hell can't I just keep my mouth shut?

Carter smiles and describes some mashed potato dish that sounds straight up weird, and I nod politely. "Well, that's nice for you, that you got Layla to cook for you. Sounds great," I say, trying my best to sound unaffected.

Carter smirks and takes another bite of his food while Dad smiles down at his plate. I'm acting jealous and it's showing, and I hate that I can't control my reaction.

Carter yawns just as we finish up dinner, and I involuntarily glare at him. "Looks like you didn't get much sleep last night," I say through gritted teeth, unable to help myself.

"No, barely slept a wink. Kept getting distracted by the view," Carter says, grinning.

My heart jerks painfully and I blanch. I look down at my plate, stricken. My stomach twists with jealousy and I bite down on my lip to reel it in.

I rise from my seat the second Carter takes his last bite and I grab all of our plates, taking them to the kitchen with me. I dump them in the sink and rinse them angrily, needing an outlet for all the anguish I'm feeling. I know the staff will take care of this if I just leave it in the sink, but I need something to do. I sigh and shake my head. I should be happy for him, but I'm just not. I can't be.

I drop my head against the kitchen counter as soon as I'm done. I'm losing it. It hurts so much more than I thought it would.

I inhale deeply and brace myself before walking back into the dining room, only to find it empty. The veranda sliding doors are open, the curtains moving with the breeze. I hesitate slightly before walking onto the veranda, my eyes finding Carter instantly.

He's sitting on the swing, a glass of whiskey in his hands. He looks up at me, and my heart skips a beat. This man... no one has ever been able to make me feel so much with a single look.

I walk towards him and take his glass from him. I take a sip before putting his glass down. I sit down next to him and look up at the night sky. I didn't think I'd ever be back here again, sitting next to Carter.

I turn to face him, my heart racing. "Sounds like you booty called Layla," I say, unable to help myself. "Or are you guys dating officially now?"

Carter bursts out laughing and shakes his head. "I do not *booty call*," he tells me, his eyes twinkling with amusement. "Now *I'm* outraged in Spanish."

A smile tugs at my lips, but I stomp it down and cross my

arms over each other. "Hey, I wonder how Tony is doing," I say, and Carter's eyes flash with anger. "I should give him a call. See what he's up to. That'd be interesting, wouldn't it? We'd be dating siblings."

Carter straightens in his seat and pins me down with a stare. "He works for me, and if he'd like to keep his job, he'd better damn well stay away from you. He stole your first date from me. I'll be damned if I let him have anything else."

I smile at him, pleased with the little bit of possessiveness he's showing me. I lean back in my seat and look into his eyes. "You didn't answer my question," I murmur. "Were you with Layla? Are you dating her?"

Carter turns to look at me and raises his hand to my hair, brushing it out of my face gently. The way he's looking at me right now... I want more of that. I want to be the only woman he ever looks at. I'm not sure why I was so blind for so long, why I clung onto a sense of obligation, when my heart so clearly guided me in the right direction.

"Why? What would you do if I was? Why would you even care?"

I bite down on my lip and Carter's eyes follow my every movement. I swallow hard as my gaze drops to his lips. What would he do if I just kiss him right now? What if I fight for him? For what I think we could still have?

Carter cups my cheek, his thumb brushing over my lips. "I spent last night at home," he whispers. "I can still see into your room from mine. Nothing has changed, you know. I can never sleep when I go back home. I can't even get myself to close the curtains. It's like I *want* to be tortured."

My eyes widen and relief courses through me. I exhale and my entire body relaxes. I didn't even realize I was this tense. I smile at Carter, and the edges of his lips tug up.

"Wow, a real smile," he murmurs, and I grin up at him.

"I see," I say, trying my best to play it cool.

Carter smiles and pulls away. "You're awfully curious about who I spend my nights with, though."

I shake my head, my eyes wide. "Am not," I whisper.

"Are too," Carter whispers right back.

I grin at him and he smiles back at me. I turn away, my cheeks crimson. Everything he told me about what he did to Layla is still running through my mind, and it still hurts. For the first time in years, though, I feel the courage to go after what I want, selfishly.

CHAPTER 41

arter

I'm surprised when I walk into the kitchen early in the morning to find it empty. Emilia is always there already, a cup of coffee in her hands. I frown and turn the coffee machine on. I guess she's sleeping in today.

I sigh, my mood dropping immediately. My mornings with her are my favorite part of my day. On the few occasions that she hasn't been there, I've always been in a bad mood. I take a sip of coffee and lean back against the kitchen counter, my mind drifting back to last night. The jealousy in her eyes, and the way she looked at me... I want more of that.

I'm startled when Emilia walks into the kitchen, a robe covering her from head to toe. I glance at it in amusement. I'm pretty sure that robe is one of mine. When did she even steal that from me?

"Morning," she says, her cheeks flushed. She walks up to me and takes my coffee cup out of my hands, lifting it to her lips.

"Morning," I murmur, my eyes roaming over her.

"I thought I'd come for a swim with you," she says, her voice soft.

I grin at her, my fingers tracing over the collar of her robe. "I see."

Emilia frowns at me, her smile wavering. "Hey, the water *is* heated, right?"

I chuckle and brush her hair behind her ear. "Yes, Minx. It's heated."

She sighs in relief and grins up at me before putting down her coffee cup and taking my hand. I glance at our joined hands in surprise and smirk.

"Come on," she says, excitedly. "Let's go."

I let Emilia pull me through the doors. She yelps when her bare feet hit the cold stone and she turns back around, slamming into me. I laugh and wrap my arms around her.

"Second thoughts, Minx?"

She looks up at me, her hands on my chest. She flattens her palms against my skin and slides her hands up, until she's got them wrapped around my neck. I love it when she touches me like that, without abandon. Slowly but surely, she's turning back into the girl I used to know.

"Who? Me? Never."

I chuckle and lift her into my arms in one fell swoop, eliciting a yelp from her. She hangs onto me tightly and shoots me a warning look. "Don't throw me in," she warns, and I pause.

"Hmm, I hadn't thought of that, but now that you mention it..."

She narrows her eyes and I grin at her as I lower her to the floor. "Go on, get in. You'll get cold if you stay out of the water."

Emilia nods at me and looks up into my eyes hesitantly. "So... I didn't actually have swim wear," she says as she undoes the sash on her robe.

I blink at her, my heart racing. Her robe falls open, and she lets it fall off her shoulders slowly, until she's standing in front of me in black lace underwear. I bite down on my lip harshly and try my best to look away, but try as I might, I can't. She's fucking stunning. I thought she looked amazing years ago, but she looks even better now. I wish I could touch her. I wish she was still mine.

Emilia smiles in satisfaction when her robe hits the floor, and she bites down on her lip as she walks past me. I close my eyes and inhale deeply. I'm about to make a huge fool of myself with the tent in my swim shorts. Thank god they're loose shorts at least. I turn my back to her briefly to reposition myself in a feeble effort to hide how hard I am, and I shake my head. This hasn't happened to me since I was a teenager. Matter of fact, no woman other than Emilia has ever made me hard so unexpectedly. I still have no control over my body when she's around.

Emilia's eyes roam over my body curiously as I enter the water, and I'm certain there's a brief flash of disappointment when her gaze reaches my swim shorts. This Minx. She was trying to turn me on *on purpose*.

Emilia swims on her back, her eyes on the clouds in the sky. I grin at her as I do my laps. She's not even remotely swimming in a straight line, and multiple times she ends up banging her head on the edges of the pool, because she has zero spatial awareness.

I swim up to her and stop right in front of her, a huge smile on my face. I pull her up, and Emilia grins and puts her hands on my shoulder, keeping herself up as I wrap my hands around her waist. "Minx, you still can't swim for shit."

She laughs and pulls me just a little closer. I want her flush against my body, my fingers threaded through her hair.

"You know what this reminds me of?" I murmur.

Emilia grins, her cheeks bright red. "The lake."

I nod. "The lake."

The last time she and I were in the lake by the summer cabin I had her pressed up against one of the wooden posts by the pier, my cock buried deep inside her and her lips on mine. Just that memory has me getting impossibly hard.

Emilia smirks when she feels my bulge against her stomach. I thought she might move away, but she doesn't.

"I told you I'd marry you someday," I whisper.

Emilia tightens her grip on me, her smile bittersweet. "And I said *I know*."

That day was the first time I asked her to move in with me. Even then, I knew I wanted to spend the rest of my life with her. I think I still do.

I pull Emilia even closer, until her body is flush against mine, and she wraps her legs around my waist, the way she did back then. I'm rock hard and pressing right between her legs. I bite down on my lip as Emilia wraps her arms around my neck.

I drop my forehead to her shoulder and inhale deeply. "I always thought you'd be my wife by now," I murmur.

Emilia buries her hand in my hair and clutches me tightly. I lift my head to look at her, and her eyes are filled with the same intensity I'm feeling. She cups my cheek and drops her forehead to mine.

"Me too," she whispers. "For years I avoided all mention of you, scared that I'd read about you dating someone else, or even worse, marrying someone else. I wanted you to be happy, but I just... I couldn't."

I thread my fingers through her hair, the way I've been wanting to, and look into her eyes. "I'd never marry anyone that isn't you, Emilia. I haven't even had a girlfriend since you. Sure, there have been some girls, but no other woman ever got to call me *hers*, the way you always have."

Emilia looks at me, insecurity making her gaze waver. "What about Layla?"

I smile and shake my head. "No. Never. She doesn't even remotely have any rights to me. There's only ever been you for me."

Emilia looks away in guilt, and I wonder if it's Sam she's thinking about. I don't know how many men came after me, and I don't want to know.

I can't help the direction that my thoughts turn to. I can't help but think of her with Sam.

"What are we doing? I whisper. "You just broke up with your boyfriend, and your father is sick. You're vulnerable, and you're probably still heartbroken."

I'm surprised when I feel Emilia tighten her legs around me. She looks at me as though she can read my mind. As though she knows exactly what I'm thinking. "Carter," she whispers. "I'm here with you now, and there's nowhere else I'd rather be. No one else I'd rather be with."

She grabs my hand and entwines it with her own before raising it to her lips. She kisses my knuckles softly and looks at me. "You told me, didn't you?" She whispers. "You told me he couldn't touch me. That he couldn't lay a finger on me... And he hasn't."

I narrow my eyes, suddenly filled with insecurity and jealousy. I grab her hands and push them above her head. "Tell me the truth," I say, my body radiating anger. "You spent weeks sleeping next to him. I've lived with you before, Emilia. You and I have never spent a whole night together without having sex at least once. So don't fucking lie to me, Emilia. Don't look into my eyes and lie to me like that."

I sigh and pull away from her. "Come on, it's getting late," I murmur.

"Carter, no," she whispers, anguished. I push away from her and turn to get out of the pool, needing space.

The idea of Emilia with Sam ruined my mood. Just knowing that she used to be his. That he's had her, that he's probably still on her mind. It fucking kills me.

CHAPTER 42

arter

I enter my bedroom quietly, not even bothering to turn the lights on. Asher and I went out for drinks, and he spent the entire time warning me away from Emilia. I know that he's right – I know it, but my heart is refusing to get the message.

I sigh and lie back on my bed. Having Emilia back here makes it so easy to forget. When I see her smile at me, it's easy to forget about all the tears my family and I have brought to her eyes.

I frown when I hear my bedroom door open. I inhale deeply, and my heart starts to race. That perfume... Where did she get it? She hasn't been wearing it, and it's one of the things I've missed most.

Emilia walks straight to my wardrobe, not realizing that I'm lying here. She probably thinks I'm still out with Asher. I turn on my side and watch her as she opens my wardrobe and browses through my clothes. She traces over the fabric of my clothes with the tip of her fingers, and I can just about see her smile to herself. She takes one of my T-shirts off the hanger and brings it to her nose. I watch her as she inhales deeply, my heart hammering in my chest.

"Seems like you're putting a lot of thought into this thievery."

Emilia jumps, shocked. She turns to find me lying on my bed and I sit up, a wide grin on my face.

"I... You... What are you doing here?"

I laugh and run a hand through my hair. "Looks like you're stealing my lines too, Minx."

I rise to my feet and walk up to her, pausing right in front of her. I lift my hand to her face and brush her hair out of the way gently. The way she looks at me makes my heart race. I glance down at her hands and shake my head. "So, this is what you selected, huh?"

Emilia blinks and tries to hide her stolen goods behind her back, but all that does is make me chuckle. I glance at my wardrobe and smile. "I'm a bit disappointed that you didn't take one of my dress shirts," I murmur.

Emilia blushes and looks away. "I was going to," she says sheepishly. "But I figured that you'd realize I stole one."

"Now here's the thing, Emilia... I've always wanted to see you in one of them."

I look into her eyes as my hands find their way to the buttons of my shirt. Emilia's lips drop open as I undo them one by one, my eyes never leaving her. I stop halfway, and a small disappointed whimper leaves Emilia's lips. I look up at her, an intimate smirk on my face. I grab her hands and place them on my chest.

"Tell you what, Emilia... If you take this shirt off me, you can have it," I say, moving her hands to the buttons that are yet to be undone.

She looks up into my eyes, and takes a step closer. She's breathing as hard as I am and I wonder if she's feeling what I'm feeling.

Her hands tremble as she undoes the remaining buttons one by one. My shirt falls open, my abs and chest on display, and Emilia drinks me in the way she used to. I love seeing the lust in her eyes, the eagerness. For a while I was wondering whether she might still be thinking about Sam, whether she might be heartbroken, but it's obvious that I'm all she can see.

I thread my hand through her hair and pull her closer. "You never make things easy, do you? I've been trying to give you space, but you keep testing me. First you show up at the pool looking fucking irresistible, and now you sneak into my room... Are you tempting me? Are you wondering how long I'll be able to stay away? Because I am. I'm wondering."

Emilia slides her hands up my chest and around my neck, her eyes roaming over my body and lingering on my face. She smiles at me and my heart skips a beat. "Maybe," she whispers. "What if I am?"

I inhale deeply and tighten my grip on her hair. "I told myself I'd stay away from you," I whisper. "That I wouldn't be your rebound. But fucking hell, Emilia. I'll be whatever the fuck you want me to be."

Emilia grabs my hair, her eyes mirroring my own desire. "Be mine," she tells me, her voice barely above a whisper.

I groan as my lips come crashing down on hers, and Emilia moans against my lips. "Baby, I've been yours since the day I laid eyes on you."

I lift Emilia into my arms and push her against the wall. She wraps her legs around me tightly, a small sigh escaping her lips. I kiss her deeper and Emilia pulls on my hair eagerly, wanting more. I've got my dick nestled against her pussy, and it feels amazing. My hands find their way underneath her robe, and I gasp when I realize that she's naked underneath.

"Carter," she whispers, her hands moving over my body impatiently. I smile and move my lips to her neck and graze her skin with my teeth the way I know she likes. She rolls her hips against me and I grin.

Emilia pushes my shirt off my arms impatiently, and I chuckle. I tug on the sash of her robe and unravel it. I inhale deeply as her body comes into view. "How the fuck did you get even more beautiful?" I whisper.

I walk to my bed and lie her down carefully before joining her. Emilia tries to cover herself up with her hands and I shake my head. I grab her wrists and slowly move them out of the way, exposing her body. Emilia blushes and I lower my lips to her neck. "Stunning," I whisper. Emilia threads her hand through my hair and pulls my lips back to hers. How long have I waited for this? It's been years. Years of dreaming and fantasizing about finally having her back in my arms. My heart feels tight as I kiss her back.

Emilia takes her time tracing her hands over my body, and I shiver just slightly when she undoes the buttons of my suit trousers. "Off," she whispers, and I press a kiss to her lips as I make quick work of my clothes.

Emilia bites down on her lip as I tug the robe fully off. Her eyes drop to my dick and she licks her lips, her chest rising and falling rapidly. "Emilia," I whisper, and she tightens her grip on me. I kiss her harder, her tongue tangling with mine. I just can't get enough of her.

I settle between her legs and slide up against her. She's so wet already. I already know I'm not going to be able to last long. My fingers find their way between Emilia's legs and she gasps. "I want you," she whispers. "Please, Carter. I've waited for years. I can't wait for another second."

I pull back to look at her, my heart soaring. Emilia looks into my eyes and the way that she's looking at me makes me feel like crying for everything we've lost, everything we've missed out on. She still looks at me the way she did years ago, and it still makes my heart race the same way. Lying here with her, it's so easy to pretend that we're still together. That we never broke up at all.

"Emilia," I whisper, sounding heartbroken even to myself. She tightens her grip on me and pulls me closer, her lips finding mine. She kisses me the way she used to, pouring every single feeling into it. I lose myself in her and sigh when I finally pull away. "I've missed you so fucking much," I whisper. I tangle my hand through her hair and pull on it as my lips come crashing back down on hers harshly. I kiss her until we're both breathless.

I pull away to look at her and smile. I love having her in my bed. Her hair is a mess, her cheeks flushed, her lips swollen and her eyes filled with me. I reach for my trousers on the floor and fish a condom out of my wallet.

"I'm going to fuck you, Emilia," I say, and she bites down on her lip in anticipation. "I'm going to fuck you so hard you won't ever think about another man. I'm going to fuck you so good that no one will ever be able to satisfy you the way I do. I'm going to keep you coming back for more, you hear me?"

Emilia nods and swallows hard as I tangle my hand further into her hair and align myself with her. "Look at me as I stretch out your pussy, baby," I whisper, and I slowly sink deeper into her. Emilia's eyes fall closed in delight, and I'm not even halfway inside her. I pause and tighten my grip on her hair. "None of that. You look at me if you want me to fuck you, Emilia." Her eyes flutter open and her inner muscles spasm. "I want you to see *me* when I fuck you."

"I always see you," she whispers. "No matter who I'm with."

I grin at her smugly and push further into her. "Good girl," I whisper, and in one hard thrust I push all the way inside her. Emilia moans loudly and I grit my teeth in an effort to stay in control. "Still so fucking perfect," I murmur.

Emilia tightens her legs around my hips as I thrust in and out of her, my eyes on hers. "You're mine, you hear me?"

Emilia nods. "I'm yours. I've always been yours."

I nod and grab her legs, throwing them over my shoulders. I remember every single thing about her body, every angle she likes. Emilia almost loses it as I hit her G spot with every thrust.

"Carter, it's too much," she moans. I love seeing her like this. I love driving her crazy like this.

"It's never enough," I say. "I'll never get enough of you."

I increase the pace and Emilia gasps. "I can't..."

I grin at her smugly. "Then come. Come for me baby. Come on my cock."

Emilia shatters at those words and I grunt as her muscles tighten around me. I look into her eyes as I come right along with her. I lower her legs and hold myself up as I press my lips against hers. I kiss her sweetly, and the way she kisses me back makes my heart feel like it might burst.

I pull away just slightly to take care of the condom and then pull her closer. I spoon her and press my lips to her neck. Emilia fidgets slightly, obviously unsure whether she should stay or go. I smile to myself and tighten my grip on her. "You're not going anywhere," I whisper into her hair, before kissing her neck. "I've waited years to have you in my bed, and now that I've got you here, I won't let you go."

Emilia relaxes against me and I smile to myself. We fall asleep just like that, wrapped in each other, both of us happier than we've been in years.

CHAPTER 43

milia

I wake up alone and panic slightly. I glance around me, my hand gliding over Carter's side of the bed. I exhale in relief when I realize that it's still warm. Last night was perfect. It's everything I've been wanting for years, but I can't help but worry. Carter and I have always been intense, our very first kiss was when we were skinny-dipping, after all. Last night was unexpected, though. I wasn't planning on sleeping with him, but I just couldn't resist. I couldn't stay away.

I slip out of bed, my eyes falling to the shirt on the floor. I smile as I think back to the way Carter dared me to take it off him. I grab it from the floor and slip it on. It *is* mine now, after all. He did tell me that I could keep it if I took it off him. I bite down on my lip as I button it up and slip my robe on over it.

I can't remember the last time I felt this happy. I can't remember the last time I felt these butterflies. When is the last time I was unable to stop smiling? I'm grinning as I walk down the stairs, the smell of freshly made coffee coming from the kitchen.

Carter's eyes find mine as I walk in, and for a couple of seconds he is all I can see. He's in his boxers, and I want him again. I want him right here, in his kitchen. He's been driving me crazy, walking around in his swim shorts every morning. I'm done resisting. I know he wants me just as badly, and I've spent too many years feeling incomplete, empty and lonely, to stay away now.

I walk up to him and hold my hand out. Carter chuckles as he surrenders his coffee cup. I smile to myself as I bring it to my lips. I've missed him so much, and I'm done denying myself the one thing in life I want most.

"If you just had more patience, I would have brought you coffee in bed," Carter murmurs.

I take a sip of his coffee and shake my hand. "Patience isn't my strong suit."

Carter chuckles. "No shit, minx."

I grin as he pulls me closer. He undoes the sash on my robe, his lips falling open in shock when he realizes what I'm wearing underneath.

"You're wearing my shirt."

I smile and nod. "Didn't you say you always wanted to see me in one of these?"

Carter's eyes roam over my body heatedly and his hands find my waist. He pulls me closer and his lips come crashing down on mine. He lifts me onto the kitchen counter and I wrap my legs around him, the shirt riding up.

"Fuck," Carter whispers. "I want you in this."

I giggle, but he wipes my smile right off my face when his fingers find their way between my legs. "Minx," he whispers, as he drops his lips to my neck and kisses me softly. "How are you wet already?"

I smile and turn my head to whisper into his ear. "Let's just say that seeing you in your swim shorts every morning has been highly... stimulating."

Carter grins as my hand slips into his boxer shorts. "I need to get back on the pill," I whisper, and Carter nods.

"I want you bare, Emilia. I want to be able to fuck you whenever, wherever."

His words make me even wetter and I clench my thighs. My cheeks redden as I look at him. "I've never wanted that with anyone but you," I tell him.

Carter looks at me in confusion and frowns. "What do you mean?"

I look away, my cheeks burning. "I've never had anyone bare but you."

Carter looks at me in disbelief, and then he grins. "Knowing that we're still each other's one and only, even for something so small... I fucking love it."

He pulls my lips back to his, and I lose myself in him. "I've missed this," he whispers. "God, I've dreamt about these lips of yours every single night."

Carter pulls back to look at me, his hands roaming over my body impatiently. He looks at me as though he can't quite believe that I'm really here, and I feel exactly the same. I don't want to overthink this, I just want to be in this moment with him.

My hands slide from his hair to his shoulders, and I pull him closer, my movements urgent and eager. "Carter," I whisper, my heart filled with longing.

He drops his forehead to mine and inhales deeply. "Let's go back to bed, Minx."

I laugh and throw my arms around his neck. Carter lifts me into his arms and I rest my head against his shoulder, feeling intensely happy.

Carter carries me to the stairs and I run my hand over his chest, a smile on my face. We both freeze when the doorbell rings. Carter looks at me and frowns as he puts me down carefully.

"We weren't expecting anyone, were we?" He asks me, and I shake my head. He sighs and looks irritated as he walks to the front door. I lean back against the wall, my eyes following him.

Carter stiffens when he opens the door and I frown. My heart sinks when Helen comes into view, Kate in tow. Her eyes find mine, and she looks shocked. I glance down and belatedly realise that my robe is undone, and she can see that I'm wearing Carter's shirt.

I clutch my robe tightly and wrap it around me, but I'm obviously not quick enough, because Kate stares at me, the edges of her lips tipped up in amusement. She glances at Carter and grins before looking down at her feet.

"Good morning, Emilia," Helen says.

I smile tightly and glance at the stairs, wondering whether I should just make a run for it. Carter looks tense, and he looks worried. I might not want to spend any time with either Helen or Kate, but I do want to spend time with Carter, and I don't want him worrying about me.

"Good morning," I murmur, trying my best to smile at her.

Helen looks relieved, and her smile widens. She holds up a grocery bag excitedly, and my heart aches. When is the last time she smiled at me that way? Most of my memories are tinged with heartache. The last couple of months I spent here overshadow the years of good memories we have.

"I thought I might make some pancakes," she says carefully, and I can't help but wonder if she chose to make that because they're my favorite.

I glance at Carter to find him staring up at me nervously, as though he thinks I might run. He looks even more hurt than I feel, and I smile at him before turning back to Helen. I nod at her and walk into the kitchen. "Pancakes sound nice," I say, even though I really want to go back to my room.

CHAPTER 44

milia

Carter looks anxious as he follows me into the kitchen and I smile to myself. A couple of minutes of being polite to Helen and Kate is pretty much nothing if that's what it takes to make him smile. He's been amazing since I got here, and I've yet to pay him back for all he does.

He walks up to me, his eyes roaming over my body. I place my hand on his chest and lean back against the counter. "Shouldn't you get dressed?" I ask. He blinks and looks down, as though he's only just realizing that he's wearing far less than I am.

He looks into my eyes as though he's searching for something. "Will you be okay?" He asks. My smile falters and I nod. I hate that Carter thinks that I still need protection. I'm embarrassed of the person I used to be, of the girl that couldn't stand up for herself.

Carter nods and walks away, leaving me in the kitchen with Helen and Kate. I turn around and sigh. Maybe I should have gone up to my room instead. I lean back as I look at the two of them, my arms crossed over each other.

Both of them look older, and I can't help but wonder what the last couple of years have been like for them. Were they happy while I tried my best to get through every single day, feeling broken and incomplete? Did the pieces I gave up of myself make Kate whole again? Was it all worth it in the end?

I want to be better than this, but I'm filled with resentment. Being back here made me realize just how much I've been missing out on in life. I forgot it was even possible for me to be this happy. I forgot what being with Carter was like. I forgot what it was like to be myself — fully, truly. Can I even go back from here? Can I go back to a life that felt bleak in contrast?

I watch the mother-daughter duo, my heart aching. Is it possible to both love and hate someone at the same time? They've both broken my heart in different ways, yet standing here with them soothes my soul. It reminds me of some of the most precious moments in my life.

Kate carefully spreads Nutella over a pancake before sprinkling some coarse sugar over it. She rolls it up carefully and then pushes the plate my way, her hands trembling. I look up at her in surprise and blink in disbelief. I can't believe that she still remembers that this is my favorite.

"Did you poison it somehow?" I ask, unable to help myself. Kate looks stricken, but I don't have it in me to feel bad. I wouldn't actually put it past her to do just that.

"I... No... Do you — do you want me to try this first?"

I look at her through narrowed eyes. She looks so meek, so innocent. Since it's Kate, I can't tell if it's all just an act or not. I never could.

Helen looks shocked, and I wonder if she'll try to defend Kate or criticize me. Much to my surprise, she does neither. She pulls my plate towards her and smiles nervously. "This looks nice," she says, and she takes a bite, startling me.

Kate looks up and her mum gratefully and I grit my teeth.

are they just trying to make me look horrible? If so, they're definitely succeeding.

Kate looks up at me nervously, and I barely even recognize her. "Actually, Emilia... I... I'm sorry I've been avoiding you," she says.

I shake my head and cross my arms over each other. "Oh, don't be," I tell her. "I much prefer it that way. Had it been up to me, I would have left both of you standing in front of the front door."

I smile at Helen humorlessly. "But as I'm sure you would remind me, Helen," I say. "This isn't my home. It's Carter's."

Kate swallows hard as her eyes fill with tears and I look away in annoyance. Carter walks in just as a tear drops down her cheek and I laugh. "Perfect timing, as always," I murmur, my heart filled with hatred.

"What happened?" He asks cautiously, his eyes moving from me to Kate. I glance up at him, my heart breaking. One night... We've had one night together. One night, untainted by memories of the past or the reality we're facing. I should have known it could never last.

"I made your sister cry," I tell him, feeling lost. I know it won't matter what I do or say. Kate's tears will speak louder than any words I can utter. I shake my head and move to walk past him. Carter grabs my wrist and stops me. He pulls me towards him and wraps his arm around me protectively.

He looks at Kate through narrowed eyes and tightens his grip on me. "What did you do?" he asks Kate. She looks at him with wide eyes and shakes her head, and I sigh. I pull away from Carter as more tears drop down Kate's cheeks.

"I want no part of this," I tell him, before glancing at Kate. I don't even have it in me to apologize to her. I knew I should have just gone to my bedroom instead. Kate wipes away her tears furiously and shakes her head at Carter.

"She didn't do anything," she tells him, and I roll my eyes. I have neither the time nor the patience for this type of theatrics. I don't want to get involved at all. I regret speaking to her, I should have just shut up and eaten the pancake.

"Emilia," Kate says, and I shake my head as I walk away. I'm not playing this game. Not ever again.

I breathe a sigh of relief when my bedroom door closes behind me. I collapse on top of my bed and check the clock. Dad should be waking up soon. He's the one I should be focusing on, and no one else.

I sit up in surprise when my door opens and Carter walks in, a worried expression on his face. "Hey," he murmurs. He climbs into my bed and I frown at him.

"What are you doing?" I ask, confused.

He smiles and pulls me closer, wrapping his arms around me. "Didn't we say that we were going back to bed?"

"What about your mom and your sister?"

Carter's smile drops and he looks away. "I asked them to leave. I never should have let them in at all."

I shake my head and look into his eyes. He looks unhappy and worried, and I know I'm the cause of it. "Don't, Carter," I say, my voice soft. "Don't alienate your family on my behalf."

I pull away from him to look at him, and my heart twists painfully. "My time here is limited. I have no intention of staying. Whatever might be happening between us is temporary. You know that as well as I do. Maybe we shouldn't even have let it happen at all."

Carter drops his forehead to mine and inhales deeply. He threads his hand through my hair, his movements frantic. "You're crazy if you think I'll ever let you go again."

I hug him and rest my head on his shoulder, my lips nestled against his neck. "You have to. What would a relationship for us even look like? More of what happened just now? I don't want that. I don't ever want to go through that again. I can't. Besides, my entire life is in London. My entire career is

209

there. You and I... I don't know what this is, but I know it can't last."

CHAPTER 45

arter

Emilia was acting distant all day yesterday, and I regret inviting my mother and sister in. It's obvious that Emilia hates being around them, and I want her to feel at home here. I want her to consider my home *hers*.

I walk into the kitchen to find it empty and sigh. I was hoping that she'd be here, that she'd share a cup of coffee with me, if nothing else. I turn the coffee machine on, hoping she might come down soon, but she doesn't. I stare at the coffee cup that I've been using for years, every memory with Emilia still fresh in my mind. Am I being selfish by pursuing her again? I still remember the way she lost her spirit day by day, the way she'd cry herself to sleep, the way she'd bite down on her lip hard enough to draw blood when Kate's words wounded her. What am I doing, reminding her of everything she went through?

She's here for her dad. There's a reason I didn't go after her, and there's a reason she hasn't returned in years. Emilia deserves better than me. She deserves to have everything she's ever wanted, and I can't give her that. I can't ask her to live a life where she's forced to endure my family, and I can't abandon them either. She's right. Whatever there is between us is temporary, but is even that asking for too much?

My heart starts to race when I hear sounds coming from the hallway, and I turn, a smile on my face. John walks in, and my smile crumbles.

He looks at me with raised brows and then smiles. "Expecting someone else?"

I look at him through narrowed eyes and then look away. "No. Of course not."

He chuckles as he fills the kettle to make himself a cup of tea. "Emilia is usually already up by now," he says. "I thought she'd be down by now."

I sigh and nod. "Me too," I murmur without thinking.

John grins and crosses his arms over each other. "So, what's going on between you two?"

I shake my head and look down, unable to look him in the eye. This crazy old man would probably gut me if he knew what I did to his daughter just a few nights ago. "Nothing."

He smiles conspiratorially and I tense. "I'm not blind, son. I was your age once, you know? You're lucky that I like you, because the way you look at my daughter sometimes can only be described as *indecent*."

My eyes widen and I suppress a smile. "Indecent, huh?" I repeat, shaking my head. I thought I'd been quite sly, but I guess not. Then again, I've never been able to hide my feelings for Emilia.

"So, what's going on? You two dating?"

I run a hand through my hair and look at him, feeling oddly nervous. "Would you be okay with that? She just came out of a relationship, and she's said multiple times that she has no intention of staying here."

John grabs his tea cup and sits down on the chair by the

kitchen counter, his expression troubled. "I know my little girl, and I haven't seen her look truly happy in years — not until she came back home. She belongs here, and she's happy here. She's just stuck in the past because she's been running away from it for so long. I thought all she needed was a bit of time. I never expected her to stay in London. She's been running from the pain for so long that she's never had a chance to overcome it."

I sigh and shake my head. "I don't know, John. You should see her when she's around Mom and Kate. I don't want that for her. Surely you don't either?"

John nods in understanding. "I don't ever want to see my daughter in pain, and it took me years to forgive your mother. But Carter, I know Helen and Kate love her. I can see the regret in Kate's eyes, and the guilt she lives with. Everyone involved has been hurting for too long. Enough is enough."

He pauses and then looks up at me. "You too, Carter. It's always been obvious to me that you love my daughter. I knew before you even did. I've also always known that she loves you just as much, and she still does. Even now she's happy when she's with you. I can see it in her eyes, in her smile. And you? I've seen you throughout the years. I know you never got over her. How about you two stop being knuckleheads and just choose happiness? It's right there, Carter."

I smile sadly and inhale deeply. Has he known all along? Is that why he's kept an eye on me throughout the years? "It's not that simple. She won't forgive Mom and Kate. You weren't there to see her fall apart. I'm grateful you didn't have to see that, but you wouldn't be saying any of this if you did."

John takes a sip of his tea and smiles. "Do you think I'd ever forgive either your mother or sister if I thought they didn't deserve it? My daughter means the world to me, and I'd keep her far away from you and your family if I, for even a single second, thought she'd be mistreated. You'd be stupid to let her go again, Carter. You're many things, but you're not stupid."

I'm surprised that he seems to want us together, and it revives the hope I struggle to hold on to. Could she and I really make it?

"Do you love her, son?"

I look into his eyes and nod. "More than life itself."

John nods in satisfaction and smiles. "Then don't let her get away this time. I promise you, she'll forgive your mother and sister. I know my daughter. I know her heart," he says. "And I'd like to think that I know both your mother and sister quite well too. They love her, and if Emilia didn't still love them too, she wouldn't be acting the way she is. She needs time to heal, but she'll get there."

I want to hope so, but hope is in short supply for me these days. "Maybe she will. Maybe she won't. It needs to be up to her. I can't just assume she will, and I need to be okay with it if she doesn't. I'll respect her choices either way."

"But will you? Will you be okay with it if she leaves? I don't want to see either of you unhappy, Carter. Life is fragile. Trust me, I've learned that the hard way."

He sighs and shakes his head. "You know, I always knew you'd be the one that'd take my daughter away from me. It's why I was so upset when you two finally started dating. I was never worried about any other boys, but you? I knew you'd be the one for her. I knew you'd be the only man she'd love more than she loves me. And she still does, Carter. She still loves you. So don't fear the future."

John smiles at me reassuringly as he rises from his seat. I'm lost in thought as he puts his cup in the sink and walks away.

His words echo in my head for the rest of the day, and I can't figure out what the right thing to do is. I want her, but more than that, I want her to be happy. If I can't be the one to make her happy, then I need to take a step back. I can't set us on a path to destruction again. I can't be the reason she cries herself to sleep ever again.

CHAPTER 46

milia

I feel conflicted. Is it possible for your heart to feel broken, but to feel more alive than you have in years? That's how I feel. Waking up with Carter a few days ago was everything I've been dreaming of for the last couple of years. Being with him again was surreal – it was like we were never apart. The way he makes me feel and the way he touched me... It was perfection.

Just when the smallest amount of hope bloomed in my heart, Helen and Kate walked in. I saw the hope in Carter's eyes, and I didn't have the heart to walk away when I knew he wanted me to stay. It was only breakfast, but I hated every second I spent with them.

Dad tightens his grip on my hand and I turn to look at him. "What's wrong, Princess?" He asks.

I smile and shake my head. "Nothing, daddy," I tell him. I take a good look at dad and sigh. Every day he seems to get thinner, even though he's getting the best care he could possibly have. I'm worried. I know he's staying strong for me, but every day his dialysis sucks a little bit more life out of him.

My dad has always been strong and in control of everything. He's always been powerful, especially in his career. I worry that it's affecting him too much mentally to be at the mercy of his illness.

Dad wraps his arm over mine and shakes his head. "You're being quiet," he says. I feel my cheeks heat a little and look away. All I've been able to think about lately is Carter. It's been a few days since we slept together, and I keep telling myself that we can't do it again, but it's so hard to stay away. The only way I can resist him is if I physically stay away. Carter hasn't said anything, and he's been giving me space, but there's no escaping what's between us.

"It's nothing, daddy."

Dad tightens his grip on my hand and frowns. "Is it Sam? Are you still upset?"

I look at him with wide eyes and shake my head. I probably should still be upset about breaking up with Sam, but I haven't even thought of him recently. "I... No... That's not it. I'm just worried. I'm worried about you, and I'm wondering about the future. My boss said I could take as much time as I need, but eventually she'll need me back. And if I stay away too long, I'm worried that might impact my career."

Heartbreak flashes through my dad's eyes at the mention of me returning to London, and I regret bringing it up at all. He gets upset at the thought of me leaving, and the last thing he needs while he's fighting his illness is additional stress.

"I see," he says. "And you won't consider moving back home? It's been so good having you back here, I've gotten so used to you being back home, I wish you could stay."

I drop my head to my dad's shoulder and sigh. "I'm not sure I can, Dad. I worked so hard to build everything I have, and I can't give it all up now. Besides, where would I even work if I moved back here? The only large company around here is Carter's."

Dad smiles, his eyes twinkling. "What's wrong with that? You're already working there, and the boy can do with more people that he can trust. There is plenty of opportunity for growth at Clarke Reed. I read an article the other day that said Carter's company is amongst the most desirable companies to work for in the *world*."

I look away, my heart twisting painfully. The truth is that Carter gives me so much responsibility in his company that I've learned more here than I ever did at my old job. I love working with him, and the work is just more interesting. Even more so, I just love knowing that the work I do directly benefits someone I care about, that it makes a difference. At Clarke Reed I'm not just another employee, I'm someone Carter relies on for all legal advice. It's a new feeling to me – being more than just another worker bee. I adore Alice, but she and I are just that: worker bees. There's a lot of reeducation I'd have to do to formally become a lawyer here, but it'd be worth it. I'd be happier here.

I guess most of the reason that I want to go back is because I know that Carter and I can't be together. The longer I stay, the more it will hurt when I finally leave. And if I do stay to be close to my dad, it'll only be a matter of time before I'll have to see him fall for someone else. I don't think my heart can take that, but I don't think I can leave my dad either.

I'm still thinking about dad's request hours later. I slip through the sliding doors and walk to the swing on the veranda, the breeze messing up my hair. I sit down and sigh. It isn't until right at this moment that I realize I was hoping that Carter might be here. I tell myself that I want to stay away from him, yet I find myself seeking him out constantly. It's like my head and my heart are at war.

My heart flutters when the door opens and I glance up to find Carter walking in, still in his work suit. Why does he have to look so good in a suit? My eyes roam over his body, and my heart starts to race. Why is it only him that my body responds to in this way?

Carter pulls on his tie and takes a seat next to me, his thigh brushing against mine. He closes his eyes and leans back, looking tired.

"Long day?"

Carter nods and sighs. I want to take him into my arms, I want to run my hands over his body and cup his cheek so I can turn his face towards mine and kiss him.

"Are you done trying to resist me?" He asks. Carter opens his eyes and looks at me, his gaze intense. He reaches for me and buries his hand in my hair. "Because I'm done."

I look at him with wide eyes and he smiles. "If my time with you is limited, then I'm not holding back. I've spent years dreaming about you and missing you. I don't want to look back at these months that we've got together with regret. I'm done with all the regret, Emilia. For just a couple of weeks I want to have it all. Tell me you want the same."

I hesitate and Carter's expression falters. "If we're not on the same page, then let me know now. I'll stop. I won't pursue you in the slightest, I won't make you feel uncomfortable. But if you do, Emilia... Then I'm going to kiss you right now. I'm going to kiss you, and I'm going to slip that robe off your shoulders. I'm going to get you naked, right here on my veranda, and I'm going to fuck you. So, tell me, Minx. Should I stay or should I go?"

My heart is banging in my chest and even though I'm scared of what our future might hold, I'm certain of what I want right now. "Stay. I want it all too. I want it all with you."

CHAPTER 47

arter

I exhale in relief and pull her towards me impatiently. Emilia smiles against my lips and I tighten my grip on her hair. I trap her bottom lip between my teeth before kissing her fully, and Emilia moans. She wraps her hand in my hair, and I lift her up. Emilia straddles me and I run my hands over her body, tugging on her robe roughly. It slips down her shoulders and I smile smugly when I realize that she's wearing another one of my t-shirts.

"You little thief," I whisper, and she blushes. I drop my lips to her neck and kiss her gently. Emilia groans and tugs on my clothes. I love seeing her so eager, so desperate for me. She opens the buttons of my shirt and leans in, kissing my neck the way I just kissed hers.

"Carter," she whispers. She looks up at me with lust-filled eyes, and I groan. Emilia tugs on my trousers and I bite down on my lip when she wraps her hands around my cock.

"So impatient," I whisper, and her cheeks redden. She looks

up at me and grins before moving away. I groan in dissatisfaction, and Emilia blows me a kiss.

"Who's impatient now?" she asks as she drops to her knees in front of me. My dick jerks when she licks her lips, and I'm already close. Emilia looks at me as she slowly brings her lips closer, teasing the hell out of me. I thread my hand through her hair and grit my teeth.

"Baby, I need you right now," I tell her.

Emilia laughs and swirls her tongue around the tip, and a powerful wave of desire crashes through me. I jerk against her and she takes me in deeper, her mouth hot and tight. She looks up at me as she bobs her head up and down, driving me half insane. She moans, and the feeling of it has me tightening my grip on her hair.

"Minx," I whisper. She increases the pace and takes me in even deeper. Fucking hell, I can feel my dick hit the back of her throat, and then she swallows. The sensation is unreal and I moan loudly. I grab her hair and thrust my hips ups roughly, and she takes me in gladly, another moan vibrating through her throat.

"I can't," I tell her. "I want to fuck you right now, Emilia," I whimper.

She lifts her head and grins. "Say please," she tells me, and I laugh.

"Please, my love. Let me have that tight sweet pussy of yours."

Her eyes darken and she rises to her feet. I slip my hands underneath the tee she's wearing and yank her panties down, not at all surprised to find them soaking wet.

She climbs on top of me and I groan when she grabs my dick and sinks down on it without warning. "Fuck," I moan.

Emilia smiles in delight and I pull her towards me, my lips finding hers as she starts to move on top of me. I kiss her deeply, losing myself in her. Being with her is still as intense and raw as it's always been.

I move my hands to her ass and grab her tightly, eliciting a moan from her. "I need more," I tell her. "I need all of you."

She wraps her legs around me as I rise to my feet, and I turn to press her against the wall. Emilia moans loudly as I lift her legs over my shoulders and I grin. She's so fucking perfect, it's unreal.

I fuck her hard and look into her eyes as I thrust into her. "Your pussy feels so damn good, Minx," I tell her, and she bites down on her lip. "So hot, so tight. It's like you were made for me."

She pulls on my hair and I slam into her even harder. "You like this, don't you?" I whisper. "You like having your tight pussy all stretched out by me."

She nods, her eyes glazing over. "I do," she moans. "I do."

I grin and lift her a little higher, making sure I'm angling her the way I know she can barely take. I look into her eyes as I thrust into her, rubbing up against her g-spot teasingly.

"You want to come for me, don't you?"

Emilia nods and I chuckle. "But you can't, baby. I won't let you. I'm not done with you."

Her nails rake over my scalp and desperation flashes through her eyes. I love this. I love how much she wants me, and how blatantly it shows. "I'm going to fuck you all night, Emilia. All that time you stayed away, all those years I've fantasized about you... we need to make up for lost time."

I tighten my grip on her ass and thrust into her roughly, slamming into her all the way. Emilia moans and yanks my head closer, her lips coming down on my neck. She grazes my skin with her teeth and then sucks down where she knows I'm sensitive.

"Carter," she whispers, her voice husky. "I can't take it. Please, babe. Please, make me come."

I drop my forehead to hers, both of us breathing hard. My lips drop to hers, and I kiss her roughly, deeply.

"Please," she whispers, and I suck down on her lower lip before pulling away.

"Look at me," I tell her, and she does. I slow down the pace, driving her insane, keeping her right on the edge. "Tell me you won't run again. Tell me you're mine for as long as you're here."

Emilia nods and pulls me back to her. She kisses me before looking into my eyes. "I'm yours. I've always been yours."

I shake my head and tighten my grip on her ass. "Exclusively, Emilia. I don't want you looking at another man, don't want you thinking about anyone else, you hear me?"

She smiles, and I thrust into her harshly, replacing her humor with lust. "Yes. *Yes*," she groans. "I swear, Carter. Only you."

I smile in satisfaction and give her what she wants. Her inner muscles tighten around my cock, and she fucking milks me. I can't hold on and come deep inside my girl, both of us trembling. I drop my forehead to hers, feeling lightheaded as fuck. "Damn, Minx... I think I'm seeing stars."

She laughs and pulls my head towards hers. "Screw the stars," she says. "You'd better only be seeing me."

I burst out laughing and walk us back to the swing, sitting down with her in my arms, the two of us still intimately connected. "Yes, ma'am," I tell her. "You're all I can see. You always will be."

Emilia smiles in satisfaction, and my heart skips a beat. I can't remember the last time I was this happy, and I can't help but worry. I worry it won't last, and that I'll lose her all over again.

CHAPTER 48

milia

I smile at my phone, feeling strangely giddy, and Dad frowns at me. "What has you smiling like that?" he asks, startling me. My cheeks heat up and I lock my phone screen instantly. Carter has been texting me all morning, and it's got me feeling like a teenager all over again.

"Oh, it's nothing," I tell him. "I saw a funny meme online just now."

Dad looks at me as though he doesn't believe me, and then he shakes his head. "Meme. Such a stupid name," he mutters, and I burst out laughing.

"I have no idea why it's called that either, to be honest," I murmur, getting back to the research I was doing. Carter lets me work from home most days so I can spend my time with Dad, but today I kind of wish I'd gone into the office. I miss him. Last night was perfect, and I want more of those nights. I want more of this happiness that I thought I'd never experience again. I want to make the most of the time we've got together. My phone buzzes and I smile before I even unlock my phone.

Devil: *You and me. dinner. tonight. I need some quality time with you.*

I love that he still has the same phone number, even after all these years. His is the only phone number I know by heart. His, and my own.

Emilia: *What about Dad? We always have dinner with him.*

Devil: *Enzo will look after him. Don't you worry. That's what we have so much staff for, after all.*

Emilia: *I know that... I meant, what will we tell him?*

Devil: *Tell him I'm taking you out for dinner. How about 7?*

I roll my eyes and sigh.

Emilia: *I'll tell him we have a meeting or something.*

Carter doesn't reply for a minute, and I'm suddenly worried that he doesn't like me not being honest about us to dad, but how could we? We both know this is temporary.

Devil: *See you tonight, baby. Shall I pick you up at home or do you want to drive down to the tapas place?*

I smile to myself, my heart fluttering. When is the last time I was this excited to go on a date? I can't even remember.

Emilia: *I'll drive down. See you later x*

I look up to find Dad looking at me, a smile on his face. "Another meme?" he asks, and I nod awkwardly.

I glance at the clock and bite down on my lip. Dinner is in two hours or so, and I still need to get ready. Dad and I have gotten into a routine of sorts. He'll sit with me as I work during the day, taking breaks to do his personal training and whatever other errands he decides to do that day. We make sure to have lunch together, and then I sit with him and work on my laptop as he undergoes his dialysis. After that we wait for Carter to come home so we can have dinner together. We rarely deviate from our schedule, so I wonder what he'll think of having dinner by himself for once.

"Um, I just got an email about a meeting I have to attend later," I say awkwardly, avoiding his inquisitive gaze.

Dad is quiet for a while, and then he smiles. "I see. Well, you can't go in that, can you?" he says, pointing at the pajamas I'm wearing. Since I work from home, I spend most of my days wearing one of Carter's t-shirts with a pair of leggings. I glance down at my outfit and blush. "Um, yes, I'd better get ready," I murmur, my heart racing. I'm certain Dad can see straight through me, but I'm glad he isn't calling me on it.

I'm nervous as I get ready, wanting to impress Carter, but not wanting to overdo it either. I end up deciding on a tight black dress that looks great without making me look over-dressed. I pair it with heels I know Carter will love and put on some red lipstick. I twirl around in front of the mirror, my heart racing. I wonder what he'll think when he sees me.

I walk down the stairs, and Dad smiles at me when he sees me. "You look beautiful, Princess," he tells me.

I blush and kiss his cheek. "Love you, Dad," I murmur, and he smiles, looking just a touch emotional. He waves me off and I glance back at him as I walk out the door.

I'm ridiculously nervous as I drive to the tapas place. It's been years since Carter and I went on a date, and I have no idea what it might be like.

He's leaning against his car when I arrive, his face tipped up at the sky, and I pause by my car as I take him in. This man owns my entire heart. Just looking at him makes me feel so intensely happy. Words can't even explain how he makes me feel, how he's always made me feel.

Carter turns to look at me, as though he could feel my gaze on his skin, and his eyes widen. I grin as he checks me out, and my hips sway just a little more as I walk up to him. He meets me halfway and buries his hand in my hair, pulling me close impatiently. His lips come crashing down on mine hungrily, and I lose myself in him. I don't pull away until I hear someone whistle near us, and Carter drops his forehead to mine.

"You look far too beautiful tonight, Emilia," he whispers.

"I'm so tempted to skip dinner and go straight for dessert," he says as his lips trail down my neck. I giggle and take a step away, my hand entwining with his.

"Later," I promise him. There's no way I'll be able to stay away either, not when he looks this hot. My eyes roam over the suit he's wearing, and Carter grins smugly when he catches me ogling him.

He tightens his grip on my hand and raises our joined hands to his lips. He kisses the back of my hand gently before leading me to the tapas place that's been here for pretty much ever.

Mrs. Henderson, the owner, lights up when she sees us walk in together. She raises her hand to her heart and smiles widely. "My goodness, Emilia Parker and Carter Clarke," she murmurs. She opens her arms, and I hug her tightly. I spent some summers working here for her, and Carter would always come in to annoy me. Even then, Mrs. Henderson was convinced that he liked me, and she'd tease me about it endlessly. She hugs me back and pulls away to look at me, her eyes moving between Carter and me. "You're finally back, sweetheart," she says, and I nod. It's little things like these that make me feel so at home here, in a way I never did in London. It isn't just the memories either. Mrs. Henderson looks up at Carter, and she smiles so motherly, so adoringly, that my heart fills with tenderness. She's giddy as she leads us to a table. Rather than asking us for our order, she insists on surprising us, and Carter winks at me as she walks away.

"I didn't think it'd be possible, but she's more excited to see you than I am," he says, laughing. He grabs my hand and lifts it to his lips, and my heart skips a beat.

"Do you know what this reminds me of a little?" I ask, a thousand memories with Carter flitting through my mind.

He grins and presses another kiss to my hand. "La Familia,"

he murmurs, and I look up at him in surprise. How does he always know what I'm thinking?

"Yes, La Familia," I murmur, thinking back to the restaurant we used to frequent back in college. "I'd love to go back there one day, you know? I wonder if Lita will even remember us."

Carter looks away and sighs, his smile melting away. For a second he looks hurt, as though he too is thinking of everything we've missed out on.

"We'll go," I tell him. "We'll go together. Maybe we can do a little weekend break."

Carter smiles, and relief rushes through me. I don't want tonight to be tainted by memories and regrets. I just want us to be happy.

CHAPTER 49

arter

I can't get enough of her. This is exactly what we needed, a night out, just the two of us. I love John as much as I love my own father, but sometimes I do find myself wishing Emilia and I could just have the house to ourselves. She isn't trying to hide her affection for me now that we're out, but she'd be uncomfortable at home.

"The food was so good," she says, her eyes twinkling with happiness, and I smile as I signal for the bill.

Emilia looks around conspiratorially before leaning in. "Don't tell Mrs. Henderson, though, but I do still miss Lita's food."

She looks so conflicted as she whispers to me, and I can't help the way my heart overflows with happiness. She's so fucking cute, and she's mine. After all these years, she's finally mine again.

I grab her hand and lift it to my lips, kissing the tips of her fingers. "I'll take you back to Lita, baby," I tell her, and Emilia smiles. I can't wait to get out of here. I hate having this entire damn table between us. The only part of her I can reach is her hand, and I want more than that.

Emilia grins as though she knows what I'm thinking, and I chuckle. "Come here," I tell her, half rising from my seat to lean over the table. She shakes her head and meets me for a quick kiss, and I sigh in disappointment.

I wait impatiently for Mrs. Henderson to take my card, and by the time I've got it back in my hand I'm ready to throw Emilia over my shoulder. She looks at me and chuckles at my expression as she rises from her seat. I help her into her coat and keep my arm wrapped around her. She leans into me and smiles up at me, and my heart skips a beat.

Emilia and I both tense when the door opens right before we walk out, and Layla walks in. She freezes, her eyes falling to my arm around Emilia's shoulder, and she frowns.

"Emilia, Carter," she says, an insincere smile on her face.

I nod at her and pull Emilia along, not wanting to speak to her at all, but she crosses her arms over each other and blocks our way. I have a feeling Emilia isn't going to appreciate it if I shove her away, so I stay put, silently fuming.

"How is your boyfriend?" Layla asks, vindictiveness flashing through her eyes. Emilia smiles up at me and rises to her toes to kiss my cheek, catching me by surprise.

She looks back at Layla and grins. "He's standing right here. Why don't you ask him?"

Layla looks at me in disbelief and raises her brows. "What?" she says, before turning back to Emilia. "What about Sam?"

Emilia shrugs and wraps her arm around my waist. "I have no idea. He went back to London after we broke up, and we haven't spoken since. I can give you his number if you want, though."

Layla stares at Emilia and grits her teeth, and I just about manage to suppress a smile. Emilia looks at me and smiles. "Ready to go home, babe?" she says, and I nod.

I smile as Emilia pulls me past Layla. My Minx looks agitated and angry, and she glares at me as she drags me to my car. I love the way she pouts, the way she shows me all her pettiness and her jealousy. She glares at me as we reach my car, and I grin.

I push her against my car and hook her leg around my hip, my lips finding hers. I kiss her until she relaxes against me, and then I drop my forehead to hers. "Boyfriend, huh?"

Emilia pulls away from me and looks at me with wide eyes. "I... it just slipped out. I was just..."

I laugh and thread my hand through her hair. "You what? You were just being possessive? Jealous? Claiming me as yours?"

Emilia blushes and looks away, and I drop my lips to her cheek, kissing her gently. "I prefer *husband*, but I guess we can start off with boyfriend."

She gasps and pushes against my chest, shaking her head. She thinks I'm joking, but I'm not. I'm more certain now than I've ever been before. I'm making Emilia my wife. I know that there's so much standing between us, but fuck it all. I've given my family so many of my years. I've done everything I could to make them happy, to make sure Kate was healthy. John is right. Enough is enough. I'll happily move to London with Emilia, away from everything and everyone. She won't ever have to speak to them or see them if she doesn't want to. I lost out on so many years with her, and I'm not willing to spend even another second without her. I always thought she could do better than me, that she'd be happier without me, but I was wrong. She's just like me. She's still my other half, the way I am hers. I see it in the change in her since she came back home, the way she smiles at me, the way she touches me. I thought I was doing her a favor by staying away, but instead I just made us both suffer. No more. I've done what I thought was the right thing for so long, it's about time I do what is right for *me*, for *us*.

I let her go and open the car door for her, a smile on my face. She glances at my Ferrari, the car she drove here, and I wink at her. "Graham will pick it up," I tell her, and she nods, a smile on her face. Emilia looks at me and smiles as I drive us home. She grins and drops her hand to my thigh, slowly but surely inching closer to my rapidly hardening dick. I grin and take a left turn where I should be taking a right, and I park in front of the park I took Emilia to on her sixteenth birthday. It's pitch black around us, the road deserted, and I smile at her.

"It's like you can read my mind," she whispers, and I grin as I undo my seat belt. Emilia is in my lap the second I've got it off and I grin against her lips.

"I've missed you, Carter," she says, sighing. I bury my hand in her hair and kiss her, her hand roaming over my body. I smile against her lips when her hands find their way to my trousers.

"I've missed you too, Emilia. Every second of every day, Minx. You were always on my mind, always in my thoughts and in my every dream."

I caress her waist and move my hand down her thighs, and she inhales sharply when my fingers find their way between her legs. I grin when I realize she's already wet.

"Me too," she whimpers, moaning as I tease her. "I've thought of you every day, Carter. It was always you."

I watch her as she gets closer and closer, this moment so fucking precious. I want things to be like this between us forever. She shatters on my fingers and I smile as she kisses me, small whimpers escaping her lips.

Emilia grins and grabs my cock, sinking down on me hard and without warning. I moan loudly, and she smiles smugly. I hold her as close as I can as she rides me, my heart overflowing with love.

Emilia rotates her hips, making me moan again, and then she smiles. This girl. She'll drive me fucking insane.

CHAPTER 50

milia

I wake up in Carter's bed and smile to myself as he pulls me closer, still fast asleep. I snuggle into him and sigh. I've been on cloud nine all week. Things have been so perfect between us, and I couldn't be happier. I don't even mind the sneaking around we do around the house. If anything, I find it fun and exciting. I've spent every single night in Carter's bedroom, and I have a feeling Dad knows, but he's just letting us be.

I was worried that Dad would be upset, or that he wouldn't approve, but he hasn't said a thing. I guess he might be waiting until we tell him ourselves, but we haven't really talked about our future together. I told Carter that whatever was going on would be temporary, but neither one of us is acting like it will be.

I've only just about started to fall back asleep when my phone buzzes. I glance at it and frown when I realize it's the local clinic's number. I pick up, feeling anxious, my voice still sounding sleepy.

"Emilia?"

I freeze, recognizing Layla's voice. Why did it have to be her, of all people.

"Good morning, Layla."

I try to get up, but Carter groans and pulls me even closer. "Minx," he murmurs, his eyes fluttering before he falls back asleep.

Layla falls silent on the phone, and for a second I actually feel bad. She clears her throat awkwardly.

"It's about your blood tests. There was an anomaly in them," she tells me, and my heart starts to hammer in my chest. She laughs, and the sound sends chills down my spine.

"I was wondering why Carter was so adamant that you shouldn't ever see the physical files. He asked me to call you with the results, but he requested that I keep the paperwork from you. I didn't think much of it, because it's Carter, but I just had a look at your files, and something doesn't add up."

I feel uncomfortable and anxious. "What are you talking about?" I whisper, my voice shaking.

"Your blood type is A, but your father's blood type is B, and your medical file states that your mother's blood type is O."

I blink, not quite getting it. Layla sighs loudly. "I never knew you were adopted, you know? It's nice that you'd still consider organ donation for your adoptive father, but unfortunately, you aren't a match."

I sit up and push Carter away, my stomach churning. "This must be some kind of mistake," I whisper, feeling sick.

Layla pauses. "I've ran all the tests twice, Emilia. Your blood types don't match, and it's impossible for two parents with blood type B and O to have a child with blood type A. I hate having to be the one to tell you this, but I just thought something like this shouldn't be kept from you."

I don't even hear whatever else she's saying, my mind whirling. My phone drops from my hand and I start to tremble. My dad isn't my dad? How could that possibly be true?

Does he even know? Why would he take care of me for so many years if he knew? Why would he have kept me after my mother left us?

Maybe Layla is wrong, and my mother's blood type isn't O. I run a hand through my hair, and Carter shifts uneasily. I glance at him as he blinks lazily, a smile on his face as he wakes up and finds me sitting here with him.

Carter frowns and sits up when he realizes something is wrong, and I take a good look at him. Could Layla be right? Has Carter known all along?

"Emilia?" he says, sitting up. The sheets fall to his waist and he leans back against the pillows. He runs a hand through his hair, confusion clouding his eyes. "What's wrong?"

I inhale deeply and wrap my arms around myself. "Is it true?" I ask. "About my dad?"

Carter glances at my phone in my hands, his eyes widening.

"What do you mean?" he asks. I see the wheels in his mind whirling, and the way he looks at me makes my heart sink. I've seen that look in his eyes before, but I've never seen it directed at me. He looks calculative and defensive, and I've got my answer. Betrayal washes over me, and my stomach churns violently.

"Layla called," I whisper, and Carter's eyes fill with resignation. He looks down, as though he can't face me, and my heart twists painfully.

"She said there was an anomaly in my blood work. But then, you already knew that, didn't you? She said she's had the paperwork for weeks, and you asked her not to share it with me. Why, Carter? Why would you do that to me? Why would you keep something like that from me?"

He looks so lost, so heartbroken, but I have no sympathy for him. I shake my head and get out of bed, throwing my robe on as quickly as I can. Carter grabs me from behind and holds on tightly, his chin on my shoulder.

"Emilia," he whispers. He wraps his arms around me tightly, as though he's scared to let me go, to let me walk away.

He's got his hands wrapped around my waist, and I grab them tightly, holding on for just a second before forcibly removing them. I can't tell if I'm in shock, if I'm just angry or if I'm sad. I push away from Carter and grit my teeth, forcing back my tears.

"How could you?" I ask him, my voice breaking. "How could you keep something like this from me? How long have you known?"

Carter sits down on his bed and turns me so that I'm facing him. I look at him, and a tear drops down my cheek. He's the one person I always thought would have my back. The one person that would never lie to me, that would never betray me.

He runs a hand through his hair and sighs, looking just as devastated as I do. "Emilia, this is something you father intended to take to his grave with him. He didn't want you to know. I only found out when he first got sick, and at the time you and I hadn't even spoken in years."

He raises his hand to my face and swipes my tears away with his thumbs, his expression anguished. "What about when I came back? How could you have taken me to bed knowing you were keeping something like this from me?"

Carter pulls his hands away and sighs. "Minx, it wasn't my place to tell you."

I stare at him in disbelief. "So, if I hadn't found out, you would've kept this from me for the rest of our lives?"

Carter looks away and shakes his head. "I don't know, Emilia. I don't know."

I sniff and clutch my robe tightly. I don't even know how to feel. I have a million questions that I'm not even sure I want the answers to.

When Dad first told me about his diagnosis, I thought I'd be able to save his life. I thought it was only a matter of time until all tests came back positive. Would I have been able to save him if I were his real daughter?

I inhale deeply, shakily, and walk out of Carter's room. For the first time in forever, he isn't who I need right now. He isn't the person I can turn to when my world falls apart, because he had a hand in it.

CHAPTER 51

milia

I walk into my own bedroom, my entire body trembling. I can't get myself to stop. I can't get my heart to stop racing, to stop hurting. Breathing feels hard, and every few seconds I choke on another sob. My eyes fall closed, and yet another tear drops down my cheeks as I sink down to the floor, my knees hitting the cold marble floors.

I think back to my childhood, to the resentment my dad so clearly felt for my mother, the way he could barely look at me for the first couple of years after my mother left, even though he clearly loved me. I think back to all the times he took care of me when I was sick, all the times he held me when I cried. I still remember how distraught he was when I contacted my mother years ago, how upset he was when she told him I was stalking her, when all I really did was email her. Why did he keep me if I'm not even his? Why did he raise me? How long has he known? I don't understand why he never told me.

I inhale as best as I can, a sob tearing through my throat. I raise my hands to my face and allow myself to burst into tears. I don't want to cry, I don't want to feel this way. I don't want to be weak, but my heart feels so broken.

I feel arms wrap around me, and I look up, expecting to find Carter, but instead it's my Dad that looks into my eyes. He looks worried and pained, as though finding me crying hurts him more than it does me, and I start to cry even harder. Dad hugs me tightly, and I rest my head on his shoulder.

"Emilia, what happened?" he asks, sounding incredibly worried.

"Daddy," I murmur, my tears falling endlessly. I tighten my grip on him. He feels so thin, so frail. I thought I'd be able to donate my kidney to him, but that's never going to happen now. Whatever is left of my heart shatters. "I can't save you," I whisper. I never told him I got the tests done, because I was scared he'd lose hope. But now... I can't hold it in anymore. If I'd been his real daughter, I might have had a chance to save him.

Dad tenses and pulls away, grabbing my shoulders. "What?" he asks, and I see fear flash through his eyes. The door opens behind him, and Carter walks in. The two of them exchange a look, and dad looks down in resignation.

"Why...why didn't you tell me?" I ask, my voice breaking.

Dad cups my cheeks and wipes away my tears. He inhales deeply and shakes his head. "Because there was nothing to tell you. You're my daughter, Emilia. You're my little girl, my princess. I was there on the day you were born, I was there when you took your first steps, and I will be there to walk you down the aisle. You're mine in every way that matters."

I sniff, and Dad tucks my hair behind my ear gently. He smiles at me and shakes his head. "Stop crying, Princess," he says, and I pout, knowing he's about to tease me. "It's not a good look on you, sweetheart."

The edges of my lips tug up, and I try my best to stop my tears. Dad throws his arms back around me, and I rest my head on his shoulder. "This changes nothing, Emilia. You're still my daughter. You'll always be my daughter, and I'll always love you."

I try my hardest to swallow down a sob, but it escapes my lips nonetheless. "I love you, Daddy," I cry, a fresh bout of tears running down my cheeks.

Dad sighs and rubs my back gently. "I know, honey. I love you, too."

He holds me until I've somewhat calmed down, and I pull away reluctantly. I almost don't even want to ask the questions I need an answer to. Maybe if I don't ask, I can remain in denial a bit longer.

"I've known since you were three," Dad tells me. "I found out much the same way you did, actually. You'd fallen through a glass table we used to have, and you were bleeding so badly that you ended up needing a blood transfusion. I wanted to donate my blood, but I was unable to. I was distraught, initially. But in the end, I realized it didn't matter. You were my daughter, regardless of whose blood runs through your veins."

I can't imagine what might have gone through Dad's mind the day he found out. He must've been so worried for me, and to then find out something this shocking on top of it. If I'm feeling betrayed, how must Dad have felt? Was I a reminder of my mother's betrayal every time he saw me?

"Why did you... why didn't you send me to Mom? When she left, why didn't you tell her to take me too?"

Dad frowns as though the mere idea is ridiculous, and he cups my cheek. "Baby girl, you're my kiddo, my little girl. Your mom... she was never meant to become a mother. She and I probably never even should have gotten married. I'm not sure how much you even remember of her, but your mother has always been a very unique person. She's always been very care-free and impulsive, and our marriage was yet another thing she rushed into thoughtlessly. As she does with most things in her life, she ended up getting bored with me, with having a family. I guess the rush and the excitement wore off pretty quickly. I don't even know who your biological father is. I've wondered for years, but I truly don't know. It's the one thing she'd never tell me. I thought she might at some point throw it at me during an argument, but she's remained quiet about who it is. Truthfully, I had no idea she wasn't faithful to me until the day I found out you weren't biologically mine."

Dad sighs and strokes my hair. The way he looks at me makes me feel like a child all over again. "Like I said, baby girl, it doesn't matter. You're my daughter, my princess. You always will be, Emilia. I understand if this changes things for you, though. I shouldn't have kept this from you. I guess part of me was scared of how you'd react once you found out. I was scared that you might leave, that you might want to find your real father. But that is no excuse, Emilia. I'm so sorry for keeping this from you. I had no right."

I inhale shakily, another tear dropping down my cheek, and I shake my head. "Dad," I whisper. There's so much I want to say, but all that comes out of my lips are pained sobs.

I hug him tightly and try my best to calm myself down, to regulate my breathing, so I can say what I need to. "I love you, Dad. This doesn't change a thing. You'll always be my dad."

He tightens his grip on me, as though he's scared I'll slip away if he lets me go, and I rub my cheek on his shoulder, soaking his robe with my tears. I couldn't care less about who my biological father might be. I have no interest in ever finding out. My Dad is enough. He's never once made me feel like I'm not his real daughter, and that's all I could ever want.

I can't imagine what he's been through in the last couple of years. I can't believe how lucky I am to have gotten him as my Dad.

CHAPTER 52

milia

I park my dad's old car in front of our house and sit back. I couldn't even bring myself to take Carter's red sports car, the car I've come to love so much. He and I haven't spoken in days, even though he keeps trying to explain himself. Nothing he can ever say will make me feel better. It's hard enough to deal with the knowledge that my dad isn't my biological dad. I don't have the mental energy to deal with his betrayal. I can't believe he actively tried to keep this from me. If all he'd done was keep his silence, I might've understood. But this? I just don't get it.

I stare at my old house, a thousand memories flashing through my mind. All of my best memories were made here. I don't even remember much from before Dad and I moved here. I have some vague memories of my mom, but not many. I know I look a lot like her, and I remember she used to take me on unplanned trips and excursions. At the time it was exciting, and I adored her, but in hindsight it just proves what Dad told me, that she was impulsive, and maybe even reckless.

I think back to my childhood and all the times I blamed my

dad for not being there, for working too much. I wonder how hard things were for him. I wonder how hard it must have been to deal with my mother's betrayal. If I was three when he found out, so that means he ended up forgiving her and staying, because she didn't leave until I was seven. I can't imagine what it must have been like for my dad, to have his heart broken like that, twice. I wish I could go back in time and treat him better, show him a little more gratefulness. I've never lacked for anything growing up. Dad was never very affectionate when I was younger, and his recent playfulness has only really developed in the months since he got his diagnosis, but I always knew he loved me. He was always there for every big occasion, even if he was absentminded or, at times, clueless about what was going on in my life. How hard must it have been for him to have a teenage daughter?

I sigh and get out of the car. I hesitate as I walk to the garden and bite down on my lip. I glance up at the treehouse longingly. I still remember seeing it from my bedroom window on the day we moved into this house. I did then what I'm about to do now. I trespassed.

I'm not as stealthy as I used to be when I was younger, but I still manage to walk up to the treehouse without setting off any of the automatic motion detector lights in the Clarkes garden. The stair steps creak underneath me, the sound familiar and nostalgic. Even after all these years, this is where I go when I'm upset. I walk in, my eyes roaming over the interior. Everything is mostly unchanged, but it's definitely received an upgrade, because there are now light switches, and a small heater in the corner that definitely didn't used to be there. I didn't even notice any of this the last time I was here with Carter, because he was all I could see.

My heart aches as my mind fills with memories of Carter. I still remember being wrapped in his arms, right here, the temperature as low as it is now. I told him this place needed electricity, and specifically, a heater. He told me he'd get it put in for me someday, and I can't help but wonder if it's here now because he kept his promise, even though he wasn't sure if I'd ever return.

I turn the heater on and sit down in the window seat, my eyes on the starry sky. I inhale deeply as my vision begins to blur, and tears start to run down my face. I draw up my knees and drop my head on top of it, relishing in the solitude the treehouse provides me with. I've had to be so strong around Dad, because the moment I seem sad, he gets worried. But I'm so tired. So tired of everything. I'm tired of hurting, tired of the pain. I feel terrible for dad too, for everything he's been through with my mom, for the way I used to lash out at him as a teenager, and for everything he's going through today. When I came here, I was so certain that him getting better was only a matter of time, only a matter of him finally accepting a kidney donation from me. But now? What are we supposed to do now? I need to call the clinic to discuss our options, and I hate myself for procrastinating, all because I know I'd have to speak to Layla.

I sniff and try my best to stop crying, but I can't. I'm startled when I feel someone touch my shoulder, and I look up in surprise to find Kate standing next to me, a bottle of wine and two plastic cups in her hands.

She sits down on the floor and pours two glasses of wine wordlessly. She hands me one, her expression blank, and I take it with trembling hands. I raise the cup to my lips and end up emptying it in one go, drinking it as though it's a shot. Kate doesn't say anything, instead she just refills my cup. I empty that too and smile at her bitterly.

"I apologize for trespassing," I tell her, and she shakes her head, indicating that it doesn't matter. I laugh. "I guess it's fine. I bet seeing me cry like this delights your soul."

Kate looks hurt for a second and then she sighs. She doesn't say a thing as she tops my cup up again, and I wish she'd speak up. I wish she'd give me a reason to argue with her.

She takes a sip of her wine and stares at her cup. I sigh and drop my head back to my knees, another tear dropping down my cheek. I sniff loudly, my breath labored. I can't even breathe properly, because it feels like I'm still crying, even though I've tried my best to stop.

"My dad isn't my real dad," I say, unable to keep the words in. I glance at Kate and grin. "I bet that just makes your day. I don't have parents. Not real ones, anyway. My dad, the man that raised me, and the one that'll always be my *Dad*, isn't my biological father. And my mother, the woman that actually gave birth to me, well... she was never a mother to me."

"I'm sorry, Milly," she says, her eyes flashing with sympathy, and I hate it. I don't want sympathy from her.

I laugh, the sound hollow, yet slightly hysterical. "Man, this must be amazing for you. I bet you're loving every second of this. It gets better, though. You know how I found out? Layla told me."

Kate's eyes widen, and for a second I'm certain I see hatred flash through them. "That bitch," she murmurs, and it startles me so much that I laugh.

"Is *she* allowed to date Carter, or is he off-limits to her too? I could never tell if you just had a brother-complex, or if your problem was with me specifically. Maybe a bit of both. He'll probably go back to dating Layla soon enough, so you won't have to worry about me."

I empty my cup and hold it out for Kate. She frowns as she refills it for me and then refills her own cup. I sit there, staring at her, hatred and heartache clouding my vision.

"He's going to die. I'm not a match for him, so I can't donate my kidney. Your biggest wish is about to come true, Kate. I'm about to end up all alone, with no family, no real friends, nothing. You took the love of my life from me, and now you get to watch me lose everything I have left."

I take a big gulp of my wine and it burns down my throat, adding to my misery. "I regret it, you know? Even then, I chose *you*. I chose your health, your family, and Carter's happiness. What for? All it did was cost me valuable years I could've spent with my dad. I spent years feeling fucking miserable and missing Carter, missing my Dad, missing everything I left behind. I convinced myself I did the right thing, but I *didn't*. I didn't owe you shit. I didn't have to do that for you, and I regret it. I regret it so much. I regret not choosing my own happiness, and I hate you for taking so many years from me."

I burst into tears all over again and hide my face against my knees. "I hate you so much," I whisper. "I'll hate you until the day I die, Kate. I'll never ever forgive you."

Kate sighs and strokes my hair gently. "I know, Emilia," she whispers. "I know."

CHAPTER 53

milia

Carter stands by the door as I roll my suitcase through the hallway. Dad sighs and looks at me with heartbreak in his eyes. I smile at him as reassuringly as I can. "Just a few days," I murmur. "I just need a few days."

Dad brushes my hair out of my face and nods in understanding, his gaze moving from Carter to me. He hasn't asked me anything about us, but it's obvious something is wrong. We've barely spoken, and though Carter has apologized countless times, none of it makes a difference. A hundred apologies won't make me feel less betrayed, it won't unbreak my heart.

His eyes shutter closed in resignation when I walk past him. Graham nods at me and lifts my suitcase into Dad's old car for me. My heart feels heavy as I drive away.

The roads are so familiar, yet so many years have passed. For a little while I found the intense happiness that I thought was long lost. It almost feels like Carter and I are jinxed. Like we aren't meant to be together. Every time we find our way back to each other, life tears us apart somehow.

I park in front of my old house and look up at it. It feels both familiar and foreign at once. I haven't spent a single night here since coming back. I walk up to the door and unlock it, my hand trembling. I close the door behind me and sink to the floor, resting my back against the front door. I pull my knees up and drop my forehead to my knees, my arms wrapped around myself.

I inhale deeply, but my breath is shaky. I can't help but wonder how Carter could've possibly kept something this big from me. How could he have known and never told me? It makes me wonder what else he's keeping from me. I can understand white lies, but something like this?

I swallow hard and pick myself up from the floor. I walk up the stairs slowly, nostalgia hitting me right in the chest. Fresh tears roll down my cheeks when I open my bedroom door. I stand in the doorway and stare straight into Carter's bedroom. How often have we stood by our windows, communicating through them? How often have I stood where I thought I was out of view, just watching him?

I sigh and walk to my bed. I sink down on top of it, my mind replaying the memories I've made here. How often have I sat in my bedroom despising my dad, when he must have given up so much for me. I'm not even his real daughter, yet he never once made me feel like I might not be. I bet it would've been much easier for him to move on with his life had I not been there to chain him to the past. Despite that, he chose me. He cared for me and gave me everything I could've ever needed.

I bite down on my lip and sniff, not wanting to cry all over again. I squeeze my eyes closed and inhale deeply. It feels like I lost everything, when I know I haven't. Carter's betrayal, finding out I'm not Dad's real daughter, breaking up with Sam. My entire life feels like it's in disarray.

When I came here, I knew exactly who I was, where I was going in life. I was going to continue building my career slowly but surely, until I made partner at the firm I was at. I was going to keep dating Sam, until eventually we'd take the next step. My life was so carefully planned out, and it was everything I thought I needed. But in hindsight, none of it made me happy.

Since coming here I've rediscovered myself, my happiness, only to be reminded that intense happiness also puts me at risk of intense pain. In London, at least my heart was always guarded. I sigh and lie down on my bed, my eyes shuttering closed.

I miss him. I'm mad at him, but I miss him nonetheless. I miss his arms, and the way his lips feel against mine. I squeeze my pillow tightly, wishing it was Carter instead.

I'm startled out of my thoughts when the doorbell rings. I sit up in surprise and make my way down the stairs, surprised to find a Tupperware box with what looks like dinner in it on my front steps. I pick it up, my eyes darting to the house next door. I can just about see the Clarkes' front door close, Kate's hair betraying her. I pick the food up carefully and stare at the note in surprise.

I'm not sure what made you come here or what might be going on, but please have some food. An empty stomach won't make you feel better. Please take care of yourself.

PS. The food isn't poisoned
PPS. There's wine and chocolate cookies for you in the treehouse
PPPS. I promise I wasn't stalking you, but I saw you from Carter's bedroom window and you looked a little sad. I won't bother you. I hope you feel better soon.

. . .

248

The edges of my lips tug up and I stare at the door Kate just disappeared through. I hate to admit that I'm a little touched. I'm not sure what the last couple of years have looked like for Kate, but she seems to have changed. I hope it isn't just a mirage.

I glance back at my house and then I slip on my shoes and grab some cutlery before making my way to the treehouse, my food in hand. As she said, there are indeed chocolate cookies waiting for me, along with a bottle of wine.

I lift one of the cookies to my lips, my heart twisting painfully. Kate likes lemon-flavored things, while Carter prefers rich flavors. I'm the only one that likes chocolate. Helen doesn't even like chocolate, so why am I holding freshly made cookies?

I sit down on the windowsill, my dinner in my lap and the heater on. I have an entire house to myself, yet I still feel more at home here. My heart aches as I open the Tupperware box to find my favorite pasta in it. Did Helen make this, or was it Kate? Either way, I don't understand why. Why would they do this? Is this a way to make amends?

I take a bite, and another tear rolls down my cheek. My heart breaks for everything I've missed out on in the last couple of years. For everything dad is going through right now. I've been so strong for so long, but right now in this moment, it's too much. I can't hold on.

I burst into tears with my food in hand, feeling overwhelmed and lost, unsure where I stand with the people I love most, unsure if I even want to stay or go back to the life I so carefully built. Either way, it seems I stand to lose something.

CHAPTER 54

milia

I wake up feeling like I haven't slept a wink. I kept tossing and turning, overthinking everything. I ended up questioning everything I thought was important. My job in London, my trust in Carter, my dad's recovery. I feel like I've been functioning purely on hope, and it all came crashing down at once.

I sit up in bed, and I notice movement through the window from the corner of my eye. I turn to look into Carter's window, and my heart skips a beat when I see him walking into his bedroom, a towel wrapped around his waist.

Did he spend the night at his parents'? I didn't see him when I went to bed, so he must have come in after I fell asleep. I sit back and watch him for a moment, instantly thrown back to our childhood.

I didn't think I'd ever get to experience this again. I didn't think I'd ever see him through our windows again. My heart wrenches painfully and I tear my gaze away. When I look at him, I can't stay mad at him. While I don't want to be mad just for the hell of it, I need a moment to think through everything that happened. I need time to myself, to decide whether the choice Carter made is one I can live with. Whether it affects my ability to trust him.

I slip out of bed and into the shower, my thoughts on both Carter and Dad. I feel like I'm at a turning point in life, and there are some big choices ahead of me. I haven't been scared of the future in years, but right now, right here, I am.

I walk back into my bedroom absentmindedly, my thoughts whirling. I pause when I notice Carter standing by his window, a large piece of paper in his hands.

Minx, it says.

He notices me looking and turns it over.

I'm sorry.

I clutch my towel tightly, my heart aching as he bends down to write something down. He holds up three pieces of paper, one after the other.

I was wrong.

I thought I was doing the right thing.

Allow me to earn your forgiveness, please.

I inhale deeply, my heart wavering. I know Carter, and I know his heart. I know it wasn't his intention to hurt me, but that's what he did nonetheless. Sometimes it's good intentions that hurt the most.

My phone rings, Carter's name lighting up the screen, and I hesitate before picking up.

"Minx," he murmurs, and my heart skips a beat. "I'm sorry," he says, leaning against the window.

I walk up to mine and sigh. "I know you are, Carter. But that isn't enough. What hurts the most is that you knew how much this would impact me, yet you chose to make a decision on my behalf that you just didn't have the right to."

He falls silent and nods. "I know, Emilia. I can see that now, but at the time, I thought I was doing the right thing. Baby, this is something your father wanted to take to the grave. It wasn't my place to tell you. It wasn't my secret to spill. I promised your dad that you wouldn't find out through me. I love you, Emilia... but I owed your dad this, at least."

I inhale shakily. "Even after all these years, Carter, I always thought you'd be the one person that'd never keep anything from me. A lie of omission is still a lie, Carter. And this... this wasn't something small. I would've gotten over it if you'd just kept your silence, but instead of that, you purposely obstructed my access to medical files that would have told me the truth. That's not okay, Carter."

Carter rests his forehead against the window and inhales deeply. "I know, Emilia. I just didn't want you to get hurt. You've had to go through so much since coming back, that I wanted to do everything in my power to keep you from hurting any further. You're right to say it wasn't my place, and I apologize for overstepping. I had no right, and I don't know how to make this right, Emilia. I don't know how, but I'll do whatever I can to earn your forgiveness. Will you let me?"

I spent years loving him, wanting him, missing him. I can't take more of it. I close my eyes and drop my forehead to my window.

"Yes," I whisper. "I won't forgive you easily, Carter, and this isn't something I'll forget. But I... I love you. I still love you."

Carter straightens and turns away. I watch in disbelief as he walks out of his room, the call disconnecting. I stare at my phone in confusion, bitterness filling me.

I'm still staring at my phone when my bedroom door opens and Carter walks in, startling me. He walks up to me and grabs my shoulders gently, his eyes flashing.

"Say that again."

My eyes roam over his body, my heart racing. It feels like I haven't seen him in years. I lift my hand to his still wet hair and brush it out of his face before looking into his eyes.

"I love you, Carter."

He exhales and drops his forehead to mine, his arms wrapped around me. "I love you too, Emilia," he says, pulling away to look at me. "I don't know how to make this right, but I'll do anything."

I look into his eyes and my heart starts to ache. He looks so panicked, so anxious, so desperate to make things right. I cup his cheek gently, and Carter presses a soft kiss to my forehead.

"Time," I whisper. "I just need a little bit of time."

Carter nods, his fingers brushing over my hair. "Whatever you need, Minx," he says, his eyes blazing with sincerity. I look into his eyes, and I see my entire future in them. The road ahead of us might not be easy, but it's a road I want to walk with *him*. No one else will ever do.

CHAPTER 55

milia

I walk into Carter's house and Dad looks disappointed when he sees that I don't have my luggage with me. I smile at him and walk up to him to hug him. He presses a kiss to my hair and sighs. "When will you be ready to come home? It's been over a week," he says, and I smile as I pull away from him.

"I thought I *was* staying at home."

Dad sighs and shakes his head. "You certainly inherited my stubbornness," he says, shaking his head. "This is karma, I tell you."

My smile wavers, and my heart twists painfully. It's remarks like these that are the reason I never suspected anything. "Yes, Daddy," I murmur. "I sure did."

He looks at me as though he's searching for something, and I put on a brave face for him. I don't want him to know that finding out I'm not his real daughter hurts. He's told me countless times that it changes nothing, yet I struggle to act like it *is* nothing.

"One of the nurses is going on holiday next week," Dad

says, pulling me along. I nod, vaguely remembering that. "Could you please call the agency to check if they've arranged a replacement? I believe Carter said he saves all the phone numbers and information in the top drawer of his desk in his home office. There's an identification code or something on the paperwork that you'll need to give them."

I nod, and he smiles at me as I walk away. I hesitate before entering Carter's home office. It's a space I've never entered before, and I somehow feel like I'm intruding. I bite down on my lip as I walk to his desk, my eyes roaming over the space. It looks homely and well-used, unlike his office at work. I sit down in his chair and pull the top left drawer open. I frown when I find a large stack of almost identical documents, all tied together.

I pick the bundle up and swallow hard. They're plane tickets and cancellation notices, all of them for flights to London. I flip through the documents, my heart breaking when I realize the very first one was a week after I left, and then one pretty much every month since then, the flights getting more and more expensive as the years go on. The most recent ones are a few months apart, the last one three months before I got here. I bite down on my lip in an effort to keep my emotions in check, but a tear drops down my cheek nonetheless.

"Minx."

I look up to find Carter walking in, a concerned expression on his face. His gaze drops to the papers in my hands, and he freezes. The expression in his eyes tells me I wasn't meant to see this, and I put the tickets down, my hands trembling.

Carter walks up to me, a hint of uncertainty and vulnerability in his eyes. I bite down on my lip, my heart aching. Carter sighs and brushes my hair out of my face gently. "Not a day has gone by that I didn't think of you, that I didn't want to chase after you."

A tear drops down my cheek and Carter catches it with his

thumb. I rise from my seat and throw my arms around him, my tears flowing freely. Carter holds me closely, his grip tight.

"Every day I'd wonder what I'd say to you when I finally saw you again. I'd imagine how I'd get you to give me another chance, I'd think about how to make you fall for me all over again, but then I'd remember. I'd remember how much pain you were in while you were with me. I'd remember how my family treated you, how you cried yourself to sleep every night. And I couldn't do it, Emilia. I couldn't go after you knowing being with me would mean living with so many painful memories, being confronted with a part of your life you chose to leave behind. I tried so hard to respect your wishes, but I always knew I'd cave the second I laid eyes on you again. And I did."

I bury my face in his neck and hold onto him tightly. I've never felt this way before. I've never been so angry with someone, yet so certain that nothing he could ever do would make me walk away from him. This man, he's always been my entire world. "I love you," I whisper, looking up at him.

Carter sighs and takes a step closer. He drops his forehead to mine and wraps his arms around me. "I love you too, Emilia. So much. I'm sorry, baby. It's not that I was trying to keep something from you, I didn't even really see it like that. I just wanted to help your dad keep his secrets, to keep from hurting you."

I nod and slip my arms around his neck. "I know, Carter. But that doesn't make it okay."

He nods, and I can't help but smile a little. He looks so contrite, so pained. I know he'd never knowingly do something that might hurt me, and truthfully, I'm not even sure what I would've done if I were in his shoes.

I've spent so many years missing him. Now that I'm here, now that I've got him with me, I don't want to miss out on another second. "I want all of you," I whisper. "I want to fall asleep with you, but I also want to argue with you, mess with you, kiss you... Carter, I want it all with you. I'm so mad, but even so, I can't stay away from you," I murmur, my voice pained.

Carter tightens his arms around me and kisses the top of my head. "Baby, I want nothing more. I understand if you're mad at me, just don't leave me," he says, his voice trembling. "Don't ignore me the way you have. It fucking kills me when you're right here with me, yet it feels like I've lost you all over again. Don't do this to me, Emilia. Even if I deserve it, please don't. I can't take it."

I rise to my tiptoes and press a kiss to his neck. Carter's eyes fall closed and he buries his hand in my hair as I press another kiss to his skin. I didn't even realize I made him feel this way. Carter lowers his head towards mine and I tilt my head to kiss him. He holds me as though I'm precious, as though I might slip out of his hands at any second, and my heart aches.

Carter pulls away and brushes my hair out of my face gently. I sigh and place my palms on his chest, wanting to be closer to him. I've missed him so much, it's unreal. it's only been a few days, so how am I ever going to get used to life without him?

"I'm sorry, Carter. I'm sorry for staying away for so long. I'm sorry I left in the first place. I'm sorry there's so much we missed out on. There are so many years we'll never get back."

He buries his hand in my hair and tilts my head. "Emilia," he murmurs. "I will always be grateful for what you did and for the sacrifices you made. You were right, in the end. When you left, Kate ceased to have someone to blame. She was forced to confront who she'd become and what her life had turned into."

I nod and drop my head to his chest. If I'd stayed Carter and I wouldn't have lasted. His family would have torn us apart. I knew that, but it didn't make leaving any easier.

I look up at him and cup his cheek. "I'm back now," I murmur. "I'm yours, all over again."

Carter looks into my eyes, his expression vulnerable. "But you won't stay."

I inhale deeply and rise to my tiptoes, my lips finding his. I want to promise him that I will, but I can't. My career is still in London, and even though I can act civil around Kate and Helen, I can't pretend nothing ever happened.

Carter kisses me as though he's scared I might disappear again, and I hold him a little tighter. He lifts me onto his desk and steps between my legs, and I close them around him. He drops his forehead to mine and inhales shakily.

"I'm sorry, Emilia. I'm sorry for keeping secrets, for hurting you."

I nod and try my best to smile up at him. "Carter, we've spent years missing each other. I know you didn't intend to hurt me. I know that. Just promise me you won't ever do this again, please? No secrets. Not between us."

He nods and presses a kiss to my forehead. "I promise, Emilia."

I thread my hand through his hair and pull him closer, my lips finding his. This man... he owns my entire heart. But is love enough? I can't help but feel like our happiness won't be permanent. Every time we find our way back to each other, life tears us apart.

CHAPTER 56

milia

I walk into the kitchen early in the morning and lean back against the doorway to watch Carter. He's making breakfast, and he keeps rearranging the tray on the counter, over and over again. I have no doubt that he intended to bring that to me in bed.

I agreed to move back here after I found that stack of cancelled tickets in his office. It reminded me of how much time we've already lost. I can't do this to him. To us. I can't stay away when my heart reaches for him with every beat.

Part of me feels betrayed, but part of me also understands. This was never about me. I wasn't even here for years, and Carter and my dad have clearly developed a close bond. I know what Carter is like, and it shouldn't have surprised me that he wouldn't betray my father, that he'd do what he could to keep his secrets.

My eyes roam over him and I sigh. He's wearing nothing but his pajama trousers, probably because I stole the matching top.

I walk into the kitchen, and Carter freezes, his eyes widening. I smile tightly and grab the coffee from the tray he prepared, the edges of my lips turning up. "This looks nice," I murmur. Carter seems nervous and tense as I stand next to him, and I take a sip of my coffee, my eyes on him.

"I'm not mad at you anymore," I murmur, rising to my tiptoes to kiss him. He looks at me, his gaze searching. If I had any remaining doubts about Carter's feelings for me, then they're all gone now. I might have been hurting over my dad and Carter's actions, but he's been hurting right along with me. I can tell that he's scared to lose me again, that he's sorry for hurting me. I don't want him to feel this way. We've spent too long hurting.

I wrap my arms around his neck and kiss him, losing myself in him. He groans against my lips and pulls me closer, until my body is flush against his. I giggle and run my hands over his body, feeling perfectly content. Even when life hands me blow after blow, I can deal with it, so long as he's here to hold me through it.

"I missed you," he says, and I wrap my arms around his neck. Carter lifts me onto the kitchen counter and I spread my legs, closing them around him.

"I missed you too," I murmur. He threads his hand through my hair and kisses me roughly. I feel him harden against my thighs and a low moan escapes my lips.

"Let's go back to bed," I whisper. We fell asleep together last night, but I need more of him.

Carter smiles at me and lifts me into his arms, a smirk on his face.

He freezes and puts me down when we hear footsteps approach us. I take a step away from Carter just as Dad walks into the kitchen, his eyes moving from me to Carter. "You two still fighting?" he asks, and we both shake our heads. "Good," he says, nodding.

Dad sits down and Carter makes him some herbal tea as I sit down next to Dad. I wrap my arm around Dad and he drops his head to my shoulder. He's constantly tired these days. He keeps battling headaches and muscle cramps, and it kills me. His entire life revolves around his dialysis, and I know how much he hates that. I need to find a way to give my father back his life.

"Dad," I whisper. "I want to look into paired donation. If we can find someone else that needs a kidney donation, I can donate my kidney to them, while someone in their life donates one to you."

Dad freezes and grits his teeth. He turns to look at me, and for just a few seconds, he's the man I grew up with, instead of the old man he's become. When he looks at me, I see the fearless prosecutor, the stern father, the man I've always idolized. He shakes his head and pins me down with a stare. "No. I've said no before, and I still mean it. I'd rather die than have you donate a kidney. I will not have you cutting your body open. I won't have you lying on an operating table for me. It isn't happening, Emilia. If I find out that you so much as try to go through with this, I'll refuse the paired donation. I won't have it."

I inhale shakily, my eyes filling with tears. "But Daddy, I don't want to lose you. Please, can't you do this for me? *Please*."

I burst into tears and Carter runs up to me. He wraps his arms around me, and I hide my face in his chest. "Tell him, Carter," I beg. "Tell him to accept it. Please."

Carter buries his hand in my hair and grips me tightly. "John," he says, his voice pleading. "What if I do it? You won't have to worry about Emilia. Paired donation is a great idea, and I should have thought of it myself. I'll do it."

Dad rises from his seat with so much force that his chair clatters to the floor. "No. I said no, Carter. My dignity is all I have left. I'll take my own life before I let either of you take it from me."

He walks away and slams the door closed behind him, and I start sobbing, my heart shattering. I've never felt this helpless before. I don't know what to do. I don't know how to save him if he won't let me.

CHAPTER 57

milia

I walk into the kitchen early in the morning feeling exhausted. The last couple of days have just been filled with arguments and tension. Dad won't see reason, and nothing I say changes his mind about a paired donation.

I'm sitting at the kitchen table when Carter walks in, his body dripping wet. He smiles at me, and my heart skips a beat. I wish I could control the feelings he unleashes in me. I wish I could choose to focus on the anger I felt when Layla called me, but I can't. He'll smile at me, and my heart soars.

"Morning," he murmurs, and I sigh. He walks up to me and presses a kiss to my hair. My eyes drop to his chest and his abs, and I hate how good he looks. Carter smirks and bites down on his lip, as though he knows what he's doing to me, and I look away.

"Morning," I say, my eyes dropping to my coffee cup. Carter takes it from me, and I glare at him.

He smiles and cups my cheek, his thumb trailing over the

bags underneath my eyes. "Couldn't sleep?" he asks, and I shake my head.

Carter drops his forehead to mine and sighs. "He'll see reason sooner or later."

Carter leans in and kisses my cheek, and my eyes flutter closed. Even a simple kiss from him makes my heart soar.

"Are you sure you want to spend Christmas with my family?" he asks, and for a second I hesitate. Carter told me he's been hosting Christmas at his house for years now, and though he offered to cancel, I couldn't bring myself to take him up on that offer. I don't want to stand between him and his family.

"Do you think it'll be okay?" I ask carefully. I'm worried I'll mess things up again. I'm worried my presence will be enough to cast a shadow over what would otherwise be a festive day.

Carter nods and gently pushes my hair behind my ear. "Of course," he says, a smile on his face. "Don't worry so much, Minx. Everything will be great."

I'm still thinking about his words hours later, as the doorbell rings. I hope he's right. The last thing I want to do is ruin Christmas for everyone.

Helen smiles at me as she walks in, and I see the anxiety in her eyes. I've been so angry and so hurt, for so long, that I failed to see the remorse in her eyes. But it's there. I see it clearly now.

I smile back at her, genuinely this time. She might not be my favorite person, but she's treated my dad very well over the years.

Carter places his hand on my back and I smile up at him, easing the obvious concern in his eyes. He exhales in relief and wraps his arm around my shoulders, unaware of the way Helen and Kate are looking at us. My cheeks heat and I pull away from him, suddenly feeling self-conscious. Carter smiles knowingly and I shake my head. Even when we were younger, he was always touching me once we started dating, and it seems those habits haven't changed.

I follow Helen into the living room, my heart filling with nostalgia. Eight Christmases I've spent apart from Carter. There's so much we missed out on, so many years we won't ever get back.

Carter smiles at me, his eyes filled with the same sadness, the same longing, as though he too is wondering about everything we've missed out on.

William and Kate both smile up at me as I sit down, and for once, I'm not filled with hatred seeing Kate. In the few weeks since she's been here, she hasn't done a single thing that I can condemn her for, and I'm tired of the anger. I'm tired of doing this to myself, to Carter. She looks startled when I smile at her, and I look away in amusement. I wonder who she is now. I wonder who she's grown into, and what her recovery was like. It seems like she's stopped blaming me for everything that happened, and I wonder when she made that switch. My heart aches, thinking back to everything I've experienced with her. She and I grew up together. She was like a sister to me. I guess that's why it hurt so much, why it still hurts.

Helen grins and claps. "Let's do presents," she says excitedly, and I bite down on my lip. I only got presents for Dad and Carter, and I wonder if I should have gotten some for everyone else too. While I might not be ready to fully forgive them, I am ready to behave civilly on Carter and Dad's account.

Carter pulls me up and we all sit down by the tree, like we used to. "Me first," he says, pulling a little box from underneath the tree. He hands it to me and I look up in surprise as I take it from him. I unpack it carefully, and he smiles as I lift the bracelet up to take a closer look. I stare at it in awe, and he pushes my hair behind my ear carefully.

"It's a handcrafted charm bracelet," he tells me. "A little canoe, to represent the cabin by the lake. A replica of the treehouse, a little coffee cup... and a tiny little t-shirt."

I'm smiling so widely that it hurts and Carter chuckles. "If I get things my way, we'll be adding many more charms throughout the years," he whispers, and I look up at him. I wish I could just kiss him, right here, right now. No one has ever made me feel the way he does. No one has ever made me feel this seen, this cherished, this loved.

"Wow," Kate murmurs. "That's stunning," she says. She grins as Carter helps me put it on, and I glance at her in surprise. I can't believe just how much she's changed. She seems to be genuinely happy for me, for us, and I can't help but be wary.

I glance at Carter and smile. "This makes my gift look like crap," I say, my cheeks crimson.

Dad laughs and nods. "It does," Dad says, and I look at him through narrowed eyes.

"Show me," Carter says excitedly, and I hand him one of the two boxes I had in my hands.

Carter grins and opens it, revealing the cufflinks I had custom made for him. They're golden little insects that remind me of the fake cockroach prank I used to pull on him, one of our classics.

He looks at them and then looks up at me, his eyes filled with humor and affection. "I love this," he says. "Great minds, huh?" he says, winking at me.

"My turn," Dad says. I laugh and hand him his gift. He got cufflinks too, but his have his initials monogrammed on them. Dad takes the box from me, and just as he's about to open it, his face drains of color. I place my hand on his shoulder, wanting to ask him if he's okay, but before I have a chance to, he collapses.

I jump up in shock and grab Dad, panic filling my lungs, obstructing my airways. My vision starts to blur as I shake Dad, willing him to wake up. I can hear Carter on the phone, calling for a chopper, but I can't control the fear that grips me.

"Baby, it'll be okay," Carter tells me. "We'll be at the hospital in a matter of minutes."

I want to believe him, but the panic in his voice is identical to my own.

CHAPTER 58

arter

Emilia is in tears as John is taken away, and I wrap my arms around her. I clutch her tightly, needing her as much as she needs me. I'm just as scared as she is, but I don't dare let it show. "What even happened?" she asks, trying her hardest to swallow back her tears.

I shake my head. "I have no idea, Minx. This is the first time this has happened."

I see the fear in her eyes, and it breaks my heart. I wish I had answers for her, a solution. She wraps her arms around me tightly and I hold her closely, my phone to my ear. I need some damn answers, and someone better give them to me soon.

It doesn't take long for one of the directors of the hospital, Dr. Davis, to come find us to update us. Emilia straightens, and I wrap my arm around her waist.

"Mr. Clarke," he says reverently, as he damn well should. I've donated millions since John first started his treatment here. "I checked in with the doctors, and it seems Mr. Parker is being treated for cardiac arrest. They're doing all they can to save him."

Emilia bursts into tears and I wrap her in my arms, my chin on her head. "They'd better save my father-in-law," I tell him. "You don't want to find out what the consequences will be if they don't."

Emilia knows just as well as I do that renal failure combined with cardiac arrest means John's chances are slim to none. Dr. Davis swallows hard and nods. "We're doing all we can, Mr. Clarke," he says, and I nod.

I bury one hand in Emilia's hair and rub her back with the other. I hate how helpless I feel. In the last couple of years there hasn't been much that's been out of reach for me. There hasn't been much that I couldn't acquire. But this? There's nothing I can do to save John's life, and it kills me.

"How did this happen?" Emilia asks. "Did we not watch his diet close enough? Was he not exercising enough? Maybe the nurses didn't treat him well enough."

I bend down and lift her into my arms. I carry her to the private waiting room Dr. Davis prepared for us, and sit down on the sofa, Emilia in my lap. "There's nothing we could have done to prevent this, baby," I tell her. "I have the nurses work in varying dual shifts, to make sure they keep each other accountable, and so they don't get lax. I have cameras almost everywhere to keep an eye on the staff when I can't be there myself, and you and I get daily reports about your dad's health. He seemed to be doing better than his doctors expected, so I don't know what happened, my love."

Emilia trembles in my arms and I tighten my grip on her. I hate feeling like this. I hate that I can't ease her worries.

The door opens, and my parents and Kate walk in, their eyes filled with the same worries that I'm sure are reflected in mine. Kate drops down to the floor by Emilia and places her hand on Emilia's shoulder. "Do we know anything yet?"

I shake my head and hold Emilia a little tighter. Kate sighs and drops her forehead to Emilia's shoulder. She seems so hurt, so worried. It seems like all my worries about having her around Emilia were unwarranted, and I feel bad for not wanting her to return for the holidays at all.

Dr. Davis walks in, and Emilia tenses. He smiles at us, as we all exhale in relief. "Your father-in-law will be fine, Mr. Clarke," he says. He glances at Emilia and smiles. "Don't you worry, Mrs. Clarke. Your father is in the best care he could possibly receive. I've been informed that your father was put in an induced coma. He's being monitored very carefully, but the worst is behind us."

Mrs. Clarke... even in these circumstances, I like the sound of that. Emilia nods at Dr. Davis gratefully, but I know her worries won't be eased until we get to see John.

"Baby, we've been here for hours now, and we won't get to see your dad until tomorrow. I'm going to take you home, and I'll bring you back tomorrow, okay?"

Emilia looks up at me, her eyes filling with panic all over again, and I shake my head. I need to make the call here, because Emilia will try to stay if I don't stop her. I rise to my feet with her in my arms and carry her out.

"Carter," she says, her voice breaking. "We can't leave Dad here," she says, pleading, and I shake my head.

"It's hard enough to see your dad hurting, baby. I won't watch you tear yourself apart too."

I carry her up to the chopper that I have waiting for us, and it isn't until Kate lifts herself in that I realize she followed us at all. "I'm coming with you. I'm staying with you," she says, looking stubborn as hell.

Emilia looks away, as though she doesn't really care, and I sigh as I strap both myself and Emilia in. I lift Emilia back into my arms when we land on my rooftop a few minutes later.

Kate helps me open the doors, until I've got Emilia on my

bed. I glance at her, somewhat surprised. I haven't seen much of her in the last couple of years, and it seems she's changed more than I gave her credit for.

"I'm heading to the guest room," she tells me, and I nod. "Let me know if you need something."

She shuts the door behind her, and I turn back to Emilia. Her eyes are red, and she's staring into the distance absent-mindedly. She's been so strong since she got here, and even now she's holding herself together reasonably well. This is the closest I've seen her come to falling apart.

I drop down to my knees in front of her and cup her cheek. "Do you want me to draw you a bath?" I ask, unable to come up with anything else that might make her feel better.

Emilia shakes her head and looks at me, her expression so lost that my heart twists painfully. She leans in and presses a chaste kiss to my lips. "I'm fine," she says. "I'm just going to take a shower."

She rises, and my heart breaks as she walks away. I know my Minx, and I know she's going to cry her heart out in the shower.

CHAPTER 59

 arter

I walk up to my bathroom and sink down to the floor, my back to the door. I inhale deeply and close my eyes, waiting for the inevitable.

It doesn't take long before I hear sounds of Emilia choking on sobs, the sound muffled by the water. If I hadn't been sitting right here, I wouldn't have heard her.

I don't know what to do. I want to give her privacy, but I can't stand the idea of her suffering by herself. Not when I'm right here.

I bite down on my lip and rise to my feet, my hand on the doorknob. I hesitate before walking in quietly and closing the door behind me. The bathroom is all steamed up, and Emilia is on her knees in the shower. She's so lost in her pain that she doesn't even notice me.

My heart fucking breaks seeing her like this. I don't even bother undressing and walk into the shower, dropping to my knees in front of her. My clothes are soaking wet within seconds, but I couldn't care less about that. Emilia looks up at me, her eyes filled with so much sorrow. She doesn't say anything, she just wraps her arms around my neck, and I pull her close as she falls apart in my arms. "Carter," she whispers, and I bury my hand in her hair, clutching her tightly.

It's like she's been trying her best to keep from crying, and the second I threw my arms around her, she let it all go. Emilia sobs and I hold her as she falls apart. We sit there together, the water keeping us warm. I'm not even sure how much time has passed when Emilia pulls away to look at me. She sniffs and wipes her face, and my heart fills with tenderness.

"I'm sorry," she says, and I shake my head.

"Don't be, baby," I whisper.

Emilia looks at me, her eyes lingering on my soaking wet clothes, and when she looks back up at me, my heart starts to race. She places her palms on my chest and shakes her head. "I can't believe you walked in here fully dressed," she murmurs.

I glance down to find that my white shirt has become fully see-through, and I shrug. "They're just clothes, Minx. It doesn't matter."

Emilia drops her forehead to mine and inhales shakily. "What would I do without you?"

I cup her cheek and look into her eyes. "You'll always have me, no matter what."

Emilia sniffs, fresh tears filling her eyes. She throws her arms around me and I hold her tightly, my heart shattering.

"What if he doesn't make it? What if I'm left all alone in this world? Is this punishment for staying away as long as I did?"

I pull away a little to look at her and shake my head. "He'll make it, baby. Your dad is the toughest man I know. He'll defy all odds. But even if you didn't have your dad, you'll always have me, Emilia. Always. No matter what life throws at you, at us, I'm going to be there. I'll be there to pick up the parts of your broken heart. I'll be there to put the pieces back together. I will always be there."

She looks into my eyes, raw vulnerability in them, and all I want to do is reassure her. I wish she could see how much I love her.

I sigh and drop my forehead to hers. "Baby, you're my world. I will never leave you, Minx. I'll be your family, your rock, anything you need. I'll be all that you are to me."

I lower my lips to hers and kiss her softly, my heart overflowing. Emilia inhales shakily and kisses me back, deepening our kiss. Her hands roam over my body frantically, as though she's scared I might disappear if she lets go.

I thread my fingers through her hair and tilt her head, kissing her right below her ear. "I love you," I whisper, and she trembles against me. I kiss her neck, and a small whimper escapes her lips.

Emilia's fingers find the buttons on my shirt, and she undoes them slowly, her hands trembling. "You won't ever leave me, will you?" she whispers.

I shake my head and brush her hair out of her face gently. "Never, Minx. I'm yours for the rest of my days."

My shirt falls open and Emilia's breath hitches. "Will you always love me?" she asks, and I nod.

"For as long as my heart beats."

Emilia rises to her feet and pulls me up with her. She reaches up and wraps her arms around my neck. The way she's touching me, the desperation in her eyes... it's got me feeling emotional in a way I never expected.

Emilia rises to her tiptoes and kisses me, her movements rough. I kiss her back and lift her into my arms. She wraps her legs around me as I push her against the wall, the shower spraying down on us. The way she moves against me, the little moans that escape her lips. I need her, but this is more than physical.

"Tell me you'll always be mine," she whispers, her voice breaking.

I grab her chin and drop my forehead to hers. "I'm yours, Minx. I've been yours from the second I first laid eyes on you all those years ago. I will always be yours."

She's breathing hard as she reaches for my suit trousers, the button flying off as she pulls on it. Her eyes fall closed as she wraps her hand around my dick, and I groan.

"Will you always want me?" she whispers, aligning my dick perfectly. One thrust, and I'll be inside her.

"Always, Emilia. I'll always want you. You're always the most beautiful woman I've ever seen. You always will be."

Her lips find mine and she kisses me with the same desperation I'm feeling. I cup her neck, my thumb caressing her throat. There's no way this woman wasn't made for me. There's no way she isn't the one. She looks into my eyes, and I just know she's feeling what I do. Even as the world falls apart around us, we're each other's rock, each other's salvation.

Her movements are frantic and there's desperation in her eyes, as though she needs me to make her feel better when sorrow surrounds her. I grab her wrists and pin them against the wall above her head. "Tell me what you want, Emilia."

"You," she says. "Just you, Carter."

She tightens her legs around me and wraps her arms around my neck. She moans when I push into her slightly.

"More," she whispers.

I look into her eyes as I push all the way in, her muscles contracting around me.

I take my time with her, pulling almost all the way out before pushing back in, and her eyes shutter closed.

"Look at me," I groan. Her eyes find mine and I lean in to kiss her, my lips lingering on hers.

"You and me, Emilia... we'll always have each other."

I thrust back into her and she moans, her eyes filled with what can only be described as love.

"Carter," she whispers. "Only you... only you can mend my heart when I think it's beyond repair."

Her fingers graze my scalp and I increase the pace, fucking my girl harder, rougher. Giving her all of me. She moans into my ear and I struggle to hold on. I love it when I get her to lose control like this. When the world around us melts away, until there's nothing but *us*.

She tightens her grip on my hair as her muscles tighten around me, a low moan escaping her lips. I drop my forehead to hers as my own release follows shortly after hers. We're both panting, identical smiles on our faces.

Emilia turns the shower off and I carry her out, wrapping her in a large towel. I take my time drying her off before lifting her back into my arms. She clutches onto me as I carry her to bed.

"I love you, Carter," she says.

I smile as I get into bed with her. I wrap her in my arms and she cuddles up to me, fitting against me perfectly.

"I love you too, Emilia," I murmur.

Emilia falls asleep in my arms, and despite the rough day we've had, I feel at peace. So long as we're together, there's nothing we can't get through.

CHAPTER 60

milia

Carter and I are both exhausted as we walk into the kitchen early in the morning. As if in sync, we both freeze when we find a full breakfast spread on the kitchen bar.

I look up to find Kate wringing her hands, a tight smile on her face. "I made you breakfast," she says, her gaze dropping to her feet. "Enjoy," she adds, before moving past me. Her stomach growls before she can make a dash for it, and Carter stops her in her tracks, his hand on her shoulder.

"You haven't eaten yet?" he asks. Kate bites down on her lip nervously and shakes her head, her gaze darting towards me.

I sit down in my usual spot and take a sip of the coffee she made me. "Come join us," I say, my voice soft. I'm not even remotely hungry, and all I really want is to get to the hospital as soon as possible, but I know it won't make a difference. We won't be able to see Dad yet.

Kate looks at me in surprise and hesitates before nodding. She takes a seat and I watch as Carter reaches for the cupboard above his head, grabbing the mug Dad likes to drink from. He holds it in his hands, a startled expression on his face, before putting it back slowly. My heart twists painfully. Carter makes Dad a cup of herbal tea most mornings, and not being able to do it today probably devastates him. He inhales deeply as his expression drops, and I rise from my seat. I walk up to him and hug him from behind, my cheek against his shoulder blade.

"He's going to be okay," I murmur. "Before you know it, you'll be making him cups of herbal tea again, and he'll try to scare away the nurses."

Carter turns around and wraps his arm around me while burying his free hand in my hair. "Yes," he says. "He will."

I smile at him and grab his hand to lead him back to his seat. I've been so lost in my own sadness that I forgot how hard this must be on Carter too. He and Dad have grown so close over the last couple of years.

Kate fills up our plates for us as soon as we sit down, and I blink in surprise.

"You both need to eat something," she says hesitantly. "It'll probably be a long day."

I nod in agreement and take a bite of the pancakes she made. It doesn't escape my notice that she's made a combination of foods that I love. I'm surprised she still remembers my likes and dislikes. Even my coffee is made the way I usually have it. I only manage a few bites, too worried to be able to eat.

"You need to eat, Milly," Kate murmurs, and I frown at her.

"Why are you doing this?" I ask, confused. "Why are you here at all?"

She looks down at her plate, seemingly gathering herself, before she looks back up at me. "I just wanted to be there for both of you. I just thought it might help if I made myself useful somehow. I forgot just how much staff Carter has."

I bite down on my lip as I take her in. She looks older and insecure in a way she never used to. Her eyes are kinder than they've ever been before, and she seems contrite.

"Emilia, I never had a chance to say this, but I'm so genuinely sorry for everything I've put you through. For every bit of blame, every toxic word, every bond I've broken. Nothing I can say will adequately convey my regret, so I wanted to show you. I'm not doing very well at that, I guess."

I look away. "No, you're not."

I rise from my seat and walk away. I'm not in the mood to reminisce. I purposely left her and that part of my life behind. I have enough on my mind without being burdened by her guilt.

I walk onto the veranda, the cold air biting against my skin. Carter follows me out and wraps his arms around me from behind. I lean into him, and he presses a kiss to my cheek.

"I called the director of the hospital. We'll be allowed to go see your dad before visiting hours."

I turn around, my eyes wide. "Really?"

Carter nods and presses a gentle kiss to my forehead. I hug him tightly, and he caresses my hair as he holds me.

"I'll go grab my coat," I murmur, and Carter nods.

Thirty minutes later we're walking into the hospital, both of us scared and anxious. Carter holds my hand in his, and I clutch onto him tightly.

The director of the hospital, Dr. Davis, meets us at the ICU unit and takes us through the hygiene measures we'll need to take to access my dad's room. "He's stable," he says. "We're still keeping him in an induced coma, but he'll wake later today."

I nod at him, and he hesitates. "I have some news to share with you too, Emilia," he says, a small smile on his face. "We found a donor for your father. All tests have cleared. It's a match."

I freeze, my hand rising to my heart. "A donor?" I whisper, in disbelief. "But is transplantation even possible in Dad's current condition?"

"It's an anonymous living donor, so we don't need to rush into the operation," he says, and I frown.

"What does that even mean? That's not possible, is it?" As far as I'm aware living donors are always family members or friends, and they're never anonymous.

Dr. Davis hesitates and then shakes his head. "It's rare, but it's possible. I'll discuss the procedure with the cardiologist in charge of your father's current condition, as well as the other doctors that will be operating, including the transplant surgeon and the transplant nephrologist. We'll discuss the risks, and if your father is cleared by the team, we'll go ahead with the procedure."

I nod, my heart racing. Dr. Davis waves us off as we walk into Dad's room, and I bite down on my lip in an effort to keep it together. He's hooked up to so many machines, and it all looks horrifying. It makes me feel like I lost him, even though he's still here. I barely recognize him.

I sit down by his bed, tears in my eyes. "Hi, Daddy," I murmur, hoping he can somehow hear me. "They found a donor. You're going to be fine. You're going to get all better. I can't wait to speak to you again later today. I've missed you, Dad, so please wake up soon."

Carter drops his hand to my shoulder and I look up at him. He looks as distraught as I do. I lean into him as I tell Dad about Carter almost making him a cup of tea in the morning, not realizing he wasn't there.

Carter and I sit there with him for hours, awaiting the moment he opens his eyes again. The relief I feel when he finally does is surreal.

"Dad," I whisper.

He blinks, and the medical staff performs countless tests on him, but his eyes are on me, his expression calm and collected.

We're going to be just fine. I'm sure of it.

CHAPTER 61

arter

Emilia is so nervous that she looks like she might be sick. "It'll be fine, Minx," I whisper. "This is everything we've been hoping for."

She nods and presses a kiss to her dad's cheek. John tightens his grip on her hand and smiles at her, but I see the worry in his eyes. It's been three weeks since he was hospitalized, and he's finally been given permission to go through with the kidney transplantation, but considering his health, it's far riskier than it would otherwise be.

Emilia blinks, tears rapidly gathering in her eyes, and my heart clenches painfully. I hate seeing her like this. I wrap my arm around her waist and hold her tightly. She's trembling, her skin cold.

"We'll see you in just a couple of hours, John," I say, and he nods at me. He lifts Emilia's hand to his lips and presses a kiss to the back of her hand.

I turn to escort Emilia out before she starts crying, but John stops me. "Carter, a word please," he says. I nod at him and

Emilia frowns. John shakes his head at her. "Just a couple of minutes, Princess. Like Carter said, I'll see you later. Don't worry too much, okay? These doctors all know what they're doing."

Emilia looks at me, and I can tell she doesn't want to leave, but she nods nonetheless. She walks to the door and turns back around, taking another good look at her dad before walking out.

John exhales, the bravado leaving him the second the door closes behind Emilia. I smile at him, but I fail to hide my own worries.

"Look after her," John says, his tone pleading. "If I don't make it... Carter, please. If I don't end up waking up again, please take care of my little girl. Don't let her be alone. Don't let her push you away."

I shake my head and sit down beside his bed. "You'll wake up, John. Everything is going to be fine. Don't you worry."

John shakes his head and grabs my hand. "My health isn't what it was even just a few weeks ago. Even if the chance of something going wrong isn't that big, the chance is still there. Promise me you'll take care of my daughter. Promise me you'll be there if she ends up having to bury me."

My chest feels tight as I inhale, a small shiver of panic restricting my lungs. I tighten my grip on his hand and try my best to smile at him. "I will, John. I'm never letting her go again. I'll be there for her, no matter what."

John nods at me as the nurses walk into the room to wheel his bed away. My stomach is in knots as I walk out to join Emilia. I need to be strong for her today, but I'm barely hanging on by a thread myself. She looks at me and I open my arms up for her. She slams into me and I close my arms around her tightly. Her breathing is shaky and I rub her back gently, my lips pressed to the top of her head.

I look around the empty waiting room and hold Emilia

tighter. I can't help but be disappointed that my parents and Kate didn't show up today. I thought the relationship between Emilia and them was slowly mending, but it looks like I was wrong.

Emilia presses her forehead against my chest and I thread my hands through her hair. "He'll be fine, won't he?" she murmurs, and I nod.

"Of course, Minx. He's got the very best doctors money can buy. We've done everything we can. It'll be okay. In just a few hours he'll be teasing you about your ugly crying face."

She huffs, a small smile on her face, and I breathe a sigh of relief.

"Your face is an ugly crying face," she says, pouting, and I laugh.

"I love you," I whisper.

Her smile melts away slowly, replaced by a look of sincerity. She slides her arms up, around my neck, and rises to her tiptoes. "I love you more," she whispers, her lips brushing against mine.

I tighten my grip on her hair and kiss her harder, needing her with every fiber of my being. Our kiss is slow, intense, every emotion poured into it. It's need, it's desire, it's everything.

I drop my forehead to hers, both of us breathing hard, both of us emotional. "Everything is going to be fine," I repeat, and she nods.

Emilia and I stay like that for hours, just in each other's arms, neither one of us speaking more than a few words. It's like we're both holding our breath.

Emilia's grip on my hand tightens when the doctors walk in. They smile, and we both slump in our seats.

"Mr. Clarke, Ms. Parker, everything went well," Dr. Davis says. He turns to Emilia and smiles. "Your father has asked for you already. Please allow me to escort you to his room."

Emilia bursts into tears and I smile as I pull her closer. I press a kiss to her temple as I thank the doctors, and they all grin. Emilia is a wreck as we're led to her father's hospital room, and though I'm keeping it together quite well, internally I'm just as much of a mess.

John is smiling as we walk in, and Emilia starts crying even harder. John laughs at her, just like I thought he would, and holds his hand out for her. She grabs it and lifts it to his face, and John smiles at her, tears in his eyes.

"Princess, there's nothing I won't do to spend more years with you."

Emilia nods, her hands trembling. "I know, Daddy. I'm never going to leave you alone again. I won't leave again. I'm so sorry. I'm so sorry we lost so many years. I'll stay with you forever."

John looks at me and bursts out laughing. "Not if Carter has anything to say about it," he says, winking at Emilia.

She blushes, and I know we're going to be just fine.

CHAPTER 62

milia

Dad and I stand in his dialysis room with huge grins on our faces. It's been two weeks since his surgery, and his body seems to be accepting the transplant. He's still on medication, but he's doing well. Thanks to the medical care Carter was able to provide, Dad got to do most of his recovery here at home. It's astounding how different he looks these days. Even though he's still healing, he looks so much healthier. There's a spring in his step that he'd lost. His smiles are wider, and the fear that I used to see in his eyes is gone. He's filled with life now, and it feels like I truly have my dad back.

"I can't believe I won't ever have to be hooked up to these machines again," Dad says. "I thought I'd spend my last days in this room."

I drop my head to Dad's shoulder, a flash of sorrow coming over me. He hid his fears so well.

"I can't wait to donate all this equipment."

I straighten when I hear Carter's voice behind me, a smile spreading across my cheeks involuntarily. He slips his arm around my waist and I melt into him subconsciously. He looks at me and smiles.

"We can remodel this entire room," he tells me, and I grin. He's been doing this a lot. He keeps saying *us* and *ours*, and it makes me giddy every single time.

Dad smiles. "Looks like I'll be able to walk you down the aisle after all," Dad says, his eyes moving from me to Carter.

My eyes widen and I take a step away from Carter self-consciously, my cheeks heating. Carter and I haven't really spoken about our future together. When we got together I told him that whatever we had would be temporary, but as time passed that all changed. I've told Dad that I won't leave him again, but Carter and I haven't actually spoken about what the future might hold for us. Every time I've wanted to have that talk, life interrupted.

"What should we do with the room?" he asks, and Dad grins.

"Turn it into a nursery, of course," Dad says.

I look at Dad in outrage, my cheeks bright red. I can't believe he just said that.

"I'm not getting any younger," he says, looking at Carter, a dead serious expression on his face. "I need cute grandchildren to play with. To spoil."

I hold my hand up. "Um, what about me? *I'm* cute. You can spoil me."

Dad looks at me in dismay and then turns back to Carter, dismissing me. I don't know whether to laugh or cry, and I end up shaking my head. "Carter isn't even married yet. He can't give you grandchildren."

My stomach twists painfully at the thought of him having children with anyone but me. If I'd left like I was planning to, he eventually would have. There's no way that's happening. I'm pissed off with him just at the thought of it.

Dad crosses his arms over each other and nods. "That is a

bit of an obstacle, isn't it? I know a cute girl for you," he says, a thoughtful expression on his face, and I freeze. Carter and I haven't told Dad about us, and we haven't been affectionate in his presence, but there have been touches Dad would have had to be blind to miss.

Dad smiles at me. "That reminds me, when will you be going back to London? You've been here for months. Didn't you say your boss wanted you back?"

I look at Dad through narrowed eyes. What the hell? It sounds an awful lot like he just wants me out of the way. What for? So he can match up Carter with some girl?

The doorbell rings before I can give Dad a piece of my mind, and Carter visibly exhales in relief.

"I'd better go check that," he says, walking off in a hurry. I follow him, an irrational anger thrumming through my veins.

He opens the door and looks surprised to find his parents at his doorstep. I pause and look at them in confusion as I walk in, my heart filling with bitterness. They haven't come to check up on Dad even once since he got back from the hospital.

"Emilia," Helen says, smiling. I nod at her and glance at Carter, who's helping William carry in a box of groceries. "It's been a while since we did Sunday lunch, so I thought it might be nice to cook here instead of at ours. That would be easier for your Dad, I think."

Kate walks in, her steps slow. She looks pale, sick even. She looks up at me and stares at me for a few seconds, a relieved expression on her face. "Hi," she murmurs. "I'm glad to hear your Dad is doing well. I'm sorry I wasn't able to come visit sooner."

I frown at her and nod. My feelings about her are incredibly mixed. I'm not as mad as I used to be, but I can't forgive her either.

"You really should call before you drop by," Carter tells his mom, his gaze on me. I feel bad instantly. I just know he'd have been happy to have her over had I not been here. Is this what our life is going to be like? Carter just having to choose between his family's happiness and mine, every single day?

Kate places her hand against the wall, a drop of sweat running down her temple. She closes her eyes and drops to the floor, a small groan escaping her lips. I jump into action without thinking and wrap my arm around her, worry overtaking me.

"Kate," I whisper. "What's going on?" I press my hand against her forehead, but her temperature is fine.

Helen drops the jar she's holding, the glass shattering on the floor. She barely even notices it as it crunches underneath her shoes. She cups Kate's cheeks, her eyes wide and panicked. "Catherine," she murmurs.

Kate blinks, and a tear drops down her cheek as Helen frantically checks her body. "Are you bleeding?" she asks, her voice high. She pulls Kate's t-shirt up, revealing a large and relatively fresh sutures, and I gasp.

"It's you?" I whisper. "You're the donor?"

CHAPTER 63

milia

My mind is whirling as Carter carries Kate to Dad's treatment room. Dad's nurse, Greta, jumps into action and examines her. Kate looks anguished the entire time, her eyes moving from me to the floor, over and over again. Years may have passed, but her silence still speaks volumes to me. She never intended for me to find out.

"I just need my pain medication," she tells the nurse, and Helen nods.

Carter looks at his parents, his entire body tense. "You knew about this?"

Helen and William look down, unable to face him. "It was her decision. She's an adult. It wasn't my place to tell you."

Carter grits his teeth and shakes his head as he walks out of the room. I'm tempted to follow him, but instead I sit down next to Kate. She's trembling and shaking her head, and I turn to the nurse.

"Her dose is four pills, but she'll only take one. It's no wonder she's in pain."

Kate bursts into tears, but she's trying so hard to keep from crying that she's choking on her sobs, hurting her stomach even more.

I lean in and cup her cheeks, wiping at her tears with my thumbs. "Look at me," I say. Her eyes find mine, and she calms just a little. "You're fine, Kate. You won't get addicted to these pills. You do, however, need to take them right now. You'll hurt yourself more if you won't. You hear me?"

She nods, but I see the fear in her eyes. I look up at the nurse and sigh. "Do we have an IV we can give her?"

She shakes her head anxiously. "Her medication is very specific. We don't. I'm sorry, ma'am."

I sigh and shake my head. "It's fine," I say, holding my hand out. "Give them to me."

Greta hands me the bottle of pills and I take out three. "You've had one pill, and you're going to have three more," I tell Kate.

Kate shakes her head, panic gripping her. Her breathing is erratic, and I can tell she's on the cusp of hysteria. I grab her chin, my grip tight, and look into her eyes. "If you're going to do this, you're going to do it properly," I tell her, my tone threatening. "You see it through to the end. That includes you healing well. Did you forget who your brother is? If he wants to cut off your access to these pills he can. You think any pharmacy will sell to you? You think any dealer will dare speak to you?"

Kate's eyes clear little by little, and I can tell she's listening to me. "You're going to take these pills, and you're going to give yourself a chance to heal properly. If you're scared of the meds, I'll be there every step of the way. I'll keep them, okay? I'll only give you your doses at the exact times you're supposed to have them."

I see a spark of hope in her eyes and I smile at her. "You'd do that?" she asks, and I nod.

"I promise," I say, handing her three pills.

Kate stares at them before inhaling deeply and taking them. I hand her a glass of water, and she takes it with trembling hands.

I breathe a sigh of relief when she swallows the pills. All these years I was convinced I hated her, yet I still can't bear to see her in pain.

Someone drops a hand to my shoulder, and I look up to find Carter standing beside me. He looks much calmer now, and I relax under his touch as I turn back to face Kate.

"Why'd you do it?" I ask, my voice soft.

She looks into my eyes, and all I can see is guilt.

"I owed it to you. I... Emilia, I'm so sorry. The things I've done, the things I've said. If I was the only one that lost you then maybe, just maybe, I could accept that those were just the consequences of my actions. But it wasn't just me, Emilia. My mother makes your favorite cake every year for your birthday. Your father stares at photos of you growing up for hours. He misses you every second of every day. And Carter? Carter stopped living the second you left. He just *exists*. My selfish actions ruined so many lives, including my own. I can't turn back time, Emilia. I can't undo what I've done, and I won't ever be able to make it right. But this... this was something that might make a small difference. I might not be able to give you back the time you lost, but at least I could give you more years with your Dad. It isn't enough. It won't ever be enough. But it's the least I could do."

I stare at her, seeing her in a new light for the first time in years. I can tell the guilt she's living with wrecked her. It eats at her, at who she used to be. When I look at her, all I see is a shell of the girl I used to love like she was my own sister.

"I'm going to try my best to forgive you," I whisper. "Things won't ever be the same between us. I doubt we'll ever even have any relationship to speak of. But I'm done with the hate, the pain, the regrets. I'm done living in the past. I'll try to forgive you, Kate, but I won't ever forget what you did."

She nods and bites down on her lip as a tear runs down her cheeks.

"That includes the past, but it also includes you donating a kidney to my father. It includes the food you left on my porch, the wine in the treehouse. All of it."

My heart wrenches painfully when I look at her. She looks up sharply, disbelief and hope warring in her eyes.

I tighten my hand around her bottle of pills and hold it up for her to see. "I'm keeping this," I tell her as I rise from my seat. "I'll get one of the guest rooms prepared for you so the nurses can keep an eye on your condition. It's best if you stay here for a while. I'll give you your pills personally. Consider it a thank you for what you did for my father."

She nods at me, her eyes wide. I turn to find Carter looking at me, his eyes filled with emotions I can't quite place. He smiles at me gratefully and I look down as I walk out of the room, my heart in complete chaos, all over again.

CHAPTER 64

milia

I stand just outside Kate's bedroom door, my heart hammering in my chest. I still find it hard to believe she donated a kidney to my father. For so many years I've hated her, convinced she'd never change. Convinced I'd never be able to forgive her. Yet here I stand, every thread of hatred slowly unravelling, reluctant gratefulness replacing it. I never thought that she might be suffering right alongside me, that the guilt might be eating her alive. I've grown so much as a person over the years, yet I was convinced she didn't. I rest my forehead against the door and inhale deeply. I'm feeling so incredibly conflicted.

I jump when I feel an arm wrap around my waist, and my eyes flutter closed when Carter's scent envelops me. He leans in, his chest against my back, and he lifts my hair out of the way. He presses a soft kiss against the back of my neck, and a shiver runs down my spine.

"Just go in," he whispers. "She'd love it if you did. You don't have to restrict yourself to only going in to give Kate her pills."

He trails a path down my neck with his nose before

pressing another kiss on the hollow of my throat. I melt against him and turn to kiss him. He smiles against my lips and deepens the kiss as I rise to my tiptoes. We're both panting by the time I pull away, smiles on both our faces.

Carter presses a kiss to my forehead, his lips lingering. "Go on," he murmurs. "Go in. I've got to run to the office. I'll see you at dinner."

I nod and rise to my tiptoes to kiss him. He pulls away reluctantly and looks at me with so much love in his eyes that my heart skips a beat. He smirks and pecks my lips one more time before walking away, leaving me standing in front of Kate's room.

I'm nervous as I knock on the door. It's obvious she didn't expect me, because she sits up in bed and then groans in pain.

"Emilia," she whispers. "I'm sorry. I thought it was Mom." She glances at the alarm clock on her bedside table and frowns. "Is it time for my meds already? I thought I had another hour."

I shake my head and walk to the chair Helen placed beside her bed. "It's not. I just thought I'd see how you were doing," I say, a tentative smile on my face.

Kate blinks in surprise and then smiles. "I'm good. Carter and you are taking such good care of me. I adore Mom, but it's so stressful to have her around. The nurses are really great."

I nod. "They were amazing with Dad too."

"How is he feeling?"

I relax in my seat, my smile genuine this time. "Honestly, it's like he's a whole new man. He's far more alive than he ever was before he got sick. He's filled with light, with happiness. I've never seen him this way." I glance at her and bite down on my lip. "And I owe it to you. Thank you, Kate."

Her eyes widen and she holds her hands up. "Oh no, don't. Don't thank me, Emilia. I... I've spent years thinking of ways to make things right, but I was too much of a coward. It was easier to run from my problems and pretend everything I did never happened. I pursued a life of my own, and I even ended up getting married, however briefly, in my pursuit of a new life. But in the meantime, Carter's life stood still. He forged ahead with his career, but much like your dad, he wasn't truly alive. Not in the way he was when you were around. The kidney donation... it's the least I could do, Emilia."

I study her and then look down at my lap. "Milly. You can call me Milly. And did you really get married?"

I look up at her to find her looking at me, hope and disbelief in her eyes. She nods slowly, a smile slowly spreading on her cheeks. "It's a long story," she murmurs.

"Let's call it even, okay?" I say.

Kate looks at me, brows raised.

"Let's both stop living in the past. It won't help either of us. I'm not going to lie to you and tell you that I no longer feel like you took some precious years from me... but if not for you, I'd have lost my father. You might have taken some years away from me, but you gave me others in return. Carter and I... we'll be okay."

Kate looks at me, curiosity lighting up her eyes. "You'll be okay? Does that mean you aren't leaving?"

I smile at her. "No, I'm not. I haven't found a way to tell him yet, though."

Kate frowns, a worried expression on her face. "You should probably tell him soon," she murmurs.

I raise my brows in question, and she blanches. "What do you mean?"

Kate looks away, but not before I catch the brief flash of panic in her eyes. I bite down on my lip as hundreds of terrible scenarios run through my mind. Is he expecting me to leave? Has he been waiting for it?

Kate looks at me and shakes her head. "Nothing like that," she says. "You still wear the exact same expression when you're overthinking things," she says, a smile on her face. "It's just...

he's already bought a plot of land in London. Asher and he are gathering more investors so they can expand their company to England... so Carter can be with you."

I stare at her in disbelief. "What?"

Kate nods. "The boss I currently work for, Alyssa Devereaux, is one of his investors. She and her husband are investing in Carter's London office," she says. "I totally understand it too. You've sacrificed so much for us, it's about time someone does the same for you."

I run a hand through my hair, my heart racing. "But there's nothing there for me. It's just a job. I've been far happier working for Clarke Reed. Besides, my dad is here and he loves it here. He won't want to leave, and truthfully, neither do I."

Kate bites down on her lip and nods. "You should talk to him, I think. From what I understand, he wanted to surprise you with all of this, so you wouldn't have a chance to say no. I think he wanted to keep you from making another sacrifice by staying here for him."

I smile to myself and shake my head. "This man," I murmur, and Kate grins at me.

"You know what he's like," she says. "When it comes to you, he's always been dramatic."

I smirk and cross my arms over each other. "I guess it's my turn to be truly dramatic," I say, a mischievous smile on my face.

Kate looks at me, apprehension in her eyes. "Oh, Milly," she murmurs. "What are you planning now?"

I rise to my feet, my heart hammering in my chest. "You'll find out soon enough. Do me a favor, though. Call Carter in exactly one hour and tell him to come home. Be dramatic."

CHAPTER 65

arter

I glance at my watch, my stomach fluttering. I need everything to be perfect tonight. It feels like I've been planning this for half my life.

My phone rings, and I frown when I realize it's Kate. "Hey," I murmur, a tinge of worry coursing through me. She rarely calls me, and when she does, something is often wrong.

"Carter," she says, her voice soft. "Um, it's Emilia. She's, uh, she's acting a bit strange. I'm not sure how to explain. Can you please come home? I don't know what's going on."

I freeze. "What do you mean?" I ask, unease running down my spine. "You need to explain better, Kate. How is she acting weird?" I ask as I rush towards my car.

I hear some rustling, and then the call ends. I glance at my phone in disbelief and call her back, but her phone is turned off.

I'm worried sick as I rush home, and my unease builds as I walk into the house to find it entirely empty and dark. I walk towards the stairs and pause in surprise. There's a path of candles leading up the stairs, and near every candle I find a photo of Emilia and me. It starts off with photos of us as children, and as I walk up the stairs, the photos cover our teenage years, before leading to our time in college by the time I reach the top of the stairs.

My heart is racing as I follow the path to my bedroom, the room I've very much come to consider jointly mine and Emilia's. I laugh at the items on the floor. In between the candles are fake little cockroaches, sticky notes with a car drawn on, and even a bottle of Nair. I'm biting down on my lip to stay in control over my emotions as I open my bedroom door.

Emilia is standing in the middle of our room, looking like an absolute vision amongst the dozens of candles. She's wearing a red evening gown that looks stunning on her, and my heart skips a beat.

She smiles at me nervously and I walk up to her, equally nervous. Emilia slides her arms up my chest and around my neck. She pulls me closer and I bend down, my lips hovering over hers. Her eyes flutter closed and she rises to her tiptoes, her lips brushing against mine. I exhale in delight when she kisses me, her tongue darting over my lips. I deepen our kiss, wanting all of her. She's got me feeling emotional and needy. Emilia pulls away with a smile on her face, her arms around my neck. She looks into my eyes with so much love that I can't help but count my blessings.

"Carter Clarke," she whispers. "You and I have made so many memories together. You were my first nemesis, my first kiss, my first lover, my one and only love. We've been through so much together, and repeatedly, life has tried to tear us apart. For a little while, it did. But what's eight years compared to a lifetime?"

She pulls away a little, her palms sliding down my chest. She grabs my hand and cradles it in both of hers, pulling our joined hands to her lips. She kisses my knuckles and looks up at me, and I see my future in her eyes.

"Right here in this house is where I want to make the rest of our memories. Carter, will you spend the rest of your life making memories with me? Carter... will you marry me?"

I grin and drop my forehead to hers. This girl... I bury my shaking hands in her hair and pull her in for a kiss roughly. I kiss her with all I've got, eliciting a moan from her. By the time I pull away she's panting, her eyes glassy with lust. "Yes, Minx," I murmur. "I told you I'd marry you years ago. I always knew I would."

I bend down and lift her into my arms. She gasps and I grin as I carry her out of our bedroom. I find Kate and John hovering by the door, both of them jumping when I open the door. I narrow my eyes at Kate, but the effect is diminished by the huge grin I'm wearing. "I'll deal with you later," I say, but she doesn't look intimidated in the slightest.

I walk past both of them with Emilia in my arms, and John shouts, "and?", after which Kate shouts, "did he say yes?"

I carry Emilia out of the house before she can even reply. She giggles as I place her in the passenger seat of my car. I press a kiss to her lips as I buckle her in, and she's beaming.

She turns to look at me as I step into the car, and she takes my fucking breath away. She's so beautiful, even more so tonight.

"Where are we going?" she asks, and I shake my head.

"Not very far, Minx."

She smiles at me and bites down on her lip. "Do I get to call you my fiancé now?"

My heart skips a beat and I grin at her, nodding. "Yes, but not for long."

Emilia frowns and I smirk at her. "You'll be calling me husband soon."

She laughs, her head tipped back, and my heart skips a

beat. She looks around in wonder when I park in front of my parents' house and I grin as I walk around the car. I lift her back into my arms and walk straight to the treehouse.

Emilia's eyes widen, and she grins at me. "What are we doing here? You know your house is big enough for privacy, right? Even if Kate and Dad are there."

I laugh and shake my head. "I love the way your mind works," I whisper. "*Ours*. It's our house."

I carry her up the stairs carefully, not releasing her until we reach the top. I put her down carefully and grin as she walks in, her eyes twinkling with curiosity.

Emilia opens the door and gasps. I smirk and follow her in, my eyes falling to the hundreds of roses that fill the space. It took me hours to set this all up, and the roses cut my hands a few times, but it was so worth it to see the look in her eyes. Against the wall, in large letters crafted from roses, are the words *Marry Me?*, fairy lights lighting up to the room, making everything look magical.

Emilia's eyes fill with tears, and I pull her in a bit further. "Emilia," I murmur, a huge smile on my face. "You've always had a knack for ruining my plans, no matter how well laid out they might be. Today is no exception, and though it shouldn't surprise me, it did. You both surprised and delighted me. You've always had that effect on me. Your beauty, your intellect, your heart, none of it ever ceases to surprise me. I don't think it ever will. I always hoped I'd get to ask you to marry me one day, and if I did, I knew it'd be here, where it all started. You've been my *first* in every way that matters, and I want you to be every *last*, too."

I drop down to my knees in the middle of the treehouse, and a tear rolls down her cheek. I pull a diamond engagement ring out of my pocket and hold it up, the light making it sparkle beautifully.

"Emilia Parker," I murmur. "I have loved you all my life. Will you do me the honor of becoming my wife?"

She bursts into tears and nods. "Yes, Carter. A thousand times, yes."

I smile as I slip the ring onto her finger. "Finally," I murmur. "I've been wanting to put a ring on you since you were sixteen."

She bursts out laughing and drops down to her knees. Emilia wraps her arms around me and kisses me. I kiss her back, my heart truly at ease for the first time in years. She's finally truly mine, and if she goes anywhere at all, I'm going with her.

CHAPTER 66

milia

"Are you ready?" Kate asks, a smile on her face. I nod, and she opens my bedroom door. Dad's eyes widen as soon as he sees me in my wedding dress, and tears fill his eyes. Helen and William follow him in, both of them just as emotional as Dad is. My emotions overwhelm me and I inhale shakily as a tear drops down Dad's cheek.

"You look beautiful, Princess," he whispers. I sniff and open up my arms as Dad walks up to me. I hug him tightly, a tear running down my face.

Helen walks up to us and nervously touches my hair, her hands trembling as she fixes my updo. She looks like she's been crying all morning, her eyes shimmering with happiness. I thought my wedding day would be the happiest day of *my* life, but it looks like Kate and Helen might be happier than I am. I chuckle to myself as Helen sniffs yet again.

"Her hair is fine," William says, his voice suspiciously shaky. He pats my hair and smiles at me, his eyes filled with the same happiness I see in my own father's eyes. He claps Dad on his back, and Dad squeezes me a little tighter. "I'll take her away before she starts fussing over you," he says, grabbing Helen's hand. The two of them have tried their best to be involved in the wedding, and though I didn't expect it to happen, Helen and I have grown much closer. Nothing is as it used to be, but the bonds I thought were long lost are on the mend.

William leads a reluctant Helen away, and Kate closes the door behind them as I hug my Dad a little tighter. My dad being able to walk me down the aisle today is a dream come true. I'm feeling so incredibly blessed, so happy, and without Kate this might not have been possible.

Kate smiles, but I can tell her eyes are glistening with tears too. "You'll ruin your makeup," she says, and I smile at her, my head resting on Dad's shoulder. Slowly but surely, she and I were able to mend our relationship. Things aren't what they used to be, but there's no animosity between us anymore. As a gesture of goodwill, I asked her to be my maid of honor, and it's brought us closer than I expected. She's supported me every step of the way, and nothing was ever too much. I didn't think it'd happen, but I'm glad she'll become my sister-in-law. We have a long way to go, but we're getting there, one step at a time.

"I love you, Daddy," I murmur. "You're the first man I ever loved, and you always will be."

Dad sniffs loudly, but he can't keep his sob in. He pulls away from me and buries his face in his hands.

I hold his shoulders, trying my best to hold back my own tears. "I'm not going anywhere, Dad. You're only a ten-minute drive away, and if you ever want to, you can just come stay with us. We've left your room just as it was."

He nods and tries his hardest to pull himself together. Dad cups my cheek gently and swipes my stray tears away with his thumb. "I love you, too. You'll always be my little girl, Emilia."

I nod and take Dad's hand. We both inhale deeply before walking towards the garden. Carter and I opted to get married in our garden, and the decorators have done a magnificent job transforming it into a floral paradise. It's everything I could've ever wished for. It's small and intimate, and it's *us*.

We pause at the start of the aisle, and my eyes find Carter's. I see him gasp, his eyes widening. He looks as emotional as I'm feeling, and I smile at him. I've waited for this day my entire life. I watch as Asher teases Carter, but he doesn't take his eyes off me for a single second.

Dad holds me tightly as we walk down the aisle, and his hands are shaking when he places my hand in Carter's. Their eyes meet and a silent exchange I'm not privy to ensues before Dad lets go of my hand. He smiles at me and takes a seat, and the whole world fades away. All I can see is Carter, and the butterflies in my stomach go wild.

"You look breathtaking," he says, and I blush.

"You don't look so bad yourself," I whisper.

Carter chuckles, and together, we turn towards the officiant, our hands joined. Neither one of us lasts more than a second before our eyes are back on each other.

We both opted to write our own vows, and my eyes fill with tears as Carter turns to me.

"Emilia, I swear I'll love you and cherish you for all eternity, long after I take my last breath. Throughout the growth and changes we'll face in life, I will always prioritize you and I'll never take you for granted. I promise to work with you to foster and cherish a relationship of equality, knowing that together we will build a life that will be far better than either of us could imagine or achieve alone. I'll always provide for you, and I promise to never run out of t-shirts for you to steal."

My eyes fill with tears as a sharp laugh escapes my lips. Carter smiles at me and tightens his grip on my hands.

"I promise to be your safe space and I promise to always be on your team," he says. "As your husband, I promise to be faithful and to never give up on you or on us. I know that whatever the future may hold, we'll face it together, and I vow to stand by you through both good and bad times, in sickness and in health. I love every bit of the version of you standing in front of me right now, and I promise to love the person you are yet to become. I will love you even if you hide fake cockroaches in our bed, I will love you when you inevitably stick post it notes all over my favorite car, and I will love you even if you cause me to lose all my hair – *again*."

Our guests burst out laughing, many of them remembering our old antics. Carter raises our joined hands to his lips and presses a soft kiss to the back of my hand. I smile at him, tears in my eyes.

"Carter, before anything else, you are and always will be my best friend. You've laughed with me, cried with me and you've grown with me throughout the years, and I vow to keep doing that with you for the rest of our lives, even as time and life changes us both. I vow to not only grow old together, but to *grow* together."

His eyes fill with tears as he looks at me, his expression telling me that he can barely believe we really made it, that we're really standing here together.

"I promise to be your family, and as a family, I promise to work with you to create a home filled with love, laughter, and compassion. I promise I'll always put you first, and for as long as I live, you'll be the only one for me, through sickness and health, for richer or poorer. No matter what life throws at us, I'll never leave your side, and I'll be *on* your side. I promise to love and cherish you for the rest of time, and I'll spend every day showing you just how much I love you. I will love you even if you almost get me arrested on account of illegal possession of *oregano*, and for the rest of our lives, I'll drink salty coffee with a smile on my face, grateful that it's you I get to spend my years with."

Carter's looks away for a second, gathering his emotions. I

smile at him, my heart filled to the brim with happiness. The officiant clears his throat, but I can't take my eyes off my husband-to-be.

"Emilia Parker, do you take Carter Clarke to be your wedded husband?" he asks.

I look into Carter's eyes, and for a second he looks nervous. I grin and nod. "I do."

"Carter Clarke, do you take Emilia Parker to be your wedded —"

"I do," Carter says, just as the officiant says, "wife."

Our guests burst out laughing, and so do I.

The priest smiles at us and nods. "Then with the powers vested in me, I proclaim you husband and wife. You may kiss the bride."

Carter grabs my waist and sweeps me off my feet, his lips finding mine. Loud cheering erupts around us, and I smile against his lips.

"Finally," he murmurs. "At last, you're Mrs. Emilia Clarke. My wife."

Carter cups the back of my neck and kisses me properly, deeply. The cheers around us get louder, and so does the beating of my heart.

I smile at him, my arms around his neck. "And you're finally my husband, Carter Clarke. I knew fate would lead us back to each other. You're my destiny, Carter. You always have been."

The End

EXCLUSIVE EXTRA CONTENT

Don't want Emilia and Carter's story to end?

You can find an exclusive epilogue and other bonus scenes here: https://BookHip.com/TJKLHL

AFTERWORD

Thank you from the bottom of my heart for following Emilia and Carter's story. Their story had been running through my mind for months, and I'm so happy they finally got a voice.

I truly hope you enjoyed this novel and would absolutely love it if you left a review. Reviews are the highest compliment an author can receive, and they truly do impact our careers. I've once heard it be likened to giving staff a tip in restaurants, and at the time I thought it was funny, but it's kind of true!

I truly enjoy hearing from readers, and if you'd like to stay in touch with me, you can do so here:

- Newsletter: sendfox.com/catharinamaura
- Instagram: instagram.com/catharinamaura/
- Facebook: facebook.com/catharinamaura
- Amazon: amazon.com/author/catharinamaura
- BookBub: bookbub.com/profile/catharina-maura

I'm most active in my Facebook Inner Circle reader group.

This is where I ask for input on my novels, where I share giveaways and do cover reveals. Come hang out with me at facebook.com/groups/catharinamaura

ALSO BY CATHARINA MAURA

Until You: A Brother's Best Friend Romance

Left without a job and evicted from the house she so carefully turned into a home, Aria is offered two choices: move back in with her brother... or take the job her brother's best friend offers her.

Their lives weren't meant to collide — but everything changes when Grayson realizes that Aria is the mysterious woman behind a wildly popular vigilante platform.

She's the woman he's been falling for online, the one whose coding skills outdo his, the one he's been trying to track down.

It's her. And she's off-limits.

———

Forever After All: A Marriage Of Convenience Novel

Desperate and out of options, Elena Rousseau walks into a gentlemen's club, ready to sell her body in a last attempt to save her mother's life.

She didn't expect Alexander Kennedy to be there, and she certainly didn't expect him to propose a marriage of convenience instead.

Marrying Alexander means knowingly becoming a tool in his revenge plan. But what choice does she have?

Better the devil you know than the one you don't.

———

The Tie That Binds: A Marriage Of Convenience Novel

A father's last wish results in a marriage of *in*convenience.

When Alyssa Moriani loses her father, she's faced with an impossible choice: fulfil her father's last wish and marry Daniel Devereaux, her best friend's older brother... or lose her father's company to the one person that'll burn everything she's worked for to the ground.

Her marriage to Daniel was never meant to be more than a business arrangement. They were never meant to be so perfect together, and they were definitely never meant to fall in love. After all, they started their marriage with an end date in sight.

ACKNOWLEDGMENTS

This book wouldn't be what it is without the following people: Ashley, Tammy, Patricia, Jo, Lidón, and Abigail.

Thank you for all you do for me, ladies. I am forever grateful to have you on my team.

I'd thank my amazing husband too, but he's never going to read this. I love you babe — you really should read one of my books sometime. Or, you know, *any* book.

Made in the USA
Coppell, TX
12 August 2022

81297270R00187